12 MONTHS TO LIVE

For a preview of upcoming books and information about the author, visit JamesPatterson.com or find him on Facebook, Twitter, or Instagram.

12 MONTHS TO LIVE

James Patterson
and Mike Lupica

Little, Brown and Company
New York Boston London

Little, Brown and Company
Hachette Book Group
1290 Avenue of the Americas, New York, NY 10104
littlebrown.com

First Edition: September 2023

Little, Brown and Company is a division of Hachette Book Group, Inc. The Little, Brown name and logo are trademarks of Hachette Book Group, Inc.

The publisher is not responsible for websites (or their content) that are not owned by the publisher.

The Hachette Speakers Bureau provides a wide range of authors for speaking events. To find out more, go to hachettespeakersbureau.com or call (866) 376-6591.

ISBN 9780316405690 (hc) / 9780316570640 (large print)
LCCN is available at the Library of Congress

Printing 1, 2023

LSC-C

Printed in the United States of America

For my favorite New York lawyer,
Tom Harvey. And Dr. Todd Gersten.
Both Mr. Patterson and I thank them for their
generosity in the writing of our book. —M.L.

12 MONTHS TO LIVE

ONE

"FOR *THE* LAST TIME," my client says to me. "I. Did. Not. Kill. Those. People."

He adds, "You have to believe me. I didn't do it."

The opposing counsel will refer to him as "the defendant." It's a way of putting him in a box, since opposing counsel absolutely believe he *did* kill all those people. The victims. The Gates family. Father. Mother. And teenage daughter. All shot in the head. Sometime in the middle of the last night of their lives. Whoever did it, and the state says my client did, had to have used a suppressor.

"Rob," I say, "I might have mentioned this before: I. Don't. Give. A. Shit."

Rob is Rob Jacobson, heir to a legendary publishing house and also owner of the biggest real estate company in the Hamptons. Life was good for Rob until he ended up in jail, but that's true for pretty much everybody, rich or poor. Guilty or innocent. I've defended both.

Me? I'm Jane. Jane Smith. It's not an assumed name, even though I might be wishing it were by the end of this trial.

There was a time when I would have been trying to keep somebody like Rob Jacobson away from the needle, back when New

York was still a death penalty state. Now it's my job to help him beat a life sentence. Starting tomorrow. Suffolk County Court, Riverhead, New York. Maybe forty-five minutes from where Rob Jacobson stands accused of shooting the Gates family dead.

That's forty-five minutes with no traffic. Good luck with that.

"I've told you this before," he says. "It's important to me that you believe me."

No surprise there. He's been conditioned his entire life to people telling him what he wants to hear. It's another perk that's come with being a Jacobson.

Until now, that is.

We are in one of the attorney rooms down the hall from the courtroom. My client and me. Long window at the other end of the room where the guard can keep an eye on us. Not for my safety, I tell myself. Rob Jacobson's. Maybe the guard can tell from my body language that I occasionally feel the urge to strangle him.

He's wearing his orange jumpsuit. I'm in the same dark-gray skirt and jacket I'll be wearing tomorrow. What I think of as my sincerity suit.

"Important to *you*," I say, "not to me. I need twelve people to believe you. And I'm not one of the twelve."

"You have to know that I'm not capable of doing something like this."

"Sure. Let's go with that."

"You sound sarcastic," he says.

"No. I *am* sarcastic."

This is our last pretrial meeting, one he's asked for and that is a complete waste of time. Mine, not his. He looks for any excuse to get out of his cell at the Riverhead Correctional Facility for even an hour and has insisted on going over once more what he calls "our game plan."

Our—I run into a lot of that.

I've tried to explain to him that any lawyer who allows his or her client to run the show ought to save everybody a lot of time and effort—and a boatload of the state's money—and drive the client straight to Attica or Green Haven Correctional. But Rob Jacobson never listens. Lifelong affliction, as far as I can tell.

"Rob, you don't just want me to believe you. You want me to like you."

"Is there something so wrong with that?" he asks.

"This is a murder trial," I tell him. "Not a dating app."

Looks-wise he reminds me of George Clooney. But all good-looking guys with salt-and-pepper hair remind me of George. If I had met him several years ago and could have gotten him to stay still long enough, I might have married him.

But only if I had been between marriages at the time.

"Stop me if you've heard me say this before, but I was set up."

I sigh. It's louder than I intended. "Okay. Stop."

"I *was*," he says. "Set up. Nothing else makes sense."

"Now, you stop me if you've heard this one from me before. Set up by whom? And with your DNA and fingerprints sprinkled around that house like pixie dust?"

"That's for you to find out," he says. "One of the reasons I hired you is because I was told you're as good a detective as you are a lawyer. You and your guy."

Jimmy Cunniff. Ex-NYPD, the way I'm ex-NYPD, even if I only lasted a grand total of eight months as a street cop, before lasting barely longer than that as a licensed private investigator. It was why I'd served as my own investigator for the first few years after I'd gotten my law degree. Then I'd hired Jimmy, and finally started delegating, almost as a last resort.

"Not to put too fine a point on things," I say to him, "we're not just good. We happen to be the best. Which *is* why you hired both of us."

"And why I'm counting on you to find the real killers eventually. So people will know I'm innocent."

I lean forward and smile at him.

"Rob? Do me a favor and never talk about the real killers ever again."

"I'm not O.J.," he says.

"Well, yeah, he only killed two people."

I see his face change now. See something in his eyes that I don't much like. But then I don't much like him. Something else I run into a lot.

He slowly regains his composure. And the rich-guy certainty that this is all some kind of big mistake. "Sometimes I wonder whose side you're on."

"Yours."

"So despite how much you like giving me a hard time, you do believe I'm telling you the truth."

"Who said anything about the truth?" I ask.

TWO

GREGG McCALL, NASSAU COUNTY district attorney, is waiting for me outside the courthouse.

Rob Jacobson has been taken back to the jail and I'm finally on my way back to my little saltbox house in Amagansett, east of East Hampton, maybe twenty miles from Montauk and land's end.

A tourist one night wandered into the tavern Jimmy Cunniff owns down at the end of Main Street in Sag Harbor, where Jimmy says it's been, in one form or another, practically since the town was a whaling port. The visitor asked what came after Montauk. He was talking to the bartender, but I happened to be on the stool next to his.

"Portugal," I said.

But now the trip home is going to have to wait because of McCall, six foot eight, former Columbia basketball player, divorced, handsome, extremely eligible by all accounts. And an honest-to-God public servant. I've always had kind of a thing for him, even when he was still married, and even though my sport at Boston College was ice hockey. Even with his decided size advantage, I figure we could make a mixed relationship like that work, with counseling.

McCall has made the drive out here from his home in Garden City, which even on a weekday can feel like a trip to Kansas if you're heading east on the Long Island Expressway.

"Are you here to give me free legal advice?" I ask. "Because I'll take whatever you got at this point, McCall."

He smiles. It only makes him better looking.

Down, girl.

"I want to hire you," he says.

"Oh, no." I smile back at him. "Did *you* shoot somebody?"

He sits down on the courthouse steps and motions for me to join him. Just the two of us out here. Tomorrow will be different. That's when the circus comes to town.

"I want to hire you and Jimmy, even though I can't officially say that I'm hiring you," he says. "And even though I'm aware that you're kind of busy right now."

"I'd only be too busy if I had a life," I say.

"You don't have one? You're great at what you do. And if I can make another observation without getting MeToo'ed, you happen to be great looking."

Down, girl.

"I keep trying to have one. A life. But somehow it never seems to take." I don't even pause before asking, "Are you going to now tell me what you want to hire me for even though you can't technically hire me, or should we order Uber Eats?"

"You get right to it, don't you?" McCall asks.

"Unless this is a billable hour. In which case, take as much time as you need."

He crosses amazingly long legs out in front of him. I notice he's wearing scuffed old loafers. Somehow they make me like him even more. I've never gotten the sense that he's trying too hard, even when I've watched him killing it a few times on Court TV.

"Remember the three people who got shot in Garden City?" he asks. "Six months before Jacobson is accused of wiping out the Gates family."

"I do. Brutal."

Three senseless deaths that time, too. The Carson family. Father, mother, daughter, a sophomore cheerleader at Garden City High. I don't know why I remember the cheerleader piece. But it's stayed with me. A robbery gone wrong. Gone bad and gone tragically wrong.

"Well, you probably also know that the father's mother never let it go until she finally passed," he says, "even though there was never an arrest or even a suspect worth a shit."

"I remember Grandma," I say. "There was a time when she was on TV so much I kept waiting for her to start selling steak knives."

McCall grins. "Well, it turns out Grandma was right."

"She kept saying it wasn't random, that her son's family had been targeted, even though she wouldn't come out and say why. She finally told me why but said that if I went public with it, she'd sue me all the way back to the Ivy League."

"But you're going to tell me."

"Her son gambled. Frequently and badly, as it turns out."

"And not with DraftKings, I take it."

"With Bobby Salvatore, who is still running the biggest book in this part of the world."

"Jimmy's mentioned him a few times in the past. Bad man, right?"

"Very."

"And you guys missed this?"

"Why do you think I'm here?"

"But upstanding district attorneys like yourself aren't allowed to hire people like Jimmy and me to run side investigations."

"We're not. But I promised Grandma," he says. "And there's an exception I believe would cover it."

"The case was never closed, I take it."

"But we'd gotten nothing new in all this time until a guy in another investigation dropped Salvatore's name on us."

"And here you are."

"Here I am."

"I don't mean to be coarse, McCall, but I gotta ask: who pays?"

"Don't worry about it," he says.

"I'm a worrier."

"Grandma liked to plan ahead," he says. "She was ready to go when we found out about the Salvatore connection. When I took it to her, she said, 'I told you so,' and wrote a check. She told me that she was willing to pay whatever it took to find out who took her family."

"This sounds like your crusade, not mine."

"Come on, think of the fun," Gregg McCall says. "While you're trying to get your guy off here, you can help me put somebody else away."

I know all about McCall by now. He's more than just a kick-ass prosecutor. He's also tough and honest. Didn't even go to Columbia on an athletic scholarship. Earned himself one for academics. Could have gone to a big basketball school. His parents were set on him being Ivy League. Worked his way to pay for the rest of college. The opposite of the golden boy I'm currently representing, all in all.

"I know we're supposed to be on opposing sides," McCall says. "But if I can make an exception..."

I finish his thought. "So can I."

"I'm asking you to help me do something we should have done at the time. Find the truth."

"You ought to know that my client just now asked me if

I thought he was telling the truth. I told him that I wasn't interested in the truth." I shrug. "But I lied."

"If you agree to do this, we'll kind of be strange bedfellows."

"You wish," I say.

Actually, *I* wish.

"I know asking you to take on something extra right now is crazy," he says.

"Kind of my thing."

THREE

ON MY WAY HOME, I call Jimmy Cunniff at the tavern. He used to get drunk there in summers when he'd get a couple of days off and need to get out of the city, day-trip to the beach and party at night. Now he owns the business, but not the building, though his landlord is not just an old friend but also someone, in Jimmy's words, who's not rent-gouging scum.

A Hamptons rarity, if you must know.

Jimmy's not just an ex-cop, having been booted out of the NYPD for what he will maintain until Jesus comes back was a righteous shooting, and killing, of a drug dealer named Angel Reyes. He's also a former Golden Gloves boxer and, back in the day, someone who had short stories published in long-gone literary magazines. The beer people should have put Jimmy out there as the most interesting man in the world.

He's also my best friend.

I tell him about Gregg McCall's visit, and his offer, and him telling me we can name our own price, within reason, because Grandma is paying.

"You think we can handle two at once?" Jimmy asks.

"We've done it before."

"Not like with these two," he says, and I know he's right about that.

"Two triple homicides," Jimmy Cunniff says. "But not twice the fun."

"Who knows, maybe solving one will show us how to solve the other. Maybe we'll even slog our way to the truth. Look at it that way."

"I don't know why you even had to ask if I was on board," Jimmy says. "You knew I'd be in as soon as you were. And you were in as soon as McCall asked you to be."

"Kind of."

"Stop here and we'll celebrate," he says.

I tell Jimmy I'll take a rain check. I have to go straight home; I need to train.

"Wait, you're still fixed on doing that crazy biathlon, even now?"

"I just informed Mr. McCall that crazy is kind of my thing," I say.

"Mine, too."

"There's that."

"Are you doing this thing for McCall because you want to or because the hunky DA is the one who asked you to?"

"What is this, a grand jury?"

"Gonna take that as a yes on the hunk."

"Hard no, actually," I say. "I couldn't do that to him."

"Do what?"

"Me," I say.

There was a little slowdown at the light in Wainscott, but now Route 27 is wide-open as I make my way east.

"For one thing," I tell Jimmy, "Gregg McCall seems so happy."

"Wait," Jimmy says. "Both your ex-husbands are happy."

"Now they are."

FOUR

MY TWO-BEDROOM SALTBOX is at the end of a cul-de-sac past the train tracks for the Long Island Railroad. North side of the highway, as we like to say Out Here. The less glamorous side, especially as close to the trains as I am.

My neighbors are mostly year-rounders. Fine with me. Summer People make me want to run back to my apartment in the West Village and hide out there until fall.

There is still enough light when I've changed into my Mets sweatshirt, the late-spring temperature down in the fifties tonight. I put on my running shoes, grab my air rifle, and get back into the car to head a few miles north and east of my house to the area known as the Springs. My favorite hiking trail runs through a rural area by Gardiners Bay.

Competing in a no-snow biathlon is the goal of my endless training. Trail running. Shooting. More running. More shooting. A perfect event for a loner like me, and one who prides herself on being a good shot. My dad taught me. He's the one who started calling me Calamity Jane when he saw what I could do at the range.

Little did he know that carrying a gun would one day

become a necessary part of my job. Just not in court. Though sometimes I wish.

I park my Prius Prime in a small, secluded lot near Three Mile Harbor and start jogging deep into the woods. I've placed small targets on trees maybe half a mile apart.

Fancy people don't go to this remote corner of the Hamptons, maybe because they can't find a party, or a photographer. The sound of the air rifle being fired won't scare the decent people out here, who don't hike or jog in the early evening. If somebody does make a call, by now just about all the local cops know it's me. Calamity Jane.

I use the stopwatch on my phone to log my times. I'm determined to enter the late-summer biathlon in Pennsylvania, an event Jimmy has sworn only I have ever heard about. Or care about. He asked why I didn't go for the real biathlon.

"If you ever see me on skis, find my real gun and shoot *me* with it."

I know I'm only competing against myself. But I've been a jock my whole life, from age ten when I beat all the boys and won Long Island's NFL Punt, Pass, and Kick contest, telling my dad I was going to be the first girl ever to quarterback the Jets. I remember him grinning and saying, "Honey, we've had plenty of those on the Jets since Joe Namath was our QB."

Later I was Hockey East Rookie of the Year at BC. That was also where I really learned how to fight. And haven't stopped since. Fighting for rich clients, not-so-rich ones, fighting when I'm doing pro bono work back in the city for victims who deserve a chance. And deserve being repped by somebody like me. Fighting with prosecutors, judges, even the cops sometimes, as much as I generally love cops, maybe because of an ex-cop like Jimmy Cunniff.

Occasionally fighting with two husbands.

Makes no difference to me.

You want to have a fight?

Let's drop the gloves and do this.

I'm feeling it even more than usual tonight, pushing myself, hitting my targets like a champion. I stop at the end of the trail, kneel, empty the gun one final time. Twelve hundred BBs fired in all.

But I'm not done. Not yet. Still feeling it. *Let's do this.* I reload. Hit all the targets on the way back, sorry I've run out of light. And BBs. What's the old line? Rage against the dying of the light? I wasn't much of a poet, but my father, Jack, the Marine and career bartender, liked Dylan Thomas. Maybe because of the way the guy could drink. My mother, Mary, who spent so much of her marriage waiting for my father to come from the bar, having long ago buried her dreams of being a writer, had died of ovarian cancer when I was ten. I'd always thought I had gotten my humanity from her, my sense of fairness, of making things right. It was different with my father the Marine, who always taught me that if you weren't the one on the attack, the other guy was. His own definition of humanity, just with much harder edges. He lasted longer than our mom did, until he dropped dead of a heart attack one night on a barroom floor.

It's dark by the time I get back to the car. I'm thinking about having one cold one with Jimmy. But then I think about making the half-hour drive over to the bar in Sag Harbor and back, and how I really do need a good night's sleep, knowing I'm going to be a little busy in the morning, even before I head to court.

I drink my last bottle of water, get behind the wheel, toss the rifle onto the back seat, knowing my real gun, the Glock, is locked safely in the glove compartment. I have a second one at home. A girl can't have too many.

I feel like I used to feel in college, the night before a big game. I think about what the room will look like tomorrow. What it will feel like. Where Rob Jacobson will be and where I'll be and where the jury will be.

I've got my opening statement committed to memory. Even so, I pull up the copy stored on my phone. I slide the seat back, lean back, begin to read it over again, keep reading until I feel my eyes starting to close.

When I wake up, it's morning.

FIVE

SHIT, SHIT, *SHIT*.

I look at my watch.

Six thirty.

I am putting the car in motion before I'm even fully awake. I have enough time, barely, to get back to the house, shower, get into my sincerity suit, and still make my eight o'clock appointment in Southampton before heading to court.

When I get to Southampton, I pull up to the small, one-story building across from Town Hall where I am meeting with one of my best friends in the world, Samantha Wylie.

Sam has been my best friend since we attended the same junior high school up-island in Patchogue before my father couldn't take it any longer and moved us back to the city.

She is a truly great beauty, tall and blond and happily married—the bitch—with two kids, both in college, one in pre-law and the other in pre-med. Even more annoying, at least to me, and just to make her picture more perfect, she and her husband have two labradoodles.

"You've never been much of a dog person," she once said. "But what do you possibly have against labradoodles?"

"I don't know," I told her. "There's just something about them that's always pissed me off."

We both laughed that day at how silly I sounded. I'm not afraid to do silly with her. And I'd done more laughing, about more silly stuff, with Sam Wylie than with anybody who'd managed to stay in my life for very long, including two ex-husbands.

But there's something wrong today—I know it from the moment I am inside her office. And I find myself, in the moment, wishing I *had* rescheduled.

She isn't my pal Sam today; she's not the girl with whom I used to sneak beers on sleepovers.

She's Dr. Samantha Wylie.

SIX

TODAY'S APPOINTMENT IS SUPPOSED to be strictly routine, the follow-up Sam, being Sam, has always mandated to review test results after my annual physical. I keep telling her that the only reason she makes me come back is because she misses me.

"How are Rusty and Dusty?" I ask when I sit down.

Rusty and Dusty aren't the labradoodles' names. Just what I've always called them.

No reaction. "I got your test results back."

"You don't have to tell me," I say. "I'm in better shape than Wonder Woman. The new hot one."

She opens the folder in front of her and spreads out x-rays and lab reports. Sam had finally taken some pictures and done her tests because of what I had originally described to her as a persistent pain in the neck. And a bump back there that I hadn't noticed until a couple of weeks ago. The one she biopsied.

I feel the small, dark, cold place inside me begin to grow.

Then she starts to talk. And I wish, for the life of me, I could process, even *hear*, everything she is saying.

But I don't hear very much after "brain and neck cancer."

She pauses.

"It's further along than I'd prefer."

"Same. I thought you said I just pulled something working with my hand weights."

"You pulled a bad card, Jane, is what you did," she says. "I can't lie to you."

"Go ahead and lie a little. I won't stop you."

My next words sound monumentally dumb the moment they are out of my mouth.

"This can't happen today."

"There's never a good time, or a good way, to give someone news like this. Especially to someone you love."

She asks if I want to see the pictures. I tell her I'll save them for the scrapbook.

I try to smile. Put up a false front. Be a tough guy.

Be Jane.

Be *me*.

She's now talking about squamous cells that have spread into the lymph nodes.

"When I was a kid, I thought they were limp nodes," I say. I flop my wrist in a limp way. "I think I'd rather have some of them."

No reaction.

"Come on. That's funny."

"None of this is funny," Sam Wylie says. "And we both know it."

"What am I supposed to do? Cry?"

"If you want to."

"I don't," I say. "Cry, I mean."

"I do," Sam Wylie says.

She's talking slowly, patiently, but all I hear are the words running together, about chemo and targeted radiation and immunotherapy and the advances they've made with that, that there are ways to slow the disease for as long as possible.

"Am I hearing the word 'cure' in there anywhere?" I ask.

"In some cases," she says after a pause I don't like even a little bit.

Then she circles back to how we'll probably start with chemo when the time comes. I'm already shaking my head.

No, no, *no*.

"You can't have my hair. You've talked about what great hair I have even when it was as big as it was back in high school. No kidding—you're not getting it without a fight, Sam."

My hair is brown, shoulder-length, with streaks I was talked into by the woman who cuts my hair when I'm not trimming the bangs myself.

Now Sam is the one acting as if she hasn't heard a word I just said.

"Jane, you can't put this off, at least not for very long."

"Watch me."

"I know this is a shock."

I cut her off. "Am I dying in the next few weeks?" I ask.

I'm aware that I'm out of my chair. Feeling dizzy once I'm vertical again. Feeling the way Jimmy says he used to feel after he got tagged in a fight.

But still standing.

"Of course not."

"Then I have a case to try."

I'm at the door now, asking the only question I care to have answered.

"How long?"

She gives me a long look. "There's never a precise metric," she says.

"Try."

"Worst case? A year."

"No."

Now she manages a small smile. *"No?"*

"Not taking that deal."

"I can't knock down the sentence," she says. "I'm not a judge."

"Kind of," I say. "Judge, jury, hopefully not executioner."

"I'm so sorry."

"I want more than a year, since this is already sounding like the worst case I've ever taken."

She hesitates. "You sound like you're plea-bargaining here."

She makes a show of putting the x-rays and test results back in the folder, as if looking for something to do with her hands.

"How about fourteen months?"

"C'mon. You have to be able to do better than that."

"No, Jane. I can't and still be honest with you."

I tell her that deal I'll take. "We lawyers call this a negotiated settlement," I say, and then leave her office, knowing I now have to make one more important stop before court.

SEVEN

I KNOW SOMETHING THAT only the regulars at Jimmy Cunniff's tavern know, that it's open to them in the morning, even with the blinds facing Main Street drawn. And the sign in the front door window turned to CLOSED.

You go through the back door, and once you do, you can find at least a couple of hard-core cases drinking coffee with their whiskey. Or having coffee with whiskey added. Or having their first cold beer of the day. There is no hard-and-fast rule about when Jimmy or one of his bartenders opens up. If someone is inside getting ready to work, they might unlock the door the first time they hear somebody outside tapping on the window.

By the way? I'm not a hard-core drinker.

But I need a short one this morning, and I need it now.

So I come in through the back and see Jimmy standing at the front end of the bar, staring up at the television showing highlights of last night's Yankees game. I hear him curse. Even though he's Yankees and I'm Mets, we've managed to keep the baseball separate from our working relationship, at least so far.

He makes his way down the bar. "I'm almost positive you're supposed to be somewhere right now."

"Decided I need a quick shot of courage. And knew where I could get it."

He snorts. "There you go, acting like this case is a matter of life or death or something."

He turns without me asking and grabs a bottle of Bushmills and a glass and smiles at me from underneath a nose he broke—between boxing and bar fights as a teenager in this very spot—countless times. The nose makes a hard right about halfway down before cutting back to the left. I've always thought of it as a bit of an architectural wonder.

"And don't let this go to your head," he says as he pours, "but you need a glass of courage less than anybody I know. Present company included."

He pours some Bushmills into his coffee mug, then stares at me. "Hey. You okay?"

"Brilliant."

"You know something I don't about today?" he asks.

I grin. "Lots."

He's talking about the trial. I'm not.

Tell him.

Sit him down at a table and tell him.

If I'm going to tell anybody what Sam Wylie just told me, it's Jimmy.

Tell him now.

I throw down the whiskey instead.

What my old man used to call the breakfast of champions when mom was dying of cancer in front of our eyes.

Jimmy raises his coffee mug. "You got this, Janie."

Yeah, I think. *I got it, all right.*

EIGHT

I CRANK UP GREEN DAY all the way to Riverhead, driving fast when I can, trying to focus on where I'm going and not where I just came from. And what I just came from.

Thinking this:

Maybe in my case, not Rob Jacobson's—my life—New York State hasn't abolished the death penalty after all.

"Control what you can control," Jimmy always says, "and let God take care of the rest of the shit."

He can be such a poetic bastard.

But wait.

This is Her idea of taking care of me?

The scene outside the courthouse when I arrive is just as wild as it would be if Rob Jacobson's trial were being held at Criminal Court on Centre Street in the city, as if they moved all the color and pageantry and BS this far east.

I see by the satellite trucks that all of the networks are represented. All the local New York channels. I see some newspaper people I recognize, the fortunate few who still have jobs. But only a few. The rest shouting questions at me as I make my way across Court Street look as if they're here representing a school paper, or have stopped on their way to Driver's Ed.

I answer a few questions. Might as well start working them now, out here in what always feels to me like an open-air courtroom.

"Did he do it, Jane?" a voice shouts at me from down below.

"Wouldn't be here if he did."

"But isn't the evidence overwhelming, Jane?" I hear a woman's voice say.

"Whoa. Are you here reporting or prosecuting?"

Then I'm gone, and through security. I suspect that Rob Jacobson is already waiting for me inside the courtroom. Ten forty-five now. A late start today.

But as I make my way down the hallway I feel myself getting the spins. Take a fast right into the ladies' room. Blessedly, it's empty. I get past the door and lean against the wall inside and feel myself start to slide down it before I stop myself.

For the second time this morning I feel as if I can't breathe.

Fourteen months.

I think about splashing some water on my face but remember at the last second that I would be making a stupid mess out of a makeup job I'd been pretty proud of when I left the house. Can't have that, not when I'm ready for my close-up. So I reach down and turn on the cold water and cup my hand and drink some.

Stare at myself in the mirror. Same face I saw in the mirror at home before I rushed over to Sam Wylie's office. But the only thing really the same now is the job. The trial that begins in a few minutes, ready or not.

For some reason, I think about the movie *All That Jazz.* Roy Scheider, who lived in the Hamptons at the end of his life, played Bob Fosse, even though his character had a different name. Joe something. But a director and choreographer, like Fosse. And when it was time to get to work, he'd look in mirror, smile brightly, and say, "It's showtime, folks!"

I don't usually go for old movies. But there has always been something about this one, even if it was made before I was born. Or maybe because I saw Scheider on the beach a few times.

I'm the one looking into the mirror now.

"Showtime, folks," I say, forcing a smile.

When I turn around, there is a woman staring at me from across the room. I hadn't heard her come in.

"What are *you* looking at?"

NINE

NO JUMPSUIT FOR ROB JACOBSON today. He's wearing a suit that I'm thinking might have cost more than my Prius Prime. As I take a closer look at him, I decide I'm not the only one at the table wearing makeup.

"Well," he says, leaning toward me, "the ball's about to go up, isn't it?"

I am briefly back in Sam Wylie's office.

"I'm sorry...what?"

"The ball in Times Square on New Year's Eve. You ever do that? I did it a couple of times when I was a kid."

"Yeah. That's where I always wanted to be on amateur night."

I'm taking out my yellow legal pad and pens and the manila folder that contains the printout of my opening statement. I went through it one last time the night before, start to finish, not rushing it, wanting to make sure I had it down cold, knowing I had a doctor's appointment early in the morning.

My favorite leather bag was a gift from my first husband. Unless it was my second. When I have everything I need out of the bag, I turn to face my client.

"And to be clear, Rob," I say, unable to stop myself, "the ball *drops* on New Year's Eve. It's the balloon that goes up. It's a military expression my old man used."

I can feel his eyes on me as I begin to underline the phrases and moments from my statement I want to step on when the time comes.

"You are some piece of work. You know that, right?"

"Actually, I do."

I look around the room. Jury over to our right, already in their seats. The clerk's small desk in front of the judge's bench. Spectators behind Rob Jacobson and me. His wife, Claire, is in the first row, staring straight ahead, as if her eyes are fixed on the world she had before this trial became her world, and her husband's. I turn to look at her. She nods at me without changing expression. And Jimmy Cunniff likes to talk about *my* resting bitch face.

Less than five hours since I woke up in the car. Less than three since I got the news from Sam Wylie. Time flies.

Two minutes to eleven.

Showtime.

I know how punctual Judge Jackson Prentice III is. At eleven on the dot the door will open and he will come walking in and the balloon will go up and the ball really will drop.

It's already been the longest day of my life, and yet I feel myself smiling. Feel my right knee bouncing up and down under the table. Feel the kinetic energy in the room changing, and the air, as if a switch is about to be thrown. I used to feel this way before hockey games. Or when I was walking down an alley or up some stairs, sometimes with Jimmy, sometimes not, looking for a bad guy. Or a witness we'd tracked down.

The door to the right of the bench opens.

Judge Jackson Prentice is walking so quickly toward his bench he's almost running, as if he can feel the same energy in the room that I can.

"All rise!" the clerk shouts.

I can't believe how alive I feel.

TEN

I'VE TRIED OTHER MURDER cases before. Never like this one. The Hamptons. A made-for-TV mystery. A lot of front pages at the *Post* and *Daily News* and *Newsday,* the tabloids, from the moment it became clear that Rob Jacobson was the only suspect.

Had he done it?

And if he had done it, *why* had he?

Why was Jacobson's DNA all over the Gateses' rental house, including on the beds in the master bedroom and the daughter's? Why did an eyewitness have him speeding away on the night in question from a home he said he'd never been inside?

The Suffolk County district attorney, a publicity hound and ambitious as hell, is Kevin Ahearn. Jimmy has already taken to calling him Front Page Ahearn. I know, though I've never gone up against him, that his record on convictions is as spotless as mine is on acquittals. Which makes him, from where I sit, a very bad man.

And a meticulous one. The first few minutes of his folksy presentation, getting it in early that he grew up in Greenport, over on the North Shore, as if he himself could have been among the jury pool, have me thinking I should have packed a lunch.

Then, as I knew he would, he takes a shrewd turn, detailing the state's case against Rob Jacobson without once mentioning his name. Rob is "THE DEFENDANT." Emphasis intended.

"His is a world apart," Ahearn says. "Sagaponack and an opulent town house on the Upper West Side of Manhattan, and the exclusive Dalton School over on the other side of Central Park. The world where the defendant became convinced he could buy anything he wanted."

Ahearn pauses.

"Anything, in this case, except an acquittal," Ahearn says.

He introduces the Gates family, sharing their Instagram stories about this being the first time they had ever rented a summerhouse in the Hamptons, the summer Mitch and Kathy Gates celebrated their twentieth wedding anniversary in late July with their teenage daughter, before they were found dead in that house.

"The defendant took everything away from them," Ahearn says. "And on one terrible night, that family and all of its history was gone. And their dream summer had turned into a nightmare."

I'm not watching him now. I'm watching the jury. The guy *is* very good. And has their full attention with the story he's telling and the way he's telling it, concluding with a guarantee.

"My esteemed opponent will talk, probably at length, about the lack of motive. But what she will really be doing is shouting at you from the other side of a mountain of evidence against the defendant."

Ahearn isn't a big guy. Trim, gray-haired, blue suit that looks—and not by accident, I'm guessing—as if it could use a good steaming. But he's definitely got a big courtroom voice. Using it to full advantage now.

"My friends, I will leave you with this: facts are very stubborn things."

One last pause.

"Almost as stubborn as the state's pursuit of justice in this case, one that will inevitably end with a conviction," he says. "When we have concluded our business in this courtroom, this won't be about celebrity and it won't be about money. It will be about the facts. And about something that you have probably noticed is under attack in this country but still matters: *the truth.*"

I am already getting out of my seat as he is sitting down, walking across to the empty witness stand, smiling, then turning to the jury.

And applauding. Loudly, and enthusiastically.

From my right I immediately hear the gavel of Judge Jackson Prentice III, who is clearly and enthusiastically displeased. With me.

"Really, Ms. Smith? This isn't a show."

Yeah, Judge, it is.

Sometimes all *it is.*

But I don't say that. Instead, I say: "I'm so sorry, Your Honor. I was so impressed by opposing counsel's performance that I couldn't contain myself. Even you have to admit that was some great story he just told to the men and women who will eventually acquit Rob Jacobson *because* of the facts of this case."

I walk over to the jury box now and lean over, elbows resting on the partition. I'm directly in front of an older guy who reminds me of David Letterman after Dave grew the mountain-man beard. I smile. He smiles.

"But as skilled a prosecutor as Mr. Ahearn is, he is something much more than that," I say. "He is a fabulist, one who wants you to believe that suddenly a lack of motive doesn't matter.

But it does, ladies and gentlemen. It *always* does, despite all those facts Mr. Ahearn was bragging about the same way he frequently brags about his conviction rate."

"Your Honor," Ahearn says.

I hold up a hand, turn to him, and wink.

"Low-hanging fruit."

Then I'm moving again.

"That fatal flaw for Mr. Ahearn, you should pardon the expression, happens to be why this one isn't going into his win column."

Now it's my voice that's rising, as I am feeling the jazzed adrenaline that always starts to rise when I'm the one taking control of the room.

"There. Is. No. Motive. Here."

Back to the jury box, walking slowly in front of them. Smiling again.

"Now, it's abundantly clear that somebody went to an awful lot of trouble to make the police and Mr. Ahearn believe that Rob Jacobson, with no personal history of violence, murdered Mitch and Kathy and Laurel Gates."

I don't mention that most violent crimes are actually committed by first offenders, because that doesn't help Mrs. Smith's daughter Jane at all.

"Somebody brutally murdered three innocent people," I say. "But that doesn't mean you have to send an innocent man to prison for the rest of his life."

I spend some time explaining away the trace evidence, and how easy it would have been to have planted it—somebody could have done it, but it sure as hell wouldn't have been easy—and then I throw some shade on the idea that on a night heavy with marine layer the black Mercedes that was spotted leaving the Gateses' rental house even belonged to Rob

Jacobson, the car driving in an area, I point out, where black Mercedes seem to be spawning like rabbits.

Time to wrap it up.

"Mr. Ahearn and I actually agree on something," I say. "And so, I am certain, do all of you. This truly is a monstrous crime. But so, too, ladies and gentlemen, *would* be the crime of convicting an innocent man."

I sit back down.

No applause for me when I finish.

But I'm thinking that maybe there should be.

ELEVEN

KEVIN AHEARN HAS JUST finished questioning his first witness, the first cop on the scene the night of the murders, when Judge Jackson Prentice III announces that court is being adjourned for the day.

Rob Jacobson is on his way back to his cell when Claire Jacobson asks if she can have a word. "This won't take long."

Not if I have anything to say about it.

That's what I'm thinking as I show her into the same attorney room where I'd met with her husband the day before.

"If you're looking for legal advice, I'm kind of booked up at the moment," I tell her.

"Is that supposed to be funny?"

Claire Jacobson has made it clear that even after he—or they—fired his first two attorneys, no legal dream team she could have imagined ever would have included me.

But sadly we're stuck with each other.

She has requested the meeting so she can review the day's proceedings, as if she's hosting the postgame show.

"Your theatrics seemed to fall flat with the judge, quite frankly. Maybe you need to think about a change of attitude."

In some ways, she reminds me of Sam Wylie—taller, just

as blond, elegant in ways I know I will never be. Lady of the manor. She also appears to be in glowing health. So she's got me there, too.

"If you think what you saw today were theatrics, then you better think about wearing one of my old hockey helmets the further we get into this thing."

She sighs.

Theatrically.

"Golly, *there's* good news." She shakes her head dismissively. "Judge Prentice wasn't amused, and for the record, neither was I."

I feel myself biting through my lower lip hard enough to draw blood. I'm tired, I want to get outside and do my few minutes of standup, and then head back east.

But I'm doing my best to behave. A constant challenge.

Now I sigh.

"For the record, what I did today had nothing to do with your husband, or the judge, or the prosecutor, bless his heart," I say. "And it wasn't for you. I was only addressing the jury. I'd like to have you on my side, Claire, I would. But I sure as hell want those twelve people on my side. No, check that. *Need* them on my side."

There is no change in her expression. Maybe her eyes get a little wider. But with the work she's clearly had done, it's frankly hard to tell.

"We need them on Rob's side," she says.

We.

"You must know by now, having gotten to know *him*," she continues, "that he is, despite his many shortcomings, incapable of having committed this hideous crime."

"He points that out to me on a daily basis. Sometimes hourly, when he gets the chance."

"Is that an answer?" she asks.

She checks her phone now, as if I'm the one keeping her from being somewhere.

"When it's murder, Claire, it's always a crime."

It's been a long day, and I'm too deep into it to be wasting my time on bullshit like this.

"You know I don't like you very much," she says.

"You probably won't be surprised to learn that you're not the first."

Then I tell her I really have to be going, because the media is waiting for me to explain to them what they saw today. It's just another way for me to play to the jury at the same time, even though Judge Jackson Prentice III has told them to avoid all coverage of the trial, particularly on television.

Fat chance.

"To be continued," Claire Jacobson says, leaving the room first.

"Looking forward to it," I say, but the door has already closed behind her.

As I walk through the double doors at the top of the steps, it occurs to me, and not for the first time today, the percentage of time I might have left in my life that will be spent in the company of Rob and Claire Jacobson.

The first question is shouted at me from a woman I recognize from CNN. "How do you think Mr. Ahearn did presenting the case against your client today?"

"What case?" I ask.

At least they think I'm funny.

TWELVE

AT FIERRO'S, I PICK UP a pizza, then drop the box on my kitchen counter. After I run to the ocean and back, I eat only a couple of reheated pieces with the one beer I'm allowing myself tonight. Then I turn on the Mets game and my laptop.

I will get to the coverage of the first day of the trial later. I was there, so it will be light reading.

For now I read up on neck and head cancer, and how it progresses, and how quickly. Doing what just about everybody else does these days, which means self-diagnosing on the internet.

But after too many websites educating me about too much bad shit, I finally give up.

I know what Dr. Sam has told me, that the beginning of my treatment will mean chemotherapy plus radiation, and that the worst-case scenario, depending on my own particular pathology, might eventually include loss of my voice and—even worse— a feeding tube at some point. I can only imagine how romantic that might be for Dr. Ben, the most popular vet in the area.

Sam has made it clear that I can put off starting treatment for my specific cancer, which has only progressed locally so far, but hasn't metastasized. I just can't put it off for long. And I've made it clear that it's a risk I'm willing to take, because starting treatment now would mean somebody else would have to finish the trial. And that wasn't going to happen on the chance that this was the last case I was ever going to try.

"I just don't want you to do anything that reduces your best chance at being cured," Dr. Sam had said.

"Makes me even more motivated to get a fast acquittal," I'd said.

"Just know that if you don't, I'll be the one putting you in handcuffs and taking you to chemo," she had said, and then shook her head. "Still crazy."

"After all these years."

I don't fall asleep in my car tonight, just in front of the Mets. When my ringtone—the Boston College fight song—awakens me, the boys on the postgame show are breaking down the loss as if it's some kind of ballpark *CSI* episode.

It's Jimmy.

"I've been thinking on it," he says, "and the case up-island where the people got deep-fried is one we definitely take."

"I already locked it in on my way home from court."

"Without locking it in with me first?"

"I knew you wanted me to," I say. "I could hear it in your voice."

"Okay, then. So unless you got something you need me to do with Jacobson tomorrow, I'm gonna take a ride over there and meet with McCall and get after it."

"Please take me with you," I say.

"C'mon. I been reading about what happened today. Sounds like you killed it."

"That's me. A killer."

Jimmy says, "You're sure your plate's not too full for us to do the other?"

"Girl's gotta eat," I say, and end the call.

I'm about to head up to bed when I hear a familiar scratching at the back door. I throw on the porch light, unlock the door, and open it.

The dog is back.

It's a black Lab who started showing up about a week ago. No collar. Male. Moving slowly, but not limping, or in any obvious distress. I don't know a lot about dogs, but this one's coat seems to have a lot of gray in it, whatever that means. His eyes, though, seem pretty alert.

His tail is always wagging when he shows up in the yard.

It is now.

"You looking for a nice home?" I say.

His ears prick up.

"This isn't one," I say, and go back inside.

THIRTEEN

DAY THREE OF THE trial brings with it my first surprise from Kevin Ahearn.

You know what lawyers hate more than surprises in court?

Nothing.

The witness, on my list, is named Nick Morelli. He once dated Laurel Gates even though he's a little older. He's local. No college. Fishing guide. Lot of that going on out here, along with potato farming, if you're not in the business of being rich. Morelli makes his living now doing charters. One-boat guy, inherited from his father, who's beat it down to Florida by now, along with Morelli's mother. The boat's docked over at one of the commercial piers in Montauk.

I interviewed him during pretrial. So did Jimmy. A little rough around the edges. But no red flags to speak of. No alarms sounding. He doesn't want to be a part of the trial, but I make it clear he doesn't have a choice. He pushes back a little but finally lets it go.

I see him for what Ahearn wants him to be, someone testifying to the character and all-around goodness of the dead girl.

He's the first witness on Ahearn's list like that, won't be the last. Ahearn is doing what I would have done, painting a picture of Laurel Gates, all the life she had ahead of her, how popular she was. Her dreams. All that.

Right now he is taking Nick Morelli through their friendship, and their brief dating life.

I'm taking notes to keep myself busy, not sure if I even want to cross.

Now Ahearn is asking Nick Morelli when the last time was that he saw Laurel Gates.

I want to raise my hand, like I'm the smartest girl in class. I know the answer to this one, because Nick Morelli told me when I interviewed him. It was a few weeks before she died that they saw each other last, outside a place called the Stephen Talkhouse in Amagansett. Maybe a mile from my house. Bar with music. One of the few places like it for kids west of Montauk, where the real summer party scene is. The Talkhouse is so packed on summer weekends it's as if fire codes have never been invented.

I drive past there sometimes on a Saturday night and think the line outside might actually be stretching all the way to my house.

"Did you get the chance to speak to her that night?" Ahearn says to Morelli. But turning to look at me as he does.

"I was going to," Morelli says, "but she was across the street, in the parking lot next to the barbershop, while I was waiting for my Uber to show up. And she was making out with some old dude."

Wait for it.

"And you're sure it was Laurel Gates?" Ahearn says.

"I am," Morelli says. He shrugs. "I used to make out with her over there myself before we broke up."

I have to let it play out. It would be like trying to stop the waves at this point.

Even people in outer space know where this is going.

"And do you happen to know who this old dude was?" Ahearn asks.

Shit, shit, *shit.*

"Now I do."

"And do you see him in this courtroom, Nick?"

Ahearn knows exactly what he's doing. It is a couple of minutes before five o'clock. He knows the same thing that I do, that Judge Jackson Prentice III adjourns at five each day even if one of us is in mid-sentence.

Morelli points directly at Rob Jacobson. "He's sitting right there."

"Let the record show," Kevin Ahearn says, "that the witness is pointing at the defendant."

Then Morelli adds one more thing: "Laurel's dad thought I was too old for her. Funny, right?"

Ahearn nods, then says, "No further questions at this time."

No kidding. Not only is it five o'clock now. It's a Friday afternoon.

What the jury just heard from Nick Morelli isn't just the last thing they'll hear from him today. It's the last thing they'll hear from him until Monday morning, about my client making out with Laurel Gates across from the Stephen Talkhouse. A girl young enough to be his daughter. And there's not a thing I can do about it.

Ahearn winks on his way past Morelli, gets close enough to our table so that Rob Jacobson and I hear him say to us, "Spoiler alert: there's more."

Judge Jackson Prentice III breaks in. "We'll reconvene on Monday morning. For now, court is adjourned."

The clerk tells us all to rise. Prentice leaves. I can hear the buzz from the spectators behind me, like something just happened in the big game. I put a hand on Rob Jacobson's shoulder and sit him back down.

Then I sit back down myself and lean close to him so I can whisper in his ear. "You lying son of a bitch."

FOURTEEN

"I CAN EXPLAIN," ROB JACOBSON says as I nearly drag him into the attorney room. I grabbed him by the arm the last few feet in the hallway. In the moment, it's not where I'd like to grab him, and then squeeze.

"You told me you didn't know her," I say, getting up in his face the minute I've slammed the door behind us.

I see the guard watching us closely from the other side of the glass, seeing us nose to nose. Like I am about to drop the gloves. I wave him away. Like: *Get out of* my *face*.

"Please let me explain," Jacobson says.

He backs away from me until he has sat down on the other side of the table.

"Can't *wait*."

I sit down myself and carefully place my clenched fists in my lap.

"I was drunk that night," he says.

"That's your defense? To your very own defense attorney? *You're not a college boy!* You were *drunk*? Do you honestly think that's going to get you over on this? You're on trial for a triple homicide. One of them was that kid you were swapping spit with, you dumb bastard."

He holds up his hands, as if to cover up.

"I'm embarrassed that I was even *at* the Talkhouse and *was* enough of a dumb bastard to walk out with her," he says. "And just for the record? She was even drunker than I was."

I keep my hands in my lap and wait for the urge to actually strangle him this time to subside. "Are we referring to the drunk *dead* teenage girl here, Rob? That ought to play really well with the jury. I'll be sure to mention that to them first chance I get."

"I was never with her again after that one night," he says.

"Trust me when I tell you: once was enough."

"I really am sorry for not telling you about it."

"You're sorry. Got it. You're sorry. There's an old legal expression that covers this, Rob. Sorry doesn't fix the goddamn *lamp*." I stare at him across the narrow table. "Ahearn just said there's more. Do you know what he might be talking about, or is he just screwing with me?"

He hesitates briefly. But then shakes his head. "That's all there is," he says. "She finally went back across the street, and I came to my senses enough to go home."

I lean across the table. "You better not be lying to me again."

"I didn't lie to you in the first place," he says. "It's like I said. I just held back something that embarrassed the living shit out of me and hoped would never come up."

"A distinction without a difference."

"Listen," he says, "I understand that you're pissed that you have to wait all weekend to rip into him. But I know that when you do, you're going to kill the guy."

I don't get the chance.

Jimmy Cunniff calls me around noon the next day and says, "We got ourselves a situation."

FIFTEEN

JIMMY CUNNIFF IS STANDING with Kevin Ahearn, end of the dock, Montauk Marine Basin. I see the chief of police from East Hampton, Larry Calabrese, with them. In the water next to them is a trawler with "Nick O' Time" written on the bow in a fancy Old English font.

Nick Morelli's boat.

I know it's his, or used to be his, because Jimmy told me.

"Blood inside the cabin" is Jimmy's greeting to me. "And on the deck. Not a lot. But enough."

"How much is enough?"

"It's like that judge said about porn that time," Jimmy says. "You know it when you see it."

Jimmy likes to get to it. He thinks small talk is for people who need more to do.

"Jane," Larry Calabrese says to me.

"Chief."

A good guy. Good cop. I like him a lot.

Ahearn just nods.

"A perfect shitstorm," Calabrese says.

"What are the odds?" Ahearn says, squinting out at the water. "My star witness."

"Your star witness until I got to cross-examine him," I say.

"Well, counselor. Good luck with that now."

"A disappearing witness could set you up to ask for a mistrial—we both know that."

"Not happening."

"Just wanted to raise the subject."

"You plan to raise it with the judge?"

"Nope."

"Then at least we agree on something."

Ahearn somehow looks out of place here, out of court, in a short-sleeved polo and jeans and even boat shoes.

"And by the way?" Ahearn says to me. "It's like I told you in court. Morelli had more testimony to give, none of it good for you." He points at Morelli's boat now and adds, "Good fortune has goddamn smiled on the defendant in the nick of time."

"Good one," Jimmy says.

"We're not in court, Kevin. You can use his name here."

"Piss off, Jane. You know what I think? I think your guy knew it was only going to get worse for him on Monday and maybe had the money to do something about it."

"*Kill* him?"

Ahearn shrugs. "What's one more?"

"Thanks for sharing, Kevin."

"How about I share that this is all pretty goddamn convenient for you and him."

"Enough!" Chief Larry Calabrese says. "From both of you! Maybe the two of you esteemed lawyers could stop thinking about your goddamn case and think about what appears to be a suspicious and senseless death here. Unless Nick Morelli took his boat out and hit himself in the head and decided to swim to New London to get himself stitched up."

Jimmy tells me the rest of it now. Another fisherman, on his way back in, saw *Nick O' Time* drifting out past Montauk Point a few hours ago, at about the time when a lot of boats that had gone out early were already on their way back in.

"Even if Nick's not coming back in," Jimmy says, "he ain't drifting out there, especially since nobody saw a customer with him when he left the dock."

"Anyway," Calabrese says, "the other fisherman, Ed Fournier, gets as close as he can and starts yelling for Morelli. Nada. Tries to raise him on the radio they still use."

"Good luck with that," I say.

"You know somebody does this for a living?" Calabrese says.

"Knew," I say. "An uncle. My mother's brother. Passed a couple of years ago."

"So you know the cell service is for shit out on the deep blue sea," Calabrese says. "It's one of the last places on Earth where people aren't checking their phones every two minutes."

Ed Fournier is worried now, Calabrese says, and calls the Coast Guard. They come out and find that no one is on board, and there is indeed blood inside the cabin and on the deck. They bring back the boat. The Coast Guard has its search-and-rescue boats out on the water.

"Good luck with that, too," Chief Larry Calabrese says.

Ahearn has walked away. Calabrese sees one of his cops waving at him from Nick Morelli's boat, walks over, climbs aboard. It's just Jimmy Cunniff and me now, all the way at the end of the dock. I look out at the water and think of the way my uncle Sal once described Montauk to me. A small drinking town with a big fishing problem.

I'm almost certain he didn't mean this kind of problem.

"So Ahearn turns out to be right about something," I say. "What are the odds?"

"By the way?" Jimmy says. "I don't care what else Morelli

had to say about our boy. He did enough damage right after they swore him in."

"Maybe it really was only going to get worse for Jacobson."

"You ever have a witness get himself disappeared like this in the middle of a trial?" Jimmy says.

"No. Though I have thought about doing it myself once or twice. I had a good cross planned, for what it's worth."

"I'm sure you did," Jimmy says. "And I planned to grow up and play centerfield for the Yankees."

And just like that, staring out at the deep blue sea, I am thinking about what Sam Wylie told me. What was happening inside me. How long I had. Did it matter that Sam had tried to give me a heads-up about when my time was going to be up? That I'd been given notice? What kind of notice did Nick Morelli get before he went over the side?

I say to Jimmy, "If there's more bad stuff on Jacobson and the dead girl, and it's for real, Jacobson knows, and he's not telling."

"You gonna ask him about that?"

"First thing."

"You know what I think about coincidence," Jimmy says.

We're walking along the dock to the parking lot.

"I do. It's your lifelong belief that coincidence is a monumental load of crap."

On my way back home I call the sheriff's office in Riverhead, tell them who I am, tell them it's urgent that I set up a video call with my client. They say they'll ask the prisoner.

"No," I say. "*Tell* the prisoner."

The rest of the way back to the house I hear myself in Judge Jackson Prentice's courtroom saying that murder trials always come back to one thing.

Motive.

And if Nick Morelli had been about to hurt Rob Jacobson—hurt *us*—even more when he got back on the stand, who had more motive to shut him up than my client?

Maybe, I think, *he's the one who's going to end up dead in the water.*

If he isn't already, that is.

SIXTEEN

THEY ALLOWED ZOOM MEETINGS between lawyers and prisoners during COVID and are still allowing them, now that all these new variants seem to keep showing up and scaring everybody like it's the beginning of the pandemic all over again. Just not scaring me the way it did at the time, not anymore. There's no known vaccine for what is ailing me.

So now here Rob Jacobson is on my laptop screen, trying to act shocked about Nick Morelli. At this point I can't tell whether or not it's another pose from somebody who has been BS'ing people his whole life.

Maybe even me.

"What?" he says when I finish. Going for indignant now. "You think I've got a hit man on speed dial?"

"I don't know, Rob. Do you?"

"You're the one who's such a bear on motive and opportunity," he says. "Where's my motive if I didn't know what Morelli was going to say next?"

"Maybe you did know. And let's face it, he'd said plenty already."

He lets that one go.

Instead he says, "And where's my opportunity from a jail cell?"

I sigh, loudly enough to rattle the windows.

"Rob. You're rich as shit. And look at how easily you hired a hit man like me. Whether you did it or not, you had the means *to* do it."

He shakes his head, as if somehow he's going too fast for me.

"You have this all wrong," he says.

"Do I?"

"I couldn't wait for him to get back on the stand so you could rip him a new one. Why would I do anything to deprive you of the chance to do it and myself of enjoying watching you do it? So I can set myself up to get charged for another murder after I've beaten the rap on this one? Give me some credit."

I let *that* go. I am at my desk in the spare bedroom I use as a home office. Using a MacBook Pro I refuse to trade in, even as old as it is, and even though it's as heavy as a block of concrete compared to the newer, lighter models. I used to joke that I'd die before my laptop did.

It seemed much funnier at the time.

"What else did Nick Morelli know about you and Laurel Gates?" I ask.

He smiles. Of course he has a mouthful of perfect white teeth. But every time he does smile like this, going for the big one, he reminds me of a coyote I ran into one night in the Springs, when I was making another training run on the trail. The coyote showed me his teeth that night, scaring the holy living hell out of me. There was a brief standoff, both of us frozen in place, only one of us scared out of her wits, until he ran off into the woods.

I remember that killer smile now.

"You mean you want me to share the real and intimate details of my relationship with Laurel?" Jacobson says.

I suspect that he's playing. But I don't give him the satisfaction of acting surprised. Just wait.

"Well, guess what? There aren't any intimate details beyond the ones you know already."

"You're certain of that?"

"You have to believe me on this one."

No, Rob. Actually I don't.

"You need to understand something," I say to him. "If you had sex with an underage teenage girl, now deceased, and if Nick Morelli told Kevin Ahearn, you are the one who is screwed. And there is nothing I can do to unscrew you."

"But I didn't," he says.

"And you had nothing to do with Morelli's boat basically coming back without him?"

"We went over this."

"Humor me."

"Hard no on that as well," he says.

"You better be telling me the truth."

"To quote my hotshot attorney, who said anything about the truth?"

He smiles again. Same coyote smile as before until he gets up out of his chair and walks away.

"Zoom meeting has ended," I hear him say in the background.

SEVENTEEN

AHEARN GIVES A SUNDAY-NIGHT interview to Jim Acosta on CNN and tries to be cagey about what Nick Morelli's continued testimony would have been like if he wasn't missing and presumed dead.

"Are you suggesting there was even more of a relationship between Mr. Jacobson and Ms. Gates than the scene outside the Stephen Talkhouse that Mr. Morelli described?" Acosta says.

"You said that, Jim, not me."

"If there was," Acosta says, "is there a way for you to get it into the record?"

Ahearn, who is generally about as subtle as a jackhammer, tries to look coy.

"Jim, it's like I suggested in my opening statement, even if I didn't put it quite this way. Facts are as stubborn as Long Island ticks."

Instead of Nick Morelli, Ahearn's first witness on Monday morning is Officer Liam Murphy, a forensics specialist for the Southampton Police. By then Ahearn and I have met with the judge. As I suspected, he raises the idea of a mistrial because of Nick Morelli's disappearance. Kevin Ahearn tells him what he told me at Montauk, that he doesn't want one.

Neither do I.

I spent a fair amount of time—two separate pretrial inter-views—questioning Murphy about the abundant amount of DNA evidence from Rob Jacobson found at the Gateses' rental house. Like an abundance of riches for the cops and for the district attorney. A treasure chest, all in all.

Too much evidence, I've thought all along.

In too many rooms.

Too pretty a picture.

Ahearn painstakingly has Liam Murphy take the jury through all of it now, as if it's a house tour.

Finally I think they're done, and I'm ready to cross, step right up and ask Officer Liam Murphy if he's ever seen this much trace DNA at any crime scene.

But Ahearn isn't quite done.

He walks back to his table, pulls a photograph and a sheet of paper out of the folder on top of a stack of papers there, walks it past the jury and up to Judge Prentice, who covers his microphone as he and Ahearn have a brief conversation.

I stand up.

"No keeping secrets," I say.

Prentice glares at me. It's already become like a default move for him, like reaching for his gavel just about every time I object.

"Not how we address the court, Ms. Smith. At least not this one."

Ahearn turns to me. "There's no secrets being kept. I'm just about to introduce some new evidence that came into Officer Murphy's possession over the weekend."

But I'm back up.

"Your Honor, whatever this evidence is, I need to see it before we proceed."

Ahearn comes over and hands me the photograph and the piece of paper. The photo is of a BMW SUV, New York plates, parked out in front of what looks very much to me like one of the chop shops across the street from Citi Field, where my Mets play. The piece of paper is the car's registration, for a two-year-old Beemer.

Owned by Rob Jacobson.

My one and only.

I hand the photograph and the registration back to Ahearn.

"Relevance, Your Honor?"

"Mr. Ahearn believes the witness will be able to explain," Prentice says. "I'll allow this."

Ahearn walks back to the witness stand.

"Officer Murphy, could you please explain the circumstances of this car ending up in the possession of the police," Ahearn says.

"I got a call on Saturday morning from R&D Metals, which is a, uh, car warehouse on 126th Street in Queens, across from where the Mets play," Murphy says. "The car had been dropped off there last week by a, uh, anonymous third party, and sold for cash. Apparently transactions like this happen that way all the time. No names. Just money. But before they stripped the car and attempted to sell it for parts, someone at R&D decided to check the VIN and discovered that the car was once owned by the defendant."

"Objection," I say. "This is a fascinating tutorial on chop shops. But what does it possibly have to do with this case?"

"If the court will allow me to continue," Ahearn says, "I believe I can establish the relevance Ms. Smith is seeking."

"Overruled," Prentice says to me. To Ahearn he says, "Continue."

And now I am helpless, and defenseless, knowing that I am

about to learn what the jury is going to learn, in real time. Any lawyer worth anything will tell you the value of discovery, and what a useful tool it can be. Right up until it smacks you upside your head.

"Please explain to the court the findings from your forensic analysis after the car was towed out to Southampton," Ahearn says.

I'm watching Murphy. Some cops like having a spotlight on them. Some, but not all. Murphy isn't one of them. He looks like he wants this to be over.

"Well, we found a lot," Murphy says, "fingerprints and such, even though there was no way for us to know how long the automobile *hadn't* been in the defendant's possession."

"It was stolen two years ago," Jacobson whispers.

I write this down on my legal pad. "Shut up. *Now.*"

"Were you able to identify *any* of the fingerprints?" Ahearn asks Officer Murphy.

"Yes, sir, we were."

Crew cut. Square jaw. Pale blue eyes. Central casting for today's role of honest, earnest cop. Serving and protecting.

"And can you please tell the court who they belonged to?"

"The defendant," Murphy says, "which was no surprise because it was his car."

"And who else?"

"Laurel Gates," Officer Liam Murphy says.

I'm out of my chair and objecting, not even sure what I'm about to object *to*. But before I do Ahearn quickly asks, "And where did you find Miss Gates's fingerprints?"

"In the back seat," Murphy says. "In places that would indicate she was lying down back there."

"You had an objection, Ms. Smith?" Judge Prentice says.

"I'd like to approach, Your Honor."

He waves me forward. Ahearn is in lockstep with me as I head up there.

"I don't even know where to begin."

Prentice covers the microphone again. "Try."

"This is bullshit," I say, right before Prentice reaches for his gavel, overruling my objection, and Kevin Ahearn says there is one more piece of evidence he'd liked to enter into the record.

EIGHTEEN

OFFICER MURPHY IS GETTING to the good parts now. Because the evidence is a pair of panties.

Which he testifies are Laurel Gates's panties.

Pink.

Such a joy.

"Your expert and scientific opinion is that these panties did in fact belong to Miss Gates," Ahearn says.

As if he doesn't know.

It's actually a low-rise thong, in the plastic baggie that he's proudly just held aloft as if carrying the Olympic torch. The kind of lingerie that I occasionally look at but never buy. Just in case I might be the one caught dead in them someday.

"Miss Gates purchased a similar pair at Bonne Nuit in East Hampton, two years ago this Fourth of July," says Officer Murphy, as eager to please as ever. "But that wouldn't be enough for me to reach this conclusion, of course."

Of course not.

"The more important piece, if you can call it that, is some hair belonging to Miss Gates that we found in these panties."

"Convenient," I say.

"Was that an objection from you, Ms. Smith?" Ahearn says.

"More of an observation," I say. Then add, "Withdrawn."

Ahearn turns back to Officer Murphy. "Where did you find Miss Gates's undergarment?"

Oh, go ahead, I think. *Call it a thong, you dirty boy.*

"Wedged into the space between the seat back and the seat," Murphy says.

Ahearn says he has no further questions but reserves the right to redirect.

I walk toward Officer Murphy, who's been having such a nice day. But that's about to change.

"So you found this particular article of clothing in the place where people, oh, I don't know, sometimes find loose change in the back seat?"

"I suppose," Murphy says.

"But stuffed in there pretty tight. Am I right?"

"You could say," Murphy says, as if wondering where I'm going with this.

"Did you spot them because of their hot-pink color," I say, "or did you go looking for them?"

"I noticed a tiny bit of them, I guess you could say. And the color was, is, quite noticeable."

"But wedged in there pretty good."

"I think I already testified to that."

I go back to my table and sit on the end of it and cross my arms.

"Let me ask you something, Officer Murphy. Clearly the inference from both you and Mr. Ahearn, because of where Miss Gates's panties were discovered and because her fingerprints were where you said they were, that an act of, shall we say, sexual congress must have occurred between Mr. Jacobson, it being his car and all, and Miss Gates."

"I didn't say that. Neither did Mr. Ahearn, as I recall."

I ignore Murphy.

I smile.

"You ever do it in the back seat of a car, Officer?"

Ahearn bellows an objection and Prentice gavels me into silence and informs me once again that if I don't watch my language, I am on the road to a contempt citation.

"Let me ask this another way," I say to Murphy. "Is the jury supposed to believe that in a moment of unbridled passion"—I give a quick look at Jackson Prentice III and shrug helplessly— "this young woman took the time to hide her panties? For what, Officer? To recycle them later like a water bottle? Or just save them for a rainy day?"

"I'm not sure what you're asking me," Murphy says.

"Sure you do. Unless I'm alone in thinking they were planted."

"Is there a question there, Your Honor?" Ahearn says.

"I think I've already got my answer."

I'm not done with Officer Liam Murphy.

Before I am, we have taken a chain-of-custody trip together, and I've had him explain—reluctantly, I feel—just how many people could have had access to Laurel Gates's body once it was discovered the night of the murders, all the way to the morgue in Riverhead.

Along the way, I establish how easy it is, using a methodology known as dusting, for someone who knows what they're doing, to transfer fingerprints, or plant them, using powder that sticks to the oil on the tips of our fingers. I do it as quickly, and plainly, as possible, knowing how even the most thoughtful and dedicated jury members find their eyes glazing over when the subject is science.

But I am generally making the planting of prints sound as easy as taking a cookie out of a jar.

"As a forensics expert," Murphy says, almost proudly, "I can tell you it's not as easy as you're trying to make it sound."

I smile again, as if it's suddenly Christmas morning.

"As someone with a bachelor's degree in forensic science," I say, "I can tell you with great certainty that it *is* in fact that easy."

My degree is actually in criminal justice. Minor in forensics. But that's for me to know and them to find out. I'm not the one under oath here.

"One last thing. As the first one on the scene the night of the murders, were *you* ever alone with the body of Laurel Gates?"

"What are you implying?" he says.

I am so happy in the moment I want to kiss him. Just because of how defensive he sounds.

"Why, I'm not implying anything, Officer. I'm just asking a question."

"Well, yes, I was," he says. "But not long enough..."

He sounds defensive for a second time, like he's trying to clean something up. He realizes how he sounds. And the jury knows what it just heard.

I step in closer to him as a way of cutting him off.

"Long enough for what?"

"Objection," Ahearn says and Prentice sustains it.

"Withdrawn. Just one more question, Officer Murphy. From the time you did show up at the house that night along with other responding officers and right up until this moment, haven't there been enough Southampton policemen with access to the body of Laurel Gates to form a conga line?"

Ahearn bellows an objection. I withdraw one last question.

But this time I've gotten the last word in right before five o'clock, sharp.

When I sit back down, Jimmy Cunniff is where he's been all day, in the first row.

I motion him to lean forward.

"You know what we weren't talking about there at the end?" I whisper to him. "Women's underwear."

Jimmy grins and whispers back.

"Like Ahearn lost *his* panties just now."

NINETEEN

Jimmy

THE GUY JACOBSON IS a complete mutt.

Doesn't mean that he did it. Jimmy hopes he didn't, because he knows how much it will kill Jane if he did. She can always give you all the predictable lawyer BS about everybody deserving the best possible defense—usually meaning her—whether they committed the crime in question or not.

But with all her heart, and this girl has some heart, she doesn't want Jacobson to have done it.

Neither one of them do, because who wants to throw down with somebody who could have done something like this? But Jane takes these things more personal. Jane's the best there is, but she always wants to believe that she's *better* than someone who could get off a mutt that actually did it.

Whatever *it* happens to be.

Especially this Jacobson.

Like after the old tight-ass judge called it a day, before Jacobson would go back to his cell, Jimmy and Jane alone with him in the hallway, Jacobson trying to explain away not telling her about the stolen car, not thinking it mattered in the whole grand scheme of things, even if it was stolen right around the time of the murder.

More crap coincidence, Jimmy was thinking as he listened to the guy go on and on.

And on.

"It's just more of the setup," Jacobson finally said to Jane, as if Jimmy were not even there.

Jimmy couldn't listen any longer or sit this out.

"Gotta say, somebody must hate you a whole hell of a lot to go to this much trouble on a frame this elaborate."

Jacobson cocked his head to the side, a curious look on his face, as if surprised that Jimmy were even there.

"People hate me for who I am and what I have," Jacobson said. Giving Jimmy one of his big-guy smiles. Lots of teeth Jimmy once again wanted to knock down his throat. "I mean, even you hate me, don't you, Jimmy?"

"All due respect?" It always makes him want to laugh even when he's the one saying those words, knowing nothing good ever comes after them. "You're not important enough *to* me to hate."

"But you absolutely love the money I'm paying you and Jane, don't you?"

"With or without your pants on?" Jimmy said, and left the two of them there.

For the time being, Jimmy has done as much as he can do for Jane on the Jacobson case. Maybe tomorrow she'll want him to try to find out how the BMW got to the chop shop, even knowing that there is about as much bookkeeping at places like that as there is with drug deals.

It's the new case that has the old cop in Jimmy jazzed and running hot.

He remembers the feeling, and likes it, especially now that Gregg McCall is on the phone, telling him to get to Mineola ASAP, that they might have a suspect who might be good for the Carson murders. It's an ex-con, name of Artie Shore. After he served out his last sentence, aggravated assault, at Green Haven, he went back to work for his old friend Bobby Salvatore.

"With whom Hank Carson was in over his head."

"Like the deep end of the pool and he didn't know how to swim."

"It would have been helpful if your cops had found all this out a long time ago," Jimmy says. "But you already know that."

"It's like I told Jane: my guys didn't dig deep enough at the time," McCall says. "Carson managed to do a good job keeping his head down with his friends and neighbors about his gambling, so they just Keystone Copped their way into the narrative that the Carsons walked into a burglary in progress and whoever it was they walked in on lost his shit and shot them all."

McCall tells Jimmy they will have picked up Shore by the time Jimmy gets to Mineola. It's because, McCall says, a witness has come forward who suddenly remembered, all this time later, having seen Shore come out of the Carson home on Kildare Road the day before Hank Carson was taped up in the ER at Winthrop-University Hospital of Mineola for three broken ribs.

"Can I sit in when you talk to the guy?" Jimmy asks McCall. "Shore, I mean."

"You can't sit in," McCall says. "But you can sit on the other side of the window."

By now Jimmy is heading for the LIE, stepping on it.

"Guys like Salvatore, it's always the same," he said to McCall. "And for the guys working for them. If they kill you, they never get their money. So if it's Bobby Salvatore who had this done, there might be something more than a gambling debt going on here. Unless the debt was worse than we even know."

"We'll talk about it when you get here."

McCall calls him again as Jimmy is finally getting on the Meadowbrook Parkway.

"There's a problem."

"Shore did a runner?"

"I wish."

"You say a problem," Jimmy says. "How big a problem?"

He has a bad feeling about where this is going.

"Shore's not dead, is he?"

"Well, not yet."

TWENTY

AS SOON AS I get home from court, I decide to take a trail walk in the Springs.

Not a run tonight. No gun and no shooting, even if I am feeling an urge to shoot *something*.

Just a long walk on my private trail.

The temperature has dropped again, so I throw on my old maroon BC hoodie. My plan is to park the car, walk to the end of the long dirt road and back. Alone with my thoughts about my life, Jimmy on his way to see McCall.

What's left of my life, anyway.

And, I think, isn't that the almighty everlasting bitch of it all? Right now, this moment, I'm as big as I've ever been, at least professionally. Looking at a huge payday from Rob Jacobson, win, lose, or appeal. The payday for the Carson case won't be as big, I know. If I solve it, though? If Jimmy and I find out who did it and nearly got away with it? My profile goes sky-high, like I launched a rocket in the backyard.

But there's a problem with that, one that existed for me, and deeply, even before my visit to the office of Dr. Samantha Wylie:

The thought that my guy did it makes me feel as if there's more damage inside me.

Not to my neck and head.

To my goddamn heart.

Like a spear has gone through it—direct hit, right through me and out the back.

It's not just the suspicion that the bastard did it.

No, it's something even worse.

It's the fear he might get away with it.

Because of me.

Because I get him off.

You want the whole truth and nothing but?

There it is.

It's something else killing me.

Literally.

I've been thinking a lot about what I do for a living, who I am—defense lawyer—even before I took this case. Feeling as if there are too many times, *way* too many times, when I feel like I'm the one *really* playing defense. Precisely because of what I do and who I am. As complicated as the job can be, it all comes down to this simple fact, and no matter how noble we all tell ourselves we are:

Defense lawyers are scum buckets.

We are scum buckets as a class, even though "class" is hardly a word the rest of the world generally uses in reference to us. We defend people the world has already decided are criminals and get looked at as criminals ourselves.

Often with good reason.

Barry Slotnick. Remember him? He went, what, eleven years without losing a case? He defended everybody from Joe Columbo, all the way to the Supreme Court, to the subway shooter, Bernhard Goetz. F. Lee Bailey helped O.J. get off and Dr. Sam Sheppard, even if he didn't do nearly as well with a Jersey doctor, Carl Coppolino, accused of poisoning his wife to death.

I met Bailey a few times. Had drinks with him once. He told me there was a point in the Coppolino case when the good doctor said, "Lee, I didn't kill my wife."

And Bailey said, "But let's face it, Carl, you didn't do very much to keep her alive."

I didn't do it.

And guess what?

Sometimes they're telling the truth.

Just not always.

Anne Bremner. Maybe you've seen her on television. She defended Michael Jackson, and Amanda Knox. Never lost a civil case in her life.

I've never lost a case. Me. Jane Smith.

Civil or otherwise.

And yet there's still something wrong with this picture. Not the whole picture. Just too much of it. Because there is always the chance that we're all using our not insubstantial skills to set a guilty person free.

I walk my private trail in the Springs and think these thoughts in the gathering darkness. What if my client really did kill three innocent people? By all accounts, it was a very nice family, even if the daughter was a bit of a wild child. What if he did take out the whole family?

What about *that*?

So why did I take the Jacobson case? The obvious reason is because that *is* our justice system. That's the way it works. Everybody's entitled to a defense. And even though it can make me sick sometimes along with just about everybody else, the system actually works most of the time.

And I do stand to make a boatload of money, and sorry for the boat reference, Nick Morelli. The stage does happen to be enormous. On top of that, the attention this is bringing to me is even more enormous. Even if I lose the case and Jacobson is convicted, my career will have changed forever. What do they talk about in the mob? Made men? I'm a made *woman* already just being in play with Rob Jacobson.

But when I add it all up, looking at it from all possible angles, something I'm doing on practically an hourly basis, I know it comes down to this:

Because the case against him is just too perfect.

The evidence against him, evidence that keeps coming in, is just too frickin' perfect. I've looked at it from every possible angle. So has Jimmy Cunniff, who'd be skeptical about the cards in his hand even if dealt a full house in poker.

And it's even more than that.

The question I can't get out of my head, the question that Jimmy can't get out of his head even though he'd like to drop a safe on Rob Jacobson, is this:

Why?

Why would he kill those three people? Why would he kill a teenage girl even if he was drunk enough and stupid enough to practically be making out with her in the middle of Main Street and might have had sex with her in the back seat of one of his cars even though he swears he didn't?

Makes no sense.

By now I'm at the end of the trail. Time to start heading back.

I walk up to the tree with my target on it, am looking proudly at all the small holes in the bull's-eye and around it, when the first bullet hits the tree above me.

Definitely not a BB.

TWENTY-ONE

Jimmy

IT'S A SCENE JIMMY CUNNIFF knows well from his cop days, one that TV productions and the movies never get quite right. Police cars, flashing lights, roped-off lookie-loos, one rooftop sniper.

Here, outside the Eagle Rock Apartments, Jimmy spots McCall. Next to him is a tall, thin Black cop standing ramrod straight and holding a phone.

Jimmy knows the drill. One voice. The crisis negotiator's. And everybody else get the hell out of the way or else.

On the line is Artie Shore, who has barricaded himself in his fifth-floor apartment and is threatening to blow his brains out if anybody tries to get inside.

Not the movies or TV now.

Real life, Jimmy thinks.

And hopefully not death.

McCall introduces Captain Jonah Johnson. Nassau County Mobile Crisis Team. He's the point man.

Johnson puts Shore on speaker.

"I'm not going back to prison. Not happening."

"Nobody said anything about prison, Artie," Johnson says. "Mr. McCall here just wants to ask you some questions is all.

So why don't you just toss your gun right out that window and come out here and we'll all have a talk."

Before Johnson can respond, Shore adds, *"They didn't think they'd ever get caught, and now they just need somebody to take the fall."*

Who's they? Jimmy thinks.

But it's not his show.

The clock is already running down. The longer it takes, the better the chance everything turns to shit.

"We need to talk, you and me," Johnson says to Shore, "but not like this."

Then Shore ends the call.

McCall pulls Jimmy aside, keeping his voice low.

"The longer this goes, the more likely it is that we're looking at a very bad outcome," McCall says.

"Well aware," Jimmy says.

He keeps picturing a clock running down, like it's the end of a game. Only this is as far from a game as you can get.

Jimmy feels as helpless as anybody out here. All he can do is watch it play out. And hope they can get Shore back on the phone.

McCall walks Jimmy halfway up the block, tells him that it's not just the visit Shore paid to the Carson home that turned Shore into a person of interest. Hank Carson and Shore had also been seen arguing at the Cornerstone Bar on Jericho Turnpike a week before the Carson murders. The bartender had finally come forward, saying that he couldn't keep quiet any longer even though he knew who Artie Shore worked for and the risk of getting sideways with Bobby Salvatore.

"Then somebody shoots up the Carson family not long after."

"Too neat?" McCall says.

"You know what they say about things that look like they're too good to be true."

Jonah Johnson keeps trying to get Artie Shore back on the phone, without success. He says he's not going to wait much longer before going in.

Jimmy thinks: *You should be in there already.*

Nobody pays any attention to him, everybody staring at Artie's window, as he walks away from McCall, all the way up the block in the other direction, cuts across some backyards until he finds his way to Artie Shore's building, an unlocked back door.

He heads up the stairs, taking them two at a time.

Racing that clock he sees moving down toward triple zeros.

I know how to do this.

Let me talk to the guy.

He is about to knock on the door when he hears a single shot and knows he made his move too goddamn late.

TWENTY-TWO

MY OWN GUN, my trusty Glock 26, is locked safely in the glove compartment of the car, not that it would do me much good right now, not up against what I'm sure is a long gun.

I'm a gun girl. I know the sound, as I dive to the ground after the first shot and get behind the tree right before the second shot hits, shattering my target.

Then another shot, this one from a different angle, the bullet hitting the side of the tree.

I mean, whoever it is has moved. Or is moving in.

I scrabble into the bushes now, as another bullet scatters rock and dirt about six feet away from me, maybe less.

If he wants to hit me, he would have hit me already, I tell myself. It is, in the moment, the most optimistic way of looking at things, because the alternative is that he wants to frighten the hell of out me first but really is closing in, in which case I am very much a dead duck.

So duck, girl.

I get up and launch myself deeper into the bushes, branches slapping against my face, feeling as if I've been cut. Least of my problems.

I crouch where I am and yell, "If you're trying to scare me, mission accomplished."

Nothing.

Just some distant birdsong in the night, and the roar of cicadas, almost as loud as my own breathing sounds to me.

I think: *Even if somebody has heard the shots, they probably think it's the BB gun—mine—they hear all the time.*

I find another tree and lean back against it, trying to catch my breath and think, just as another shot hits the tree solidly enough that I feel the impact.

"What the hell do you want?"

Nothing.

I know I have no great options. I can run for the woods to my right, but to get there, I have to run through a clearing of at least fifty yards under the bright goodnight moon.

No gun. No phone.

Is he waiting me out, or am I waiting him out?

In the end it doesn't matter, because he's the one with the gun, and I'm the one being shot at. It's why I've never thought hunting is a sport, or much of a fair fight, because only the hunter has a gun.

I can't stay here all night—I know that.

Either he's still here or he's gone, having accomplished his mission of scaring the shit out of me. I crouch where I am and think, *You're going to die anyway.*

I just don't want to die tonight.

I told Jimmy Cunniff one time that I could find my way out of these woods blindfolded. I'm not blindfolded now, because of the light of the moon. Like I've got some compass in me, I work my way south, and east.

No more shooting.

Just all the night sounds, sounding even louder than before, especially the cicadas, covering the sound of me making my way slowly through the woods.

I don't know how long it takes me to get back to the small parking lot. It feels as if it might have taken an hour.

Who is he?

Or, on a more optimistic note, who was he?

I know I've pissed off a lot of people in my career. This is the first time that somebody has started shooting at me. Whether they wanted to miss me or not.

The shooter, I know, could be almost anybody in town who wants to see Rob Jacobson go down for this, and that includes even the rich people breathing the same air as him.

By the time I get to the car, my breathing has returned to normal. The first thing I do is reach into the glove compartment for the Glock. The feel of it in my hand, the heft of it, is suddenly quite comforting.

As I come around the front of the car, I see the note pinned between one of the wipers and the windshield.

> now you know
> putting cops on trial to
> save a killer's ass could
> get YOU killed.

Underneath:

> he did it, bitch.

I stand there looking at the note and think that maybe I am a gold-plated scum bucket after all.

He *did* do it, didn't he?

TWENTY-THREE

TUESDAY, SECOND WEEK OF the trial, Ahearn's first witness is Gus Hennessy.

Hennessy owns a real estate company on the East End, this part of the world where they somehow keep finding new potato fields to sell off, as if the rows between those spuds are still paved with gold—the same high-end properties that Rob Jacobson once represented.

Hennessy and Jacobson are longtime friends. As members of the ultra-exclusive Maidstone Country Club, golf partners, guests at the same parties, boldface-name guys in the same gossip columns and in *Hamptons* magazine, they, along with their wives, feel like kings and queens of the world.

When I finished my pretrial interview of Hennessy, I asked him why he thought he was being called as a witness for the prosecution.

"Counselor, I can't lie to you."

"You sell real estate, Gus. Force yourself."

He grinned. "Your guess as to why the guy is calling me is as good as mine."

"You've got nothing that can hurt him?"

"Only a better golf game and even better listings most of the time."

Ahearn begins by taking Hennessy through his friendship with Jacobson. Hennessy even uses the line about his golf game. I'm listening but wondering where Ahearn is actually going with this.

Finally, almost offhandedly, Ahearn asks Hennessy if he is aware, knowing Rob Jacobson as well as he clearly does, of any prior relationship between the defendant and Mitch Gates before the night of the murders.

"Well," Hennessy says, "I did see them together the one time on the beach, having a big argument."

Wait . . . *what*?

I casually shift in my seat so I can shoot a quick look at my client. But he's staring straight ahead at Gus Hennessy. His buddy, in what sounded like a buddy movie just a few minutes ago.

I asked Hennessy the same pretrial question, almost word for word. About a prior relationship. He said no, they'd never met as far as he could recall. Now he's changing a story that only he and I know *was* his story with me. But why? And why now? How does changing his story help him? Because it sure as hell doesn't help my client.

I suddenly remember an old line I read once about the boxing promoter Bob Arum, after Arum had been caught in some lie.

"*Yesterday* I was lying," Arum said. "Today I'm telling the truth."

I knew I could work Hennessy over on cross. But there is nothing much I can do for the moment, which is not making me a happy girl.

"It was about a week before the shootings," he says. It's like he's trying to look anywhere in the room except at our table. "It was the beach behind our house in Amagansett. My wife and I are lucky to live on the water."

Good for them.

"Go on," Ahearn says.

"It was early evening," Hennessy says. "I'm on my deck when I suddenly hear loud voices. And when I look down the beach, I see that it's Rob and Mitch Gates."

Jacobson leans over and whispers to me, "This never happened."

I ignore him, my focus on Gus Hennessy now, knowing nothing good can come of this.

And does not.

"I hate to say this about a friend of mine," Hennessy says.

Now he looks over at our table, and shrugs, almost apologetically.

"But they were going at each other pretty hard," he continues, "right up until Rob said that if he, meaning Mitch, didn't back off, he was going to kill him."

My client is up and out of his seat before I can stop him.

"That is a goddamn lie and you know it, Gus!"

Judge Jackson Prentice III's voice is even louder in the moment.

"Sit down, Mr. Jacobson! Now."

To me, Prentice says, "Please control your client, Ms. Smith."

I think about asking for a recess. But when Ahearn resumes his questioning, Hennessy has to admit that even though he heard Jacobson threaten to kill Mitch Gates, he wasn't able to hear what came next. So I don't want to wait, *can't* wait—I want my shot at Hennessy as soon as Ahearn sits down.

And I don't want the jury to get the idea that I somehow need to regroup. Not my style. *Never* been my style.

As soon as Ahearn says he has no further questions at this time, I turn to Jimmy Cunniff in the front row, tell him what I need. He nods and walks out of the room.

I start walking toward Gus Hennessy.

When I get to him, I lean at the corner of the witness stand, almost awkwardly close to him, elbow near his microphone. I'm up on him, and in his space, and we both know it.

"That must have been some scene," I say, "your best friend and Mitch Gates going at each other that way."

"Well," Hennessy says, "Rob's not my *best* friend."

I smile at him, then at the jury. "I can tell."

"Objection!" Ahearn says.

"Withdrawn."

Then I ask Hennessy how far he thinks it is from his back deck to the beach.

"I'm not sure I know, I mean, down to the exact yardage."

I want to kiss him but am sure Ahearn would object to that, too.

"Of course you do, Mr. Hennessy," I say. "You're a big deal in the real estate business from here to the Memory Motel in Montauk. You didn't build your house. I checked when I vetted you out. You bought it. So you know exactly how far it is to the dunes, and then the water after that. And if you were to turn around and sell it, you'd pace the distance off yourself just to refresh your memory. So let me repeat: how far is it from your deck, and that view that you and your wife love the way you do, to the beach?"

He shifts slightly away from me in his seat, as if to create as much space between us as possible. But I'm already moving away from him now, to the middle of the room, facing the jury.

"How far?" I say again.

"Maybe fifty yards, more or less."

"More, actually."

"You have no way of knowing that . . ."

Now I really do want to kiss him. On the lips.

"Sure, I do. I'm a local, Mr. Hennessy. I walk that beach, the one that goes past your house, all the time. And if we all went over there now, we'd surely discover that it's closer to seventy-five yards."

I'm making it up. I do walk that part of the beach a lot but have no idea which house belongs to Gus Hennessy. But he doesn't know that and neither does the jury. And I sound so sincere it's as if I'm trying to sell him some oceanfront property now, instead of a line of total BS.

"Seriously. I'd have to check."

"No need. Was my client facing you as they were having this argument, or was Mitch Gates?"

"Mitch was facing me. Rob was facing the water."

"Shouting at the ocean, so to speak," I say.

"Objection."

"Sustained," Judge Prentice says. "Let's confine ourselves to asking questions, Ms. Smith. Would that be all right with you?"

"It would, Your Honor."

Then I'm back at Hennessy. "High tide or low tide?" I look over at Jimmy Cunniff, who is back in his seat, giving me a thumbs-up. I've never needed a second chair because I usually have Jimmy sitting not far behind me.

"I don't remember," Hennessy says.

"It was high tide. My assistant checked the tide tables while we've been having this conversation. And we both know, living near the water—though I don't live as close as you do, of course—how loud the Atlantic can get at high tide. Don't we?"

"To me the ocean is always loud," Hennessy says.

"But somehow not too loud for you to overhear words said seventy-five yards away. Isn't that right?"

Before Hennessy can answer, I say, "You ever ask my client about this argument?"

"It sounded awfully personal, like something between him and Mitch that I didn't want to get involved in."

"In all your years of close friendship with my client," I say, "did you ever hear him threaten to kill anybody else?"

"No."

"People can go their whole lives without threatening to kill somebody. Wouldn't you agree, Mr. Hennessy?"

"Yes."

"Did my client sound like he meant it?"

"I hate to say this. But in my opinion, he did."

"And you decided to come forward as a way of being a good citizen. Is that right?"

"I guess you could say that."

"So *I* guess I have only a couple of more questions, then. The first is this: why did you lie to me in your pretrial interview about having no knowledge of a prior relationship between Rob Jacobson and Mitch Gates?"

"Maybe I misunderstood what you meant about a relationship."

"Sure you did."

I turn away from Gus Hennessy now, walk past my client, all the way to the double doors at the end of the courtroom. I'm facing the door when I ask Gus Hennessy, "What took you so freaking long to remember that scene on the beach?"

Hennessy says, "I'm sorry, I didn't hear the entire question."

"I asked, what took you so long, Mr. Hennessy?"

And before he can answer this time, I raise my voice and say, "Lucky for me, since you couldn't hear me from the other side of the room with my back turned, that I didn't just threaten to kill somebody."

Ahearn objects, Prentice sustains, I tell him I'm done with this witness and sit down as Prentice tells everybody we're about to adjourn for lunch.

As I'm putting my papers back into my bag, Rob Jacobson says, "I swear to you, that never happened."

I smile at him now.

"I believe you," I say.

TWENTY-FOUR

AFTER DINNER AT HOME I decide to take a ride over to where the Jacobsons live in Sagaponack.

They live close to, but not on, the water, so I park my car at the big house on Gibson Lane so that I can take a beach walk before I drop in on Claire Jacobson, unannounced. I assume she's there, because there are plenty of lights on when I drive by the house. And I see her Blue Bentley in the driveway.

By now I know that they have two grown children. The daughter is at some culinary institute in Paris and has made it clear to her father that she would travel to the moon to keep herself away from his trial. The son, Eric, is looking for the perfect wave in the Federated States of Micronesia, last I heard.

I also know that Claire hates surprises as much as I do. So the certainty that I will piss her off by dropping in on her this way has already made the twenty-minute drive over here well worth it, and sustains me on an exceptionally long beach walk, the first half into a strong wind coming off the ocean from the west.

At the start of it I pass the house that once belonged to Billy Joel, until he decided that the Atlantic was getting closer to it every year.

Only the good die young.

Walking on the beach this way, at night, usually fills me with a sense of calm. Even peace, as rare as that is for me. Just not tonight, not while I'm carrying a gun in the side pocket of my leather bomber jacket, after what happened to me in the Springs. If somebody has followed me to the beach tonight and starts shooting, this time I'm shooting back.

But I don't spot another soul out here, coming or going.

I just pray a little bit, not a strong suit since Catholic grade school. I know I'm sick. Got the pictures to prove it. But I don't feel sick, which is the unholy bitch of it all. In a lot of ways—most ways, maybe—I feel as if I'm in the best shape of my life, and that includes professionally.

A lot of good it does me.

There was a message from Sam Wylie on my cell as I was getting into the car, one she must have left while I was in the shower. When I called her back, she said that we needed to get together and discuss treatment options.

"For what?" I said into the phone.

"Jane, does everything have to be hard with you?"

I asked her if that was a rhetorical question and lied and told her I'd call her tomorrow.

Seriously? Treatment options for what? To buy myself a couple of extra months? When I *am* feeling sick and the treatments will just make me feel sicker?

I shake my head now and lean more into the wind.

The things you think about it when it's you alone on a beach in the night.

I grin.

Low tide now.

Not even loud at all, underneath the wind.

I nearly walk all the way to Ocean Road Beach before I turn around, ready to go talk to Claire Jacobson, knowing what I want to ask her to her face. Wanting to ask her why she thinks Gus Hennessy, who swears under oath that Rob Jacobson is his friend, would go this far out of his lane to run him over with a story on which he could have given me a heads-up months ago.

Yeah, I think.

What *did* take him so freaking long?

Now he wants to kill his so-called friend.

He tried to tell Ahearn on redirect, as Ahearn tried to clean up the hot mess I'd made for him, that he'd kept silent about the scene on the beach between Jacobson and Mitch Gates for as long as he had out of loyalty to his friend. But that he just couldn't have lived with himself if he'd kept silent any longer.

He owed it to the victims, he said.

And he did sound to me about as sincere as any salesman ever did.

But selling what?

That's what I want to know.

And selling out a friend this way . . . *why?*

I am passing some hedges on the east side of Gibson Lane and about to turn up their long driveway when I see a classic little cream-colored Fiat convertible pull into it.

Top down, so I can clearly see who's behind the wheel.

"Didn't see *that* coming," I say, slipping back behind the wheel of my own car.

So I decide to stick around. Nine o'clock by now. I stay until two in the morning.

The Fiat is still there. All the lights in the house are off.

This time I don't sleep in my car. I drive home, thinking about things that might be going bump in the night.

Literally.

TWENTY-FIVE

Jimmy

JIMMY IS CERTAIN IT was a cop, and a local, who took those potshots at Jane. Certain that the codes of the blue brotherhood have come into play here, as though Jane took a shot at one of them, instead of just roughing up one of them on the witness stand.

Jimmy doesn't know all the cops on the East Hampton force. But a lot of them drink in his bar. Because Jimmy Cunniff, ex-NYPD, owns the place, they consider it a cop bar. And they'd rather drink in his town than their own, especially when they'll get at least one on the house when they come in, and sometimes more than that.

Tonight three of them are sitting around a table when he gets back from a fast meeting with McCall. The best McCall can do on the call that came in on Artie Shore's landline is that it was placed by a burner. All he has. All anybody has. Somebody said something to the poor bastard and he took himself out.

I should have tried to get up there sooner. Jimmy thinks: *It isn't just ballplayers who lose a step.*

Now he's back at his usual seat at the end of the bar, watching the three cops at the table across the room. Two of them Jimmy recognizes from the local Sag Harbor PD. But the other one, Jimmy knows, is from East Hampton. Big guy in his thirties, maybe early forties. An ex-Marine, Jimmy knows, because the guy told him one time. Mike Rousselle is his name. A hardo all the way. One of the bartenders told Jimmy that Rousselle was in the night before, mouthing off enough for everybody in the place to hear him, like he wanted them to hear, wanted them to wonder how Jimmy Cunniff's friend Jane could live with herself defending a dirtbag like Rob Jacobson.

Even managed to get a laugh out of the old joke, according to the bartender. "You know what one dead lawyer is?" Rousselle said. "A start."

Another cop at the table says something now. They all laugh. Maybe Rousselle laughs the hardest. Funny guy. Does that mean he *is* the one who shot at Jane? Jimmy is too good a cop to go anywhere near that. But does Jimmy Cunniff think it was a cop?

No, he doesn't just think.

He's sure of it.

Jane originally thought it was a long gun. Jimmy found out differently. He went out to the trail and hunted around and is convinced now that it was a Glock 17, 9mm—more than enough gun to do the job for a skilled shooter. Most police departments follow the FBI's recent determination that the 9mm makes the best service weapon because it has less recoil. And Jimmy, after Jane described where her last target was, pulled a Speer Gold Dot 9mm round out of the tree with not much work. The most common duty bullet that police departments buy. And what Jimmy himself still uses. Too expensive, and not common, for most people.

But not cops.

Could somebody like this loudmouth Rousselle have been

arrogant enough or dumb enough to use his service weapon? Doubtful. But could he have an identical backup?

Hundred percent.

Jimmy alternates between watching the Yankees play the Angels in Anaheim on one of the two TV sets above the bar. But he makes a point of staring at Rousselle every chance he gets. It's him. Jimmy *knows*. Sometimes you do. He did gang work when he started with the cops. The Westies. He would walk up to a bunch of them in Hell's Kitchen, sometimes with backup, sometimes not, and know instantly who the one was *not* to take his eyes off.

"To blue lives," Rousselle says at one point, and they all raise their mugs.

Jimmy is looking directly at him again. Now Rousselle pushes his chair back, gets up, walks over to him.

"There a problem, Cunniff?"

Tight polo shirt. Ripped. Him, not the shirt. A bodybuilder. Tats up and down both arms.

"Only because I'm watching the Yankees bullpen blow another one."

"Looks like you're spending more time watching me than the game," Rousselle says.

"Sounds to me like you're the one with the problem," Jimmy says.

"You know what I *really* got a problem with? Somebody trying to lawyer a scumbag like Rob Jacobson out of a triple homicide everybody knows he's good for. Because in my book, that makes the lawyer a scumbag, too."

"A lawyer worth shooting at?"

"What's that mean?"

"Somebody who knew what they were doing took some shots at my boss the other night in the Springs," Jimmy says.

"She get hit?"

"Just missed."

"Pity," Rousselle says.

Now they're eyeballing each other, hard.

Rousselle says, "You're saying it was me?"

He's gotten maybe a step closer. Jimmy's still on his stool.

"I wouldn't make you for a back shooter." Jimmy grins up at him. "But people are always surprising you."

It has now gotten quiet in the bar, quiet enough that the play-by-play from the set closest to Jimmy is suddenly audible to everybody in the room.

Jimmy stands. Rousselle is bigger and outweighs him. These discrepancies never bothered Jimmy Cunniff, even in the ring.

"You wanna go?" Rousselle says.

"Isn't your job keeping the peace?"

"Maybe not tonight, it's not."

One of the Sag Harbor cops comes over now and says, "Hey, guys. Come on." And walks Rousselle back to the table.

A half hour later, Rousselle leaves first, walks up Division Street, finally makes the turn into the small parking lot for Jack's Stir Brew Coffee across from the Sag Harbor station.

He's pulling his keys out of the pocket of his jeans when Jimmy shoves him hard into the side of his car, grabbing Rousselle's right arm as he does, pulling it behind him as Jimmy throws a hard, short left hook into his ribs, knowing where to hit him, feeling the air come out of Rousselle as he starts to slide down the car, but doesn't.

When Rousselle gathers himself and turns around, raising his own right fist, Jimmy steps underneath it and this time tries to put another left hook all the way through Rousselle's stomach, and sits him down.

When Rousselle can get enough air in him to speak, he says, "I am a cop, remember?"

"Not tonight."

"Who the hell do you think you are?" Rousselle says.

"The last guy around here, *last,* you want to screw with."

"I think you might have busted a rib," Rousselle says.

"Only if I'd wanted to."

"This isn't over."

"A reason to live," Jimmy says, then leans down so he's back to looking him in the eyes.

Rousselle doesn't flinch.

"It was you who shot at Jane, wasn't it?" Jimmy shakes his head in the silence, almost sadly, and says, "Big mistake."

"You're the one who just made a big mistake."

Now Jimmy smiles—he can't help himself. "Don't tell me," Jimmy says. "I just fucked with the wrong Marine."

TWENTY-SIX

AFTER COURT THE NEXT DAY, I drive to Sag Harbor, a restaurant there called Page, to have dinner with my older sister, Brigid.

Brigid still likes telling me that she always felt like I was more of a brother to her than a sister. Full disclosure? Brigid was always the pretty one. And the most popular one. Growing up, I knew more about all the New York sports teams than any boy my age. Brigid had zero interest in sports. Until she got to high school and became interested in whatever sport the cutest boys happened to be playing.

According to my father, Brigid was the smart one, because she ended up at Duke.

With Rob Jacobson.

On top of everything else, Brigid has also turned out to be a better wife than I ever was. And the mother I never turned out to be. Brigid's own perfect daughter has just graduated from Duke. Pre-med. Her husband is the principal at Pierson High School in Sag Harbor. They are all nauseatingly happy.

On the drive from Riverhead, I make up my mind, decide to tell her about my diagnosis, because even though we're not as close as she wants us to be—which means about as close as we've ever been—she's my sister. And I feel as if I should tell somebody.

Jimmy Cunniff could be the next to find out, the lucky duck. Page is a block up Main Street from Jimmy's tavern. I told him I might stop in to see him after dinner. He told me his heart just skipped a beat.

"How do you think the trial is going, I mean, so far?" Brigid says.

She's ordered white wine. I've joined her. I'm not really a white-wine girl, but I'm going out of my way to be sisterly tonight.

"I'd feel better about our chances," I say, "if my client didn't keep lying like he's trying to stay in practice."

Brigid smiles. "Rob has always been a bit dramatic."

I smile back at her. "Is that how you Dukies describe people who are so frequently full of it?"

"He's a good person."

"I'm not sure if even his own wife thinks that."

"She's never understood him."

"I know. Only you really do."

"Is that sarcasm I hear?"

"You know what they say, sis. If you have to ask."

I take a sip of wine and look out at the foot traffic on Main Street. By the middle of summer, there will be nights when Main Street in Sag Harbor looks more crowded than Fifth Avenue at Christmastime.

Turning back to her, I say, "Are you sure you never slept with him?"

"How many times are you going to ask me that exact same question?"

"Maybe until you come clean about doing the dirty deed?"

I smile. She sighs.

"We are friends and have been since we both got to Duke. He certainly needed a friend back then."

She is referring to the fact—part of Jacobson's personal history and permanent record—that his father, Robinson Jacobson Jr., shot his teenage mistress and then himself when Rob was a senior at Dalton. If it sounds like a television movie, it's because it became one.

"So that explains the kind of shitheel he has so often been since?"

"Well, I know you're being your usual cynical self," Brigid says, "but even you have to admit it certainly provides some context."

"Bridge, in my world, there are reasons and there are excuses. You may think there are reasons why he's lived his life a certain way. But it doesn't excuse him, at least not in my book. You can look this up, but there are a lot of sons with dirtbag fathers who don't end up locked up for a triple homicide."

Brigid sips a little of her own wine. She is a world-class sipper, my sister. She could make a single glass of wine last through two courses and dessert.

"According to you, arrests aren't convictions," she says now. "If they were, you wouldn't make nearly as much money as you do plying your noble trade."

"Now who's being sarcastic?"

"Me!"

"We having any fun yet?"

We're silent now, as our entrees are delivered to the table. Like a bell has rung and we've retreated, at least temporarily, to neutral corners.

"You know, sometimes I get the idea that you like him more than you like me."

"I don't want to hurt your feelings."

"You? Never!"

"But sometimes it's almost as if you go out of your way to make me not like you."

"Because I'm such a tough guy?"

"You said it. Not me."

Don't be a tough guy now.

Tell her.

"I need to tell you something," I say.

TWENTY-SEVEN

SHE PUTS DOWN HER fork and stares at me. Maybe it's the tone of my voice. Maybe she sees from across the table some change in my body language.

She really is the pretty one, I think.

Even now.

I wait.

And then chicken out.

Some tough guy.

"I need you to stop visiting him at the jail. It's not a good optic for either one of you."

"He's not a killer," she says. "And he's still my friend. And I'm not going to be one of the friends who has abandoned him, the way even his own children have, those spoiled twits."

"This isn't about him. It's about you. You need to be as far away from him, and from all this, as possible."

"Are you telling me as my sister or as his lawyer?"

"Little of this," I say, "little of that."

"How about this? How about I'll think about it?"

I can't help myself. I laugh. In the moment it feels surprisingly good.

"My experience with my older sister is that has always meant no."

"I've grown," she says.

"I haven't."

"No shit," she says, and then we both laugh.

The waiter clears our plates. He asks if we'd like to look at dessert menus. We both say no. I ask for a check and tell her I'm paying.

"We'll split it," she says.

"How about I think about it?"

We both laugh again.

Tell her, I think again, but I know that somehow the moment has passed. Instead I ask her the same question as every time we talk, even though she's repeatedly told me to stop.

"How are you feeling?"

She smiles. And somehow, despite everything, looks as beautiful to me as ever.

"You mean for someone with cancer?" Brigid says. "Not half bad."

TWENTY-EIGHT

I DON'T STOP AT Jimmy's after saying good night to my sister and giving her a hug. I drive home and the whole way back think about my sister.

She was diagnosed with an aggressive form of non-Hodgkin's lymphoma six years ago. The original prognosis was for her to live out five years with it, tops.

So in addition to everything else, Brigid might turn out to be even better at cancer than I am.

I still don't know why I didn't tell her about my own diagnosis, and prognosis, despite my best intentions before dinner.

Or maybe I do.

Maybe I'm not going to allow myself to turn into some kind of cliché, the one about not letting cancer define you. Because guess what. It's not *going* to be a cliché with me. I'm not *going* to let my goddamn disease define me, at least not until this trial is over.

I'm going to keep playing my game, as scared as I am.

Scared to death.

But I can only imagine if it gets out somehow, in the middle of a trial like this one:

Defense attorney Jane Smith, battling cancer, comma...

Nope. Not happening. Not with me, it's not, I tell myself as I pull into my driveway.

When I get out of the car, I see that the dog is back.

Front porch this time, not back. Big, sad eyes staring at me. Tail wagging.

"I thought we had an understanding," I say.

Really big eyes. But still giving me the happy wave of the tail.

At least somebody is happy to see me.

"I know what you're thinking: you can win me over with a charm offensive. But you and me? This...is...not...happening."

I step over him, put my key in the lock, go inside.

Close the door behind me.

Put my bag on the front hall table, take out my gun, put it in the top drawer.

I am about to check my phone for messages, having had it on silent all the way home so I could listen to Keith Urban, when I walk back to the door and open it.

And then say to the dog what I've always hated saying to anybody.

"You win."

I get him a bowl of water. Then I open the refrigerator, chop up some leftover chicken into a bowl of rice and heat it all up in the microwave.

The dog is right behind me the whole time.

"You're an idiot."

Not talking to the dog.

Talking to myself.

After he finishes eating, I tell him that I might as well give him a name.

Rip.

Rest in peace.

TWENTY-NINE

LATE THE NEXT MORNING Ahearn calls Otis Miller to the stand.

Nick Morelli, the fisherman still missing and presumed dead, really wasn't Ahearn's star witness.

Otis Miller, though, is. Ahearn knows it. I already know it. The jury is about to find out, in the place my old man used to refer to as Macy's window.

Miller lives three doors down from the house Mitch Gates rented for his family. He's Bridgehampton, born and raised, the son of a potato farmer. Just the beginning of a pretty fascinating backstory. Prominent architect. Iraq vet, Army Intelligence, finally checked out with a Purple Heart and PTSD as parting gifts. He's written in the *East Hampton Star* about that, and openly about being a recovering alcoholic, and one who'd come home from the war addicted to opioids before rehab. He even writes long, intelligent letters to the *Star* about everything he thinks is wrong with the Hamptons, which is a lot.

I am always comparing good-looking guys to actors. Otis Miller isn't as pretty as Pierce Brosnan, the James Bond before the most recent one. But he reminds me a little of Brosnan. A lot of silver hair. Beard. Good tan. Hard body.

All in all, my kind of guy.

Just not today.

Because Otis Miller is up there trying to kill me—and killing my client in the process.

He is testifying now that on one of his long, nightly walks around the neighborhood, ones that sometimes take him all the way into town and back, he nearly got hit by a car that came flying out of the Gateses' driveway, spitting gravel and forcing Miller to dive for safety into the bushes in front of the rental house.

He found out the next morning what had happened inside the house. He hadn't heard shots; no one else in the neighborhood had, either.

But there was more than enough light, because of a full moon—I know this the same way Ahearn does, because Jimmy and I have checked—for Otis Miller to see Rob Jacobson behind the wheel of that car, a black Mercedes.

"You're certain of this," Kevin Ahearn says.

"I have lived here my whole life. I have built houses that Mr. Jacobson has sold. By now I know what he looks like, even without the ads."

"Did you think it was unusual," Ahearn says, "Mr. Jacobson driving that quickly?"

"Like I said, I know him. He had a DUI a couple of years ago. I actually thought he might be drunk."

"Objection!" I'm standing. "Your Honor, to call that conjecture is insulting to actual conjecture."

"Sustained."

Ahearn asks Miller, "Had you ever seen Mr. Jacobson, or his car, in the vicinity of the Gateses' house before this?"

"No, sir. But that doesn't mean that he hadn't been."

"Objection," I say, not even bothering to rise this time.

"Sustained," Prentice says. "Mr. Miller, please try to answer the questions without editorializing."

"I'm sorry, sir."

Miller is still a good soldier.

"So we're clear, and so the jury is clear," Ahearn says. "There is no doubt, Mr. Miller, that the man you saw driving that car was Rob Jacobson?"

"None."

"No further questions," Ahearn says.

My turn.

In that moment, as someone with cancer, I'm the one not feeling half bad.

THIRTY

MILLER IS CLEARLY A solid guy. A good guy. But he is about to find out what I learned in law school about criminal procedure. *In the end, witnesses need to know they're playing in a hardball league,* the professor said. *It's up to them whether or not to wear a helmet.*

"Good morning, Mr. Miller," I say.

"Good morning."

"Would you care to hazard a guess about just how many black Mercedes there are on the South Fork of eastern Long Island?"

"I wouldn't, actually. Hazard a guess, I mean."

"So no editorial opinion about that?"

"Objection," Ahearn says.

Prentice makes a motion, telling him to sit down. "I'll allow it. Proceed, Ms. Smith."

"Well, Mr. Miller, my math might be slightly off, but I'm guessing there are about a million cars exactly like that." I turn to the jury and grin. "None of which ever allow you to make a left-hand turn, am I right?"

I'm answered with a tiny ripple of laughter.

"But somehow, Mr. Miller, you seem convinced that this one was driven by my client."

"Because I saw him behind the wheel."

"In the dark. As you were diving for your life, correct?"

"It was him."

I turn away from him, and just loudly enough for the jury to hear say, "Sure it was."

I walk back to my table and sit on the end of it.

"Do you walk the same route every night, Mr. Miller?"

"It varies."

"Almost like a one-man neighborhood watch. Am I right?"

"That's your interpretation, not mine."

Don't respond. Don't care.

About to get to it.

"The reason I ask," I say, my tone completely casual, "is because there's something else I'm wondering: do you ever stop in and say hello to some of your neighbors?"

He hesitates now, just slightly. I'm sure I'm the only one seeing it as a poker tell. Maybe he knows where I'm going, too.

"If they're outside," he says, "maybe sitting out on a front porch, I might stop for a short conversation."

"Conversation." I nod.

"Yes."

"And you testified just now to Mr. Ahearn that you had become friendly with the Gates family that summer. Isn't that right?"

"Yes. They're good people." He stops himself. "*Were* good people."

"And knowing them as you did, you certainly noticed that Kathy Gates was quite an attractive woman, didn't you?"

Wait for it.

"Objection, Your Honor," Ahearn says, almost bored, as if objecting is the most obvious thing in the world.

"Sustained. Wherever we're headed with this, Ms. Smith, let's accelerate the process."

"Absolutely, Your Honor."

I turn back to Otis Miller.

"Isn't it true, Mr. Miller," I say, and casually, "that the reason you were outside that particular rental house on that particular evening was because you expected Kathy Gates to be alone?"

Another objection, also sustained, vigorously, by the judge.

"I find your tone insulting," Miller says to me.

"You're not the first."

"Ms. *Smith*."

"I apologize, Your Honor."

Back to Otis Miller.

"I'd appreciate it if you would please answer my question, one I will now amplify somewhat. Did you think Kathy Gates would be alone that night, and were you actually on your way to the house to see her?"

"No!" Miller says.

I look at him. He had been having such a nice ride. Maybe he thought it would continue all the way to our lunch break.

I'm thinking, *Read the room, dude.*

"Then let me put it another way. Isn't it true that you and Kathy Gates had been having an affair for much of that summer?"

Jimmy had canvassed the Gateses' neighbors. One had told him about seeing Otis Miller and Kathy Gates on the beach that summer, Miller's arm around her. Miller's next-door neighbor, a woman named Patsy Freedman, had said that she was out walking her dog very late one night, after one in the morning, and saw Kathy Gates show up at Miller's front door. One of the bartenders Jimmy knew at Bobby Van's in Bridgehampton had seen Miller and Kathy Gates having dinner that summer, just the two of them, same corner table, more than once. Same with a bartender at Pierre's, up Main Street from Van's.

Hardly ironclad proof of an affair. Or that it's true. Sometimes in court you just want things to be true, as a way of stirring the pot. Or muddying the water. Or just to get a reaction out of a witness.

I get one as Miller comes halfway out of his chair.

"No!" he shouts, with much more force than before, as Ahearn is shouting out another objection.

Only to his amazement, and mine, this one is overruled.

"I'll allow this," Prentice says. "And please control yourself, Mr. Miller."

Not on my account.

"I was not having an affair with Kathy Gates. No matter how many ways you ask the question."

"Just to be clear, then, Mr. Miller. Just on the chance that I would present two witnesses in this case who would testify that you and Kathy Gates were more than friends, those two people would be lying?"

"Yes," Miller says. "She was *not* having an affair with me."

"Let's leave that there for now and move on."

"About time," Kevin Ahearn says, and he gets gaveled into silence by the judge for a change.

"Do you ever carry a gun with you on your late-night tours of the neighborhood?" I ask Miller now.

"No."

"Are you sure of that? Because about six months before the Gates family was murdered, didn't you stop a burglary at a home about a half mile down the road from yours because you *did* have your gun with you? A Glock, the *East Hampton Star* reported at the time, as I recall—9mm."

"Yes," he says. "But that was a period in the off-season when there had been a series of break-ins in our area. So I was carrying a gun then, but no longer."

Yesterday I was lying.

"Thank you for clearing that up. So you carried a gun?"

"Objection," Ahearn says. "Asked and answered."

"Sustained."

I walk back toward the witness stand.

"Isn't it quite possible, Mr. Miller, that on the night of the murders, when Mitch Gates and his daughter, Laurel, planned to surprise Kathy Gates by coming home early from a college visit to Boston, that Mitch walked in on you with his wife—Laurel's mother?"

"Not then. Not ever."

"You think this is funny, Mr. Miller?"

"No," he says. "But I think you are."

"And isn't it quite possible with your well-documented issues with post-traumatic stress disorder that when he attacked you, you shot him and then everybody else in the house to cover up what was quite literally a crime of passion?"

Again I expect anger from him. This time he doesn't answer right away, as if he's unsure.

"No, no, no. No matter how many ways you try to ask the question."

"You're sure about that, Mr. Miller?"

"The only thing that I'm sure of, Ms. Smith, is that you're insane."

Finally, I think, *a man who understands me.*

THIRTY-ONE

AFTER I HAVE BEEN dressed down by Judge Jackson Prentice III in his chambers to the delight of Kevin Ahearn, we go back into court. It's a few minutes after five o'clock, but before he calls it a day, Prentice wants to reiterate to the jury that they are to disregard my last exchange with Otis Miller. Right before I go out to face the media.

They throw some punches this time, because of the way the day ended, but none land, or knock the smile off my face. I tell them, in different ways, that lawyers are allowed to present an alternative version of events, and that today underscored what I've identified as the core of our case:

Reasonable doubt.

Then, on heavy legs, I walk down the steps and toward the parking lot. I wouldn't admit this to anybody, not even Jimmy, certainly not Dr. Sam Wylie, but I am starting to feel fatigued at the end of the long days, what I suspect is a lot more than normal courtroom fatigue. Sam told me it might start to happen, sooner rather than later. I feel it happening now.

I am talked out, at least for this one day, and am thinking only about a hot bath and a cold beer.

When I see Claire Jacobson standing next to my car, my first thought is that getting into the barrel with the ice maiden is the last thing I need.

Or maybe it's the perfect time, as tired as I am, for the conversation I've been putting off having with her.

She opens with a friendly smile for a change, though it's frankly not her best look.

"We had a good day."

We.

"Congratulations."

"You know, Claire. There's an old legal expression that I think might go all the way back to Oliver Wendell Holmes: if you keep throwing shit against the wall, maybe some of it will stick."

"I'm not sure I ever heard that one attributed to him."

"Google it."

"Well, anyway," she says, "I just wanted to tell you myself how well I think you did. And that perhaps I was wrong about you."

"Get a grip."

She shakes her head, as if I've somehow disappointed her again. As if they should have stayed with one of the white-shoe firms they originally hired.

"Before you go," I say, "is there anything that you know that I don't? Anything that might help your husband?"

"I'm quite sure I don't know what you're talking about."

"Anything that might possibly compromise the prosecutor's case?"

"You're the one who's supposed to be defending my husband. Not me."

"So there's nothing."

She stares at me. "I'm not one of your witnesses."

"Well," I say, "not yet."

The next sound I hear in the parking lot is the *click, click, click* of her expensive and extremely high heels—the kind I never even attempt to wear—as she heads for her Bentley.

But she's not quite done with me, as it turns out, and suddenly she wheels and comes walking back to where I'm searching my bag for my keys.

"While you're being so vigilant," she says, "and so concerned about my husband and what might or might not help him, why don't you ask *your* sister what she was doing with *my* husband the night of the murders."

THIRTY-TWO

THE NEXT MORNING BEFORE WORK, I finally take Rip in to see Dr. Ben Kalinsky. The reason is obvious. I don't know enough about dogs—don't know *dogshit* about dogs.

I just know he's old, and that there is something definitely wrong with this dog.

He's been eating since I took him in. I've managed to find time to walk him twice a day, once early, once late, though not at anything resembling a high speed. Or even exercise. When I'm in court, I have neighbors come by to let him out, make sure he has fresh water until I get home.

Occasionally I find myself wondering who's going to be around longer, me or the dog.

My money is actually on him, but it's a fluid situation.

"His kidneys are failing," Dr. Ben says in his office after he's spent over an hour examining Rip.

"Well, that doesn't sound good."

"No wonder you're such a crack investigator. You don't miss a trick."

I've known him a long time, like him a lot, though never in the way he's made it clear that he likes me. And would like me to like him. He's in his early forties, tall, skinny, a long-distance runner. Hair still dark brown. Nice, even, year-round tan despite the East End winters. Divorced. Good man, good doctor. Gentle soul. We went out on a few dates a few years ago. But they always stopped where I should have stopped the damn dog, which means at the door.

"Is he going to die?"

"Well, Jane," Dr. Ben Kalinsky says, "pretty sure we're all going to do that eventually."

"Vet humor. Can't get enough of it."

"Don't forget to tip the vet techs."

"Is there anything you can do for him?"

"Sure," he says. "He's not in terrible shape, all things considered. I make him to be about eight years old, or there-abouts. Not ancient for a Lab. But getting up there, definitely. I would recommend a high-quality diet and subcutaneous fluid injections a few times a week at least to start, more often as the disease progresses. You can easily learn how to do the injections yourself, or you can bring him by for us to do them here. Some meds might help, too, if other symptoms develop, such as vomiting or trouble urinating or high blood pressure. The fluids alone will keep him around for a while. I frankly think he's got a lot of life left in him."

Wish I could say the same, Doc.

"It's all about quality of life," he continues.

"Isn't it, though."

"I'm going to take a leap of faith that you've decided to keep him," Dr. Ben Kalinsky says.

He smiles now. It's always been the same with him, whether we run into each other at Jack's Coffee or occasionally at Jimmy Cunniff's bar, or when I've braved a long run with him over the years. He makes you feel as if you're the most important person he'll talk to all day. Maybe all week.

"It's more like the dog's decided to keep me."

"I'm glad," he says. "If he ended up at a shelter, I can't imagine anybody adopting him at the age he is, and in the shape he's in."

I smile back at him. "Seriously? I really can't decide whether I rescued him or he rescued me."

"Either way," he says. "If you'd dropped him off at the shelter, they wouldn't have waited very long before putting him down."

"They'll probably do the same with me one of these days."

He frowns. "There's an odd reference point, counselor."

"Blame it on the trial," I say. "I'm probably the one who needs meds right now. You got anything that will make me smarter?"

"I've never seen that to be an issue with you." He nods at me. "May I ask a legal question?"

I smile again. It's always been easy smiling at Ben Kalinsky. I'm trying to remember just why I never let him get anywhere with me.

"I'll have to bill you for the whole hour."

"Is there a way for me to root for my friend Jane to get an acquittal, but not Rob Jacobson?"

"Not a fan?"

"I don't know many people around here who are."

"Knock yourself out and root for me," I say. "Always good to have a dog in the fight."

"Really?"

"Blame it on the trial," I say again.

He demonstrates the injections I'll need to give Rip, during which Rip barely even blinks in response. I can do this. And he tells me to get Rip as much exercise as I possibly can while loading me up with bags of the fluids and packets of needles and tubing. Then he asks what I've been feeding the dog. I tell him. He writes out a brand name and tells me to go buy him some at the pet store in Amagansett on my way home, or else.

"What does 'or else' mean, exactly?"

He grins. "I've always wondered that."

He walks me to the car. After I have Rip and the box of extras in the back seat, he asks if I want to have dinner with him tonight after I finish at the courthouse.

To his surprise—and mine—I say yes.

"Well, I'm not gonna lie," Dr. Ben says. "Didn't see that coming."

"Caught me at a weak moment."

When I'm behind the wheel, and before I close the door, he leans down and says, "I always knew there was a dog lover inside you."

"Don't push it, Doc," I say, and drive off.

THIRTY-THREE

I HONESTLY CAN'T REMEMBER the last time I've had a real date. But I am having one tonight with Dr. Ben Kalinsky, eight thirty at the East Hampton Grill, later than he says he would have preferred but he had to perform an urgent late-afternoon surgery.

I am asking myself on the ride home from court why I agreed to go out with him. It's not that I don't enjoy his company. I do. But I also know he'll be thinking of this as a first date all over again. And definitely not our last, if he has anything to say about it.

How will he feel if he knows that I'm in much worse shape than the dog?

But I'm not telling him, either. I don't want his pity. What life I have left is going to be pity-free. I've decided that. Locked it in. I happen to have a perfect role model in my sister. Brigid doesn't want anybody's pity, either. She particularly doesn't want it now that her doctors don't like what they've seen on her most recent PET/CT scan, and are reviewing new treatment possibilities for her, more than five years after she was first diagnosed. It's why I haven't talked to her yet about what Claire Jacobson told me outside the courthouse. I'm giving my sister a pass on that for now, though certainly not forever. I'm still her sister. But I'm also Rob Jacobson's lawyer.

So if she knows something about that night, I'm going to ask her why she hasn't told me.

I walk Rip when I get home, shower, decide on a pair of white jeans that I know look good on me and a black cotton sweater, fuss with my hair more than I usually do, do a *much* better job with makeup than I usually do. There's still some time before Dr. Ben will pick me up. I decide to spend it productively, reading through a file on the Carson murders that Jimmy dropped off while I was on my way to court. We never close.

I spread out some pictures of the Carsons. Individual shots and group shots, taken by a professional photographer about six months before they all died.

I keep coming back to the girl.

I stare at her, thinking how pleased she must have been with how she looked, hair and lighting and even the outfits she chose. The pearls around her slender neck. Definitely Insta worthy, as the kids like to say.

I've had more than twice as much life as this kid had.

I think of Kathy Gates, and what might have been going on between her and Otis Miller, the sheriff of their neighborhood. And of the affair Claire Jacobson is almost certainly having with Gus Hennessy. Money and sex—still the most powerful motives in the world. I wonder what secrets Lily Carson might have died with. And who might have been motivated to have her die with those secrets.

I know Jimmy is fixed on Hank Carson, as he keeps going further and further down the rabbit hole of Carson's gambling.

But what if Hank Carson wasn't the target? I keep finding

out more secrets about Rob Jacobson the longer the trial goes. What more are we going to learn about the Carsons of Garden City before we're through?

For now, though, I put the file away and decide to focus on the fact that I am about to go out on an honest-to-God date. And be Jane the girl for a change, and not Jane the lawyer.

"Yeah, right," I say to Rip the dog. "Fat chance."

THIRTY-FOUR

Jimmy

JIMMY CUNNIFF HAS SPENT the day in Garden City, doing the kind of essential cop work he was taught to do, which means knocking on doors, and not thinking Google can help you find out who did it.

Jimmy grinds through the day without a badge. He had a counterfeit made for himself after the NYPD made him turn in his real one, along with his gun, but no need for the fake today.

When people ask, he says that he's working for Mr. McCall, the district attorney, and that has gotten him by with the good citizens of Garden City.

Jimmy has gone through his adult life saying "Long story short" a lot. Maybe too much. Jane is always telling him he overdoes it. But it's only because he gets as impatient with himself as he gets with other people, wanting them to cut to the goddamn chase. So he keeps talking to friends and neighbors of the Carsons and telling them that, long story short, he's just trying to find out what really happened to them.

And gets bubkes, as his father used to say. Hank Carson was a prince—that is the consensus, all over town. The daughter, Morgan, was a golden girl. The mother, Lily, did so much charity work they didn't know how she found time to be a wife to Hank and a mother to Morgan.

The whole town seems blessed just to have known them.

Jimmy's starting to feel blessed just knowing *about* them.

And, sure, old Hank liked to have a little action on NFL games, but who didn't? Nobody has any idea that Hank was as much as two million to the bad with Bobby Salvatore.

Jimmy calls Jane when he's in the car. She asks him how it's going.

"Still in Garden City. I need to get with McCall before I head back, see where he thinks we are, which, not for nothing, feels like nowhere right now."

He tells her he'll check back later, ends the call, shuts off the radio as a way of thinking better. Or more clearly. Or something. Mostly about Hank Carson.

Whatever he owed, why kill them all, and not just him?

THIRTY-FIVE

Jimmy

IT'S DARK BY THE time he gets to McCall's house on Kensington Road, on the south side of Garden City. Jimmy has just given serious consideration to stopping at the McDonald's he just passed on his way here, because he hasn't eaten all day and is hungry as hell. But he told McCall he'd be there by eight thirty at the latest. He can eat when he gets back east.

Jimmy sees McCall's Audi, or what he assumes is his Audi, parked in the driveway. Protected license plate in the back, with OFFICER OF THE COURT on it.

Jimmy gets out and walks up and rings the doorbell.

Waits.

Nothing.

Rings it again. He didn't tell McCall exactly when he would show up. Maybe the guy is in the shower. Or out back. Or behind a closed door somewhere, talking on the telephone.

Maybe he's dozed off. Or gone for a walk. Does he have a dog? Jimmy never asked if he has a dog. Just knows that he's living alone and has been for a while. He's a jock. Maybe he's gone for a run. Jimmy remembers him saying that he still runs, but not every day anymore; it just beats the living shit out of his creaky knees.

Jimmy finally tries the doorknob.

It's open.

"Hey, McCall," he says as he steps into the foyer. "It's your friend Jimmy Cunniff."

No response.

The house, even with the lights on, is completely still.

"Hey, McCall," Jimmy calls out again, a little louder than before. "Where you at, man?"

And even though no alarm went off when Jimmy stepped into the house, he is hearing one now anyway, the alarm inside his own brain.

He has his Smith & Wesson revolver with him, an old-school gun, holstered behind him on his belt. Is starting to reach for it with his right hand.

Too late.

THIRTY-SIX

BEN KALINSKY PICKS THE WINE. I let him because I can tell it's important to him. I know from our previous nights out together that he knows a lot about wine. He knows a lot about a lot of things, actually.

Just not me.

If he did, we wouldn't be here.

"What should we drink to?" he says after he's tasted the wine, a Cabernet. "A win for you at the trial?"

"We can do better than that. How did your surgery go?"

"The labradoodle is going to make it."

"Let's drink to that. Even if it is a labradoodle."

We do.

"You got something against them?"

I am about to tell him about my perfect doctor and her perfect dogs. But it's like they say in court. Don't open the door.

"Long story."

"Why do I get the feeling that they're all long stories with you?"

"Because they are. Longer than Russian novels sometimes."

Somehow he looks all dressed up even just wearing a white

long-sleeved shirt and jeans. We've made a deal to turn off our phones during dinner.

The East Hampton Grill is one of the best restaurants in the area, if not in the most glam location, next to the East Hampton firehouse, across from my dry cleaner on North Main, and a block from Moo Moo's Ice Cream Shop, which is so good I'm convinced it's run by the devil.

It's got the look of a New York steak house, with a brick fireplace and dark paneling and a huge mural of the US flag on one of the walls. Huge mirror over the bar. The dim lighting is pretty much perfect, which means you don't need a flashlight to read the menu.

We're at a corner table.

Against all odds, I am happy to be here.

Not just here. Here with him.

Damn. I was afraid of that.

"So how's it going?"

"Fine," I say.

Way too quickly.

He smiles. It is a sweet smile. He is a sweet man. Can a vet have a good bedside manner?

"I meant the trial."

"If one of us is going to talk shop, I'd rather it be you, Doc."

"Your shop is way more interesting. I've been following the coverage. It sounds like it's been a show."

"More like a shit show," I say.

He laughs.

"Seriously? Sometimes I think that's all it is. A show."

"That sounds pretty cynical," he says.

"And me usually such a cockeyed optimist."

We both decide to indulge ourselves and order rib-eye steaks. As we eat, I tell him how conflicted I am about Rob

Jacobson. Without going too deep into the weeds, I explain how overwhelming the evidence against him is. A palm print of Jacobson's on the coffee table in the living room. More prints on the stair railing leading down from the second floor. There was hair in one of the upstairs sinks that belongs to Jacobson. And some of Mitch Gates's blood ended up on a pair of Jacobson's fancy black On Cloud sneakers the cops confiscated from Jacobson's bedroom. What we call a "totality of evidence." He says it was all planted. It would have taken some doing.

But, I explain, it could have been done. Just by somebody who went to all the trouble in the world to make all the trouble in the world for my client.

Ben Kalinsky is a good listener. So I keep going, even after having told myself that the last thing I want to do tonight is talk shop. I tell him how I'm troubled, still, by the disappearance of Nick Morelli, just because of when it happened. And how Gus Hennessy suddenly decided to come forward about the threat he'd heard from Jacobson on the beach, the way Morelli had suddenly remembered seeing Jacobson in a lip lock with Laurel Gates.

"Lip lock?" Ben Kalinsky says.

"What can I tell you? I'm old."

"You don't look old to me tonight. You look beautiful."

"My sister is the beautiful one, remember?"

He says, "Tell anyone else who thinks that to hold my drink."

He is smiling at me again and leaning forward. I am suddenly worried that I might be blushing.

Blushing, Jane.

Is that still even a thing?

I smile back at him and say, "Down, boy."

"How about 'Thanks, Ben'?"

"Thanks, Ben."

"Now we're talking."

He pours us more wine.

"Do you think Jacobson did it?"

"No," I say.

"For real?"

"I *have* to think that, even though it rarely matters to people who do what I do for a living. Because the alternative is that I'm working my ass off trying to get an acquittal for someone who murdered an entire family in cold blood."

"Do you think you'll ever know for sure?"

"Unfortunately, there's a very good chance that I won't."

"And if you do get him off, you'll have to live with that for the rest of your life," he says.

For as long as that is.

"But I'd also have to live with it if he gets convicted and he didn't do it."

"Some job you've got," Ben Kalinsky says.

"I'd rather do labradoodle surgery any day of the week," I tell him.

Another smile. The guy's killing me with smiles.

"Sounds as if I like my patients a lot better than you like your client."

"One hundred percent," I say.

The dinner crowd has thinned out by the time we're having coffee. He seems in no rush to leave the restaurant. Neither am I. When he does drive me home, he is out his door at the same time I'm out mine and walking me to the front door.

"I don't hear anything from your guy Rip. Doesn't sound like he's much of a guard dog."

"He thinks he can snore intruders away."

"Is that what I am? An intruder?"

And then he's kissing me before I can come up with a snappy

comeback. No awkward moment with both of us wondering if it's going to happen, because it's already happening.

It turns out he's a very good kisser, the bastard.

I can't remember the last time I've been kissed like this. Or the last time I kissed back like this. But I'm giving as good as I'm getting until we both pull back, out of breath, like a couple of horny teenagers.

He starts to come in again. I gently put two hands on his chest.

"To be continued."

"We could continue inside."

"Not in front of the dog."

THIRTY-SEVEN

Jimmy

ONE OTHER TIME IN his life Jimmy has felt the barrel of a gun pressed to the back of his neck. His partner, Mickey Dunne, blew the guy's head off before the guy did the same to Jimmy.

Not a sensation you forget, though.

"Gun holstered in back, correct?" the voice behind him says.

"Why even ask if you already know the answer?" Jimmy says.

They are in the middle of the living room. Jimmy has always joked that he has alienlike hearing. Not tonight. He didn't hear the guy coming up behind him, didn't feel the air in the room changing, even as the alarm inside his head *was* going off.

Rookie mistake.

"Doesn't matter, either way. You go for it again, you're dead."

"How come I'm not dead already?"

"Because I used to do what you used to do. And because I have decided to give you a reprieve. But just this one time."

"Where's McCall?" Jimmy says.

The guy chuckles. "He decided, spur of the moment, to take a trip."

"His car is outside."

"Well, shit, that's a mystery, isn't it?"

Jimmy is reviewing his options, brain racing with them. None are any good. If he even twitches now, he's certain the guy will pull the trigger. McCall's gone, he's gone, see ya, like the Yankees announcer says when somebody hits a home run.

"You kill McCall? Seriously? A goddamn district attorney?"

The guy ignores him. From where the sound of his voice is coming, he's bigger than Jimmy. Maybe by a lot. Jimmy can smell cigarettes on him.

"I'll tell you what I told McCall when it was him and me chatting in this same room. You need to leave this Carson thing alone."

"What did McCall say to that?"

"He said that wasn't going to happen. But you know what our parents used to say, Jimmy. Actions have consequences."

"What if I'm the one saying it's not going to happen?"

He feels himself starting to sweat, even in the air-conditioning. Can hear his own shallow breathing. Trying to stay calm. But feeling his heart working its way to heart-attack speed.

I should have taken my gun out, first thing.

Too late with that, too.

The guy presses the gun harder against Jimmy's neck.

Even if I drop to the ground, I'll never get to my gun in time.

Keep him talking.

Old cop rule.

"That's not even conversation, Jimmy. Because here is the situation you now are in. You *do* leave this alone, or I kill you, and then drive straight out to Amagansett and kill her, too."

He pauses. Presses the gun again.

"Totally your call. But like I say, you have now been warned."

Then Jimmy feels the needle jabbing into his neck, right next to where the gun is.

"Wait for it," the guy says.

THIRTY-EIGHT

FOR THE PAST FEW DAYS, the disappearance of a local DA has managed to knock Rob Jacobson's trial off the front pages and push it back on the six o'clock news. Jimmy keeps telling me that Gregg McCall hasn't just disappeared, that he's gone, and that all the headlines in the world aren't going to bring him back.

The trial plods along as Ahearn's case winds down. All week there has been no real drama in court, no punches landed from either side of the aisle, no bombshells. So today is the day when I finally decide to talk to the media about Gregg McCall, even though Jimmy has begged me not to do it, and to stay the hell away from it, because he doesn't want the guy who said he was an ex-cop at McCall's house coming for me next.

I thank my partner for sharing, and then do exactly what I want to do, pretty much like always.

So when court is adjourned this Friday, at five o'clock sharp, I stand on the courthouse steps and tell the assembled media that Gregg McCall is one of the best people I have ever met, one of the most professional, one of the most decent and honorable. And that even though we made no announcement about it, Jimmy Cunniff and I have been working with McCall on the murder of the Carson family, at what was his request.

"So, Jane, you believe that Mr. McCall's disappearance is somehow linked to the Carson case?" a voice calls out when I throw it open to questions.

"Absolutely."

No jokes today, no snark, none of the old razzle-dazzle.

"Are you and Jimmy Cunniff going to continue to investigate?"

"Absolutely."

"The other triple homicide or Gregg McCall's disappearance?"

"All of it. We never close."

I take back roads tonight coming home from Riverhead—not because I'm looking to beat Friday night traffic necessarily, just because I prefer back roads. They always make it easier for me to remember what it was like before everybody seemed to decide that the world would stop spinning on its axis if they didn't rent out here in the summer.

And this ride is more peaceful, at least for me—gives me some time with the phone off and music playing to think about what will happen when Ahearn does wrap up his case and I begin to mount my defense of Rob Jacobson.

Such as it is.

And whatever it's going to be.

I know all the holes in my defense of Rob Jacobson and his occasionally cockeyed defense of himself. As much time as I have spent with him, spent listening to him, sometimes to the point where I imagine my head exploding, it occurs to me how little I really know of him. I just get the version of

Rob Jacobson that he wants to be, and the one he wants me to see, in his continuing charm offensive, almost as if he can't help himself.

I am even considering having Dr. Ben look after Rip on either Saturday or Sunday and taking a ride into the city to get myself more face time with the cops who worked the murder-suicide of Jacobson's father. I know a lot about that case by now. But I feel as if I need to know even more, as a way of knowing my client better. Or at least understanding him more than I do.

Because the thought has never been far away that if his old man was capable of a monstrous—and completely mad— crime like that, then maybe he is, too.

The teenage Rob Jacobson was the one to find the bodies. His mother was in Southampton at the time, at what was once the family estate. Rob was an only child, in his room, when he heard the first shot, according to what he told police at the time.

The kid was on his way up the stairs when he heard the second shot.

He was still there with the bodies when the cops showed up, at which point young Rob Jacobson gave them what became the money quote in the *Daily News* and the *Post,* one both of the tabs ran with for a week.

"I always wondered if there was somebody out there mean enough to kill my father," he said. "Turns out there was."

The father was a killer. Did it take some sort of great leap to think the son could be one, too, despite his proclamations of innocence and being set up?

I had another weekend to ponder that, along with other mysteries of the universe.

But for now, heading east on Scuttle Hole Road, I look in the rearview mirror and see myself smiling.

And know why.

The dog will be waiting for me when I come through the front door. Waiting to watch a tough guy like Jane Smith do a complete melt when I see him.

We haven't been together that long. But I've discovered I like having a dog. And love this particular dog.

Till death do us part.

I'm cutting across Sagg Road when Jimmy calls and informs me he's inviting himself for dinner. He asks where I am. I tell him. He tells me to get my ass home and start boiling up some water.

"Then what?"

"I got tired of waiting for you to offer to cook me dinner."

"It would be a shame for you to cheat death this week and then die of my cooking."

"Nobody has ever listed pasta as a cause of death," he says, and I tell him he doesn't watch nearly enough Scorsese movies.

I finally pull into my driveway, grab my bag off the passenger seat. And remember to take my gun out of the glove compartment. After what happened at McCall's when Jimmy walked into an empty house, I have been on high alert.

I unlock the front door, take the gun out, and say, "Honey, I'm hoooooome."

I already have a treat in my free hand.

No Rip.

I head for the kitchen, whistling and calling out his name. One of the big dog beds I've bought for him is in there.

The dog isn't.

There is a brief moment, a very bad one, when I think that perhaps the dog has curled up into a ball and died. Maybe his heart gave up before his kidneys did, even with the fluids I've been dutifully injecting under his skin as Dr. Ben prescribed. Maybe he just got too sick when he was wandering around without a place to live.

"Rip," I yell now, putting some snap into my voice. "Don't you even think about dying on me."

He's not in the kitchen, either.

It's after I've gone upstairs that I hear the whimpering from behind the closed door of my walk-in closet.

Rip is in there, a muzzle over his mouth, trembling, tail pointed straight down.

I've taken off the muzzle and fed him the treat I still have in my hand when I hear my phone, still in the bag that's over my shoulder.

"This is Jane," I say.

A voice I don't recognize, a guy, says, "Now you've officially been warned, too."

"Who is this?"

"We both know the answer to that one."

"Warned about what, exactly?" I say. And then I add, "Bitch."

"About staying in your lane."

"What does that even mean?"

I want to keep him talking, on the outside chance that he might reveal something about himself.

"Here is what it means, counselor. What you need to do right now is stick with the trial."

"By the way? Pretty ballsy for you to show up here after what you did to McCall and Jimmy."

"Ballsy *and* a bitch?" the guy says. "Pick a lane on that, too, counselor."

I tell him what he can do to himself.

"And you a lady," he says.

"Not even on a good day."

"Stick with the trial," he says again. "Who knows? If you do, you might live until the end of it."

"And if I don't?"

"I'll kill your dog, too."

THIRTY-NINE

I CALL GUS HENNESSY as my first defense witness, even though he's already been called as a witness for the prosecution. I informed Judge Prentice and Kevin Ahearn of my plans on Friday afternoon so Hennessy would be in the room first thing this morning.

Now it's a couple of minutes before the judge will come walking through the door and it will feel like Opening Day, at least to me, all over again.

In the words of the great Jimmy Cunniff, former boxer, the preliminaries are officially over. It really is time for the main event.

Not Ahearn's case.

Mine.

I've considered circling back to attacking the physical evidence, throwing more shade on the prints and hair and all the rest of it than I have already. But I am saving that for later, the way I am saving round two with Otis Miller.

Today I'm opening with Rob Jacobson's so-called friend Gus. When Jacobson asks me why I'm leading off with Gus Hennessy, I simply tell him, "You'll have to wait and see along with everybody else."

"What if I order you to tell me? Being the one writing the big checks to you and all."

"Then I will once again have to remind you that I'm the one driving this bus. And Rob? You need to hope it's not the prison bus."

I go over the notes I made this morning in bed, awake at 5 a.m., ready to go as soon as my eyes were open, even before Rip was awake. I'm not one of those lawyers who likes to script all the questions beforehand. Or know all the questions I'll end up asking.

I ultimately approach every cross-examination as a conversation with the witness, one that can never be scripted out entirely, even though I so often know what to expect from the person on the stand.

Basically I'm driving that bus, too.

I might not always know exactly where we're going to end up, the witness and me. No defense lawyer does. Sometimes a witness will surprise the hell out of me and make me feel as if I've suddenly been hit on my blind side.

But one of the reasons I've never lost a case is because I've managed to keep those hard hits to a minimum.

I smile to myself as I see the clock hit nine exactly, thinking that the defense is about to play offense now, in a big way.

That's the plan, anyway.

"All rise," the clerk says.

I practically knock my chair over as I jump out of it.

I don't have cancer today.

FORTY

GUS HENNESSY IS ALL business casual. Blue blazer, open-necked tattersall shirt. But then his whole attitude seems to be casual today, as if he wants everyone in the room to think there's nowhere he'd rather be in the whole world than on this witness stand, talking to me.

He knows better. Because Gus knows he isn't sitting at the club now, chopping it up with his boys. He *is* on the stand in a murder trial.

"Good *morning,* Mr. Hennessy."

"Good morning."

I take a couple of minutes to remind him of his previous testimony as Ahearn's witness, about the argument between Rob Jacobson and Mitch Gates he says he heard on the beach.

"You recall all that, correct?"

"I do."

"Given this do-over," I say, "would you care to amend any of that testimony?"

"I don't see this as a do-over, Ms. Smith."

"Of course you don't. I'm just wondering if, given time to reflect, you're standing strong on your version of that event."

He smiles, as if about to close a deal, as if about to tell me that while the property he's trying to sell me is only one acre, it really looks like two.

"It's not my version of things. It's what happened."

"Of course it is!"

I smile back at him.

"I was wondering, Mr. Hennessy, just how your real estate business is doing these days."

"Objection," I hear from behind me.

"Sustained," Judge Jackson Prentice says.

"Your Honor, I don't mean to sound as if I'm objecting to Mr. Ahearn's objection, but there's a point to this line of questioning, if you'll allow it."

"I'll allow it, Ms. Smith. But please *get* to it."

"Would you like me to repeat the question?" I say to Hennessy.

"No," he says, "and I'll be happy to answer it. We've been lucky enough, as everybody's come out of the pandemic, to be doing quite well. There's bigger shops than mine out here. But not many."

"And you'd have to admit," I say, "that you've been helped, at least partially, by the fact that Mr. Jacobson's real estate business has suffered over this same amount of time, him being in jail and having been charged with murder."

"Rob's company is still active."

"But the name attached to it is a name now attached to a monstrous triple homicide. So while *his* shop remains open, I can give you the numbers to show how business has suffered, if you'd care to hear them. Yours and his."

"Objection," Ahearn says. More of a shout this time. "Really, Your Honor? This is opposing counsel's idea of getting to it?"

"Overruled," Prentice says. "But I'm running out of patience, Ms. Smith."

"Almost there, Your Honor. I promise."

I turn back to Hennessy.

"So to put a bow on this subject, and just as a practical matter, what's bad for my client has been good for you."

"Not just me," Gus Hennessy says.

I smile again. "Of course not!"

I walk back toward my table, pivot when I get there. In all ways.

"Other than what you say you heard on the beach that night, did you ever hear your pal Rob Jacobson threaten anybody?"

I am covering old ground. You have to sometimes. The jury doesn't remember everything. And sometimes you can get a quisling like Gus Hennessy to contradict himself.

"I mean, I guess not," he says.

"You *guess* not?" I say. "With a memory like yours, especially for dialogue, I have to believe you'd remember something like that."

"Objection," Ahearn says. "Even being sarcastic, she's clearly badgering the witness."

"Sustained."

"Let me rephrase, Mr. Hennessy. In all the years that you have known my client, socialized with him, golfed with him, been the kind of friend to him you maintain you are, have you ever seen him come close to another threat, or any manner of physical altercation?"

"I frankly don't see how that has anything to do with what I saw and heard on the beach that night."

At this point, I am no longer smiling at him.

"Here's how this works, Mr. Hennessy. I ask the questions and you answer them."

Ahearn doesn't object. Prentice lets me go.

"No," he says.

His face has reddened, just slightly. Suddenly he's acting much less like a real estate biggie on the go.

"No to what?"

"No, I've never seen him get into a fight."

"So no hint of violence."

"No."

"So it was just the one time you said you couldn't keep silent about, being a good citizen? Correct?"

"Correct."

"Taking a step back," I say, "you have to know how damaging to your friend your previous testimony is. You saying he threatened to kill one of the people for whose murder he is now on trial."

"Objection." Ahearn almost sounds weary. "Leading the witness."

Prentice surprises me here.

"Overruled. You can get your own chance to lead on cross, Mr. Ahearn. I'll allow it."

I like to keep moving during cross-examination. Keep the moment active. Less static. Now I walk over to my right and stand in front of the jury box. Looking at the jury members as I shrug. Back to my witness.

Who's about to really become mine.

"I have this columnist friend," I say, speaking more to the jury than to Hennessy.

I stop.

"Crazy, right? Columnists having friends?"

I get smiles. Hear a few chuckles.

"And this friend tells me all stories come from somewhere," I say. "And once they do, he's always telling me, my columnist friend, you then have to ask yourself a question: who does that story help?"

From behind me, Hennessy says, "Are you asking me that?"

I turn back to him. "No. That's not my question. But this is:

won't a conviction for my client ultimately help you more than somewhat?"

Before Hennessy can answer, Ahearn shouts out another objection. "Calls for a conclusion."

"Sustained."

I blow right through the stop sign.

"I'll rephrase," I say. "Mr. Hennessy, isn't it true that if my client *is* convicted, not only would your business improve but it also would give you a lot more time to screw around with his wife?"

FORTY-ONE

I FINALLY HAVE TO yell at Rob and Claire Jacobson as a way of getting them to stop yelling at each other.

We're in the attorney room we've used before. One I now point out to them isn't soundproofed, even if the happy couple is acting as if it is.

"Don't tell me what to do," Claire Jacobson says, wheeling on me. She adds, "You bitch."

"Thanks for noticing," I say.

"Well," Rob Jacobson says, "it takes one to know one, right?"

Claire continues to deny, at the top of her voice, that she is having an affair with Gus Hennessy, despite what I've told her and my client about Gus Hennessy pulling into their driveway in his convertible one night and not leaving until morning.

I don't know the last piece for sure. I didn't stay until dawn's early light. More something I intuited.

"It should be a new show," Jacobson says. "The Horny Housewives of the East End of Long Island."

Claire Jacobson turns back to him now. "There's nothing going on between us."

"Really? Jane here says there is. And she's an officer of the court."

"Fuck Jane," Claire Jacobson says.

"Well put."

"And even if there was something going on between us, which there isn't," Claire continues, "it's a little late for you to try to take the high ground on marital infidelity, isn't it, sweetheart? Somewhat like getting religion a little late in the church service?"

Before he can come back at her, she says, "Interesting, isn't it, that you're so quick to believe your lawyer and not your wife."

"She's not as expensive as you are, for one thing."

He turns back to me. "You couldn't give me a heads-up on this?"

"I didn't know I'd get the reaction out of you in court that I did," I say. "But it was worth taking a shot."

Rob Jacobson hadn't waited to call his wife a bitch here in the attorney room. He'd done it in open court. Shocked. Angry. Even acting embarrassed. He really had checked all the boxes I could have ever hoped he would before Judge Jackson Prentice III cleared the room and called for a recess.

"For the last time," Claire says, "there is absolutely nothing going on between Gus and me. It is a fever dream of your lawyer's. Maybe she gets off on it."

"Well, to be clear, it doesn't even take that much these days, Claire," I say. "But what I'm trying to do here is get your husband off."

"By dragging me through the mud."

"Mud *wrestling,* sounds like to me," Jacobson says. "Down and dirty."

Claire Jacobson, exasperated, says, "Gus had had too much to drink, as usual. It was late. He slept in Eric's room."

Their absent son, the surfer boy.

Rob Jacobson has calmed down considerably, I see.

"You're lying," he says evenly. "You know I can always tell when you're lying, Claire."

"I wish I could say the same about you, dear."

I am seated. They have both remained standing, on opposite sides of the long conference table. I know court will shortly be back in session. Prentice called for only a fifteen-minute recess.

"So you know, I will *never* allow you to call me as a witness," Claire Jacobson says to me now. "I know there are rules about spousal privilege."

"So there are. Most of the time it's a beautiful thing."

"You didn't need to do this," she says. "To Gus or to me."

"Actually, I did. Because your friend Gus is the one who didn't have to share his own fever dream about an argument on the beach that your husband disputes and Mitch Gates can't."

"So what do you think you've accomplished today with your hateful innuendo?" she says. "Bottom line."

"The jury now sees one of Ahearn's star witnesses as somebody who doesn't just get richer in business but maybe gets the girl, too, if your husband ends up locked up for the rest of his life."

There is a rap on the door. The clerk pokes his head in and says we're about to resume.

"So you're saying it's not just me who's lying but Gus, too?"

"To tell you the truth, Claire. I think the bitch here is him."

I think it might not be a bad exit line if I wasn't afraid to leave the two of them alone in here. So I wait for Rob Jacobson to lead us out, in a suit I haven't seen him wear before. I am about to follow him when I feel Claire's hand on my shoulder.

She whispers something in my ear then, and smiles at me,

rather smugly I think, as if she is the one with the high ground here.

Then in the hallway she takes a right instead of a left and heads for the doors leading to the street.

Before she leaves the building, she turns, as if certain I'm still watching her.

"You only think you know everything, Jane."

FORTY-TWO

Jimmy

JIMMY CUNNIFF SITS IN his car, which he's parked down the street from Jane's house.

Three in the morning. He's pulled the late shift tonight. Sometimes he and Kenny Stanton, his best bartender and an ex-cop himself, alternate.

He's not worried about missing sleep tonight. Or any night. Long story short? Jimmy Cunniff has never needed much sleep.

Jane gave him a lot of blowback, telling him she's a big girl and can take care of herself, blah, blah, blah. Jimmy finally convinced her she can't, not from this guy, whoever he is— that's his gut. He finally wore her down, mostly because on this one, she knows he's right.

Jimmy's not entirely sure he can take care of *him*self, either, as much of a cowboy as he's always been.

Somewhere out there is an ex-cop good enough to have gotten behind Jimmy, completely cool once he did, not rushing anything or giving away anything until he put the needle in Jimmy's neck, and down went Cunniff.

Jimmy didn't get himself checked out afterward, even though he felt like shit for two straight days, like he used to feel at the end of a serious bender. He figured it was etorphine, or something like it. Whatever it was, it made him feel as if he didn't want to get out of bed. He told no one, certainly not Jane, how he was feeling, just because Jane is always in better shape than a Navy SEAL.

Even now, Jimmy still feels a little fuzzy.

When he finally does catch up with this guy, which he has promised himself he will or will die trying, he'll owe him one for jabbing him that way.

On top of everything else.

I used to do what you used to do, the guy said.

He didn't mean boxing, or writing, or owning a bar.

So he'd been a cop. Or so he said. Did that mean NYPD? Or does he just know enough about Jimmy to know he's ex-NYPD?

During the past week, Jimmy has been calling guys in the department he's still good with, seeing if they can remember ever being on the job with someone who fits this asshat's profile, someone who might have the balls to kill a district attorney, and maybe a lot more people than him.

Maybe this guy was the last person Artie Shore talked to on the phone before he blew his brains out.

Maybe if he didn't kill the Carson family, he knew who did.

But none of that is what's driving Jimmy hard right now.

It's that this mutt got inside Jane's house.

He was *here*, the son of a bitch.

Even talked about killing her dog.

Jimmy thinks: *He spared the dog the way he spared me.*

But for how long?

The bar is closed by now, a couple of hours, even for the stayers. When Jimmy leaves here in a few minutes, he'll be replaced by Kenny Stanton. Retired now from the NYPD with full disability. Shot in the back by a gangbanger; recovered enough to walk again, but came out of it hooked on Oxy. Clean now for six months, he said, and Jimmy believed him. Kenny doesn't sleep much, either, said he'd honestly rather be working a stakeout than pushing drinks, all due respect. Said it reminded him of working the late show when he was still on the job.

Jimmy knows the feeling.

Would an ex-cop risk circling back to Jane's house, this close to having been there the first time?

Jimmy isn't sure. But to his mind? Everything is on the table at this point.

Because if this guy took out McCall that cleanly, made him disappear without leaving any trace evidence behind, then everything *has* to be on the table.

No other way to approach it.

Behind him he sees Kenny Stanton blink his lights to let Jimmy know he's here. Jimmy puts his car in gear. Maybe he can shut off his brain when he gets home and gets himself a couple of hours of sleep. He wants to take a ride into the city tomorrow, maybe after court, talk to his old partner, Mickey Dunne—they've been missing each other for a couple of days—see if he has any thoughts about a bad ex-cop who maybe has turned into a much, much worse one.

Jimmy is on Route 114, heading back to Sag Harbor, when he gets the call about the bar being on fire.

FORTY-THREE

Jimmy

"MAYBE WHOEVER IT WAS failed to take into consideration that the fire department is just up Main Street," Chief Eddie Thompson says to Jimmy.

"Or maybe they didn't give a shit."

"You got enemies?"

"How much time you got?"

They are standing on Main Street across from his bar. The fire has been put out, but the air down at this end of Main is still thick and heavy and lousy with smoke. Engine 3 is still out front. Two of Thompson's guys, in their black-and-yellow jackets, have just gone back inside.

"Whoever *did* do this didn't even attempt to hide what he was doing," Thompson says. "The gasoline can was right inside the front door."

He has his helmet in his hand.

"You probably don't want to hear this, but it could've been a lot worse. Hey, I thought you were pretty popular in this town."

"It's an out-of-town job."

"So you do know who did it."

"I do and I don't."

"But this out-of-town guy has it in for you."

"Very much so," Jimmy says.

"But no name."

"Not yet."

The Sag Harbor chief of police, Pete Garry, comes walking out of Jimmy's bar to where they're standing.

"Your thoughts?" Garry says to Jimmy.

Jimmy shorthands his way through the whole story about the Carsons and McCall and getting drugged and Jane's dog. He knows he's left things out. He's too tired and too pissed off to care at the moment.

"He hasn't threatened your ass enough already?" Garry says.

"Apparently not."

Garry says he'll post somebody in front and back until morning, not that he thinks it will do much good. Jimmy thanks him and looks around at the street scene as the onlookers, the ones out here in the middle of the night, begin to disperse. Thinking about how many arsonists like to come back and hide in plain sight in the crowd, wanting to watch the show.

Mostly men out here. Jimmy does see two young couples, probably having walked down from the high-end condos in what used to be the Bulova Watchcase Factory up Division Street.

All come to watch somebody try to burn Jimmy to the ground tonight.

Jimmy turns back to the bar, having paid no attention to the big guy in the New York Rangers cap, over on the west side of Main, leaning against a wall next to the laundromat over there, where a bookstore used to be.

Doesn't notice the guy walking back toward the municipal parking lot, pulling his phone out of his pocket.

Jimmy's phone chirps now.

Unknown Caller.

Jimmy knows who it is before the guy starts talking.

"You're still being a bad boy, Jimmy boy," what is now a familiar voice says. "A bad, bad boy. Making calls on me after I told you to stop."

"I'm going to do more than make calls on you," Jimmy says. "I'm going to piss on you after I find you and set *you* on fire."

The guy lets that one go.

"Hey, Jimmy. That guy you posted outside Jane's house? I hope nothing happened to him while you were rushing over here."

And disconnects the call.

FORTY-FOUR

ONE OF THE JURORS faints and gets carried out on a stretcher the next morning right before I am about to call my next witness. At which point Judge Prentice has no choice but to send everybody home for the day.

On *my* way home, I stop to inspect what turns out to be surprisingly minor damage at Jimmy's bar, which he insists will be open tonight even if he has to set up tables on the sidewalk, the way he did during COVID.

"I look at it this way," Jimmy Cunniff tells me. "I grew up in smoke-filled bars. So nothing's really changed."

He has already told me about the call he got after the fire, about what the guy said before the call ended, about how it turned out he'd been bluffing about Kenny Stanton not being safe over at my house. And, as always, what Jimmy Cunniff planned to do with this guy when he found him.

"Look on the bright side. If you do take him out, at least you'll have a good lawyer."

By one in the afternoon I am having lunch with my sister, Brigid, at an outdoor table on a beautiful spring day—Bostwick's Chowder House, on Highway 27 between Amagansett and central East Hampton.

She's having a salad. I ordered the fried clams platter.

"Fried food is going to kill you," she says.

"Wanna bet?" I fork a clam and put it on her plate.

Brigid laughs and recoils, like I've put a bug on it.

"Okay, so tell me stuff about the trial I can't read online."

She has always been thin, even before cancer. But she looks thinner than the last time we were together, and even paler than usual. She blames her coloring on our late Irish mother every time she has to make another trip to the dermatologist and have something taken off her face.

"How are you doing really?" I ask my sister.

She smiles. "Rhetorical question?"

"Maybe just a predictably dumb one."

"You're not creating an equivalency to the trial, are you, sis?"

"Just trying to get a better understanding of what it's like going through what you're going through and what I'm going to have to go through eventually. In my own predictably clumsy way."

Thinking that I'm using my own sister as a possible starter kit on cancer treatment.

"It continues to suck," she says. "My oncologist is talking about other types of treatment going forward. Which, he says, will come with their own complications and side effects."

I grab a clam with my fingers, dip it in tartar sauce, and almost defiantly plunk it into my mouth.

"So how *are* things going in the trial?"

I grin at her. "As someone said recently, it continues to suck."

I sip some iced tea, carefully place my glass on the table, push my plate to the side.

"I need to ask you something."

"If you're asking me why I never lost my hair, it's a mystery to me. Hopefully some miracle of our genetic code. Whatever it is, I'll take the win."

"Not what I was going to ask."

"Sounds serious."

"Kind of. Why didn't you tell me you were with Rob Jacobson at some point on the night those people died?"

She tilts her head slightly to the side, and frowns. "What?"

"You heard me, sis. Your immune system may be compromised, but I've never noticed any problem with your hearing."

"Did Rob tell you that?"

"His wife, actually, not that it matters."

"To me it does."

She shakes her head.

"Well, whoever told you," Brigid says, "it's not true."

"You're certain of that."

"I'm your sister. Are you saying you don't believe me?"

"I guess I'm saying that I've always believed that you and Rob were more than friends. All the way back to college."

"That witch he married has always believed the same thing. Well, sorry, but you're both wrong."

"If you were with him that night, you need to tell me, Brigid."

"I'm telling you," she says. "I wasn't."

"Brigid, I'm not here to judge."

"There's a relief."

"But he has no alibi for that night, from the time he was seen eating dinner alone at the bar at Sam's. You might be all he has."

"If I was with him. Which I wasn't."

"If Claire Jacobson said what she said to me, she likely said it to other people," I say. "And the district attorney will find out if she did."

"Everybody knows I'm Rob's friend. The DA wouldn't call me, right?"

Somehow the possibility of being called seems to frighten my sister.

"Just putting it out there."

She stares at me. "Wait," she says. "Are *you* thinking of calling me?"

"Only if you were with him."

"How many times do I have to tell you I wasn't?"

"Were you with Chris?"

Her husband. The principal.

"He was in Maine visiting his parents that week," she says. "I was home alone the whole night, doing a binge-watch of *Succession,* as I recall."

"People often make lies more elaborate than they need to."

"So you're flat-out calling me a liar now," she says.

"I'm trying to keep the friend you begged me to represent out of a life sentence."

"By trying to get your sister with cancer to admit to something she didn't do."

"Ah," I say. "The cancer card."

"Frankly didn't think I'd need it for lunch with my sister," Brigid says.

I lean forward, lowering my voice, so I'm not on social media in the next few minutes if somebody here has recognized me.

"For the last time," I say. "Were...you...with...him that night?"

"Am I under oath here? Should I find myself a good lawyer?"

I try to swallow a sigh but fail. Doesn't matter. Brigid has always seized on any change of expression with me, on the tone of my voice, even the slightest eye roll.

"Sorry I'm such a burden to you," she says.

"I am trying to help you."

"Really."

I wait.

"You know I understand him better than his wife ever could, right?"

"Well, then you also need to understand he—and I—can use all the help we can get right now."

She stares at me, through what becomes an awkwardly long silence. Maybe buying herself more time. So now it's exactly the way it was between us when we were teenagers, and I'd press her for intel on one of her dates and could see her trying to decide how much to tell me.

"I don't want to be a part of this," she says, staring off.

And with that, she starts to cry.

She cries silently, tears running down her cheeks, making no effort to wipe them away. The waiter has started for our table, ready to clear our plates. He stops, turns, heads back inside.

"You have no idea what I'm going through."

She's right. I don't. At least not yet.

She suddenly pushes back her chair and makes her way between the other tables, on her way to where she's parked her car in the back lot.

Good talk.

FORTY-FIVE

JIMMY RIDES TO COURT with me the next morning, Judge Prentice having officially been informed that juror number 10 had not, in fact, been staring into the abyss. He is a diabetic. Low blood sugar had gotten him. He spent a couple of hours at the hospital, got released, and informed the court that he would be back in his seat today.

Jimmy and I talk a little more about the fire, and the work being done at the bar, and how the Sag Harbor cops don't have a single lead.

"The only goddamn lead," Jimmy tells me, "is sitting next to you."

By now Jimmy has hired a local company that does bug sweeps, trying to find out if our guy got into Jimmy's house as easily as he did mine and planted something that would help him hear Jimmy's phone conversations. They came up with nothing. Came up with nothing at my house, too. They checked Jimmy's car. And mine. Nothing.

"Let's talk about something else before I get the ass all over again," Jimmy says.

So we talk about the trial. I ask him if he thinks I should bring back our forensics expert, Marge Florio, from John Jay College, as a way of recasting doubt on the physical evidence.

"My opinion?" Jimmy says.

"Why I'm asking."

"You'll just bore the jury with that shit and stop all the momentum you got going after the way you bounced that Hennessy around. And I think you already did knock down the evidence pretty good with the East Hampton cop, poor guy. It was like he wasn't ready to be called up to the big leagues."

I feel myself grinning at how tense he is. It's because he's in the passenger seat. He doesn't like *not* being behind the wheel. And likes my driving even less.

"We both know what our job is right now," he says. "Job one, like they say. And not for nothing, Janie? The divider line is *not* a lane."

"Front-seat driver."

"I wish," he says. "We should outfit this car like it's from Driver's Ed, and we both get a wheel."

"You're fine."

"Am I?"

"Job one," I say now. "Create doubt."

He lets me sit in on his regular poker game sometimes, even though the other guys at the table are much better cardplayers than I am. But some of the principles of poker apply to court. Always have. You want the rest of the table to believe, just by the way you're betting, that you have the cards.

Whether you do or not.

It's all about plausible doubt, standing it up as best you can. Make the jury doubt the perfect evidence. The *totality* of evidence. Make it plausible that Rob Jacobson is right, that he was set up. That someone other than him did it. Someone, anyone. Even when your client is a perfect ass—and I know

I've got one of those—that doesn't mean he did it. Make them look somewhere else.

Don't look over here.

Look over *there*.

From the Shiny Object School of Law.

I tell Jimmy that he's right. Screw the forensics expert. I'm recalling Otis Miller first today, instead of second, and I contact the clerk to inform him of that fact.

Jimmy says, "You think Miller could have done it for real?"

"Could have, sure. Actually did the deed? Nah."

"You feel bad about making him your straw man?"

"Yeah," I say. "But every time I do, I lie down until the feeling passes. There's just something about him. Like he's too eager to be the hero of our drama."

"So he gets a good smack again today?" Jimmy says.

I smile. "No plausible doubt on that at all."

"This may not be the time to ask you," Jimmy says, "but do you ever think you're going to lose a case?"

We're about to get off Sunrise Highway. Just to jam him up a little more, I wait until the last second in the left lane, check the mirror, then accelerate across the right lane and just manage to make Exit 65.

"Hail Mary," he says, "full of grace."

"Do I think about losing? All the time."

I grin.

"Just not today."

FORTY-SIX

I AM ABOUT TO get to it with Otis Miller.

Get to what Jimmy Cunniff likes to call the juicy.

I'm not winning my case today. Just trying to put some points on the board. Those scales that Lady Justice holds? They're supposed to be about fairly weighing evidence presented in court. But I've long since come to grips with the fact that I'm no lady, and I sometimes only play fair when I've run out of other good options.

"As we've discussed before," I say to Miller, "your issues with post-traumatic stress disorder are a matter of public record, are they not?"

"I thought sharing my story might help people with similar issues," he says. "Destigmatize PTSD even more than it is already. And encourage people who need help to get it."

"Very admirable of you."

"Do I detect sarcasm?" Miller asks.

"No, sir. Not with an issue like that and not with someone who served his country as honorably as you did. If that's what you heard, Mr. Miller, I apologize."

"No need."

I keep my distance from him for now, standing near the court reporter's station.

"Now, it goes without saying that we're here because my client has been accused of committing a violent crime," I say, "even though it would have to be viewed as a completely random act, as there has been no previous evidence of violence in my client's adult life."

"But Mr. Hennessy testified that Rob threatened to kill Mitch Gates, didn't he?"

I want to walk over and kiss him.

"So he did," I say. "Which leads me to a question, Mr. Miller. I'm wondering if your own struggles with PTSD ever caused you to threaten anybody. Or to engage in a random act of violence."

"Objection, Your Honor," Ahearn says. "Mr. Miller isn't the one on trial for murder here. Ms. Smith's client is."

"Sustained," Judge Prentice says.

"If you'll allow me just one more question along this line," I say. "Mr. Miller, didn't Mitch Gates tell you one night at the Turnpike Tavern to stay away from his wife? And didn't things escalate enough that the two of you ended up in a fistfight?"

"Objection," Ahearn says. "Hearsay."

"Sustained."

It's here that Miller surprises me.

"Wait, Your Honor. I'm happy to answer the question, if that's all right with you."

"You may answer the question," Judge Prentice says.

Otis Miller says, "It actually happened pretty much the way Ms. Smith described it, right around last call that night. We were the only two people in there, along with the bartender, who's an old Army friend of mine, which is why I stop by there from time to time. Mitch showed up, pretty well lit, and told me to stay away from his wife. I told him he had it all wrong. He took a swing and missed. I got my arms around him to discourage him from taking another. Cal, the bartender, got him out of there. That was the end of that."

"*Did* he have it wrong? About you and his wife?"

"He couldn't possibly have been more wrong—trust me."

"Mr. Miller, I'm going to ask you something I've asked you previously and remind you that you are still under oath here. Wasn't the reason Mitch Gates accused you of having an affair with his wife because you *were* having an affair with his wife?"

Otis Miller smiles. "We're really doing this? Again?"

"Sadly, we are."

"I actually thought you were going to drop it after I testified that first time around that this narrative is insane."

"It was me you called insane, just to be clear."

"As you just pointed out," he says, smiling again, "I *am* under oath."

"Boy, are you ever."

"For the last time," he says, "I was not having an affair with Kathy. I was her friend, at a time when she needed a friend. She had a complicated relationship with her daughter. Her husband was away a lot that summer. There was something else bothering her, I could tell, but something she never wanted to talk about, at least not with me. So I was there for her, nothing more."

"At all hours?"

"As a matter of fact, yes. If she needed someone to talk to, I was just up the road."

"How there for her would you say, exactly?" I ask.

"So here we are again," he says. "You want me to admit that I was having sex with Kathy Gates, no matter how many times

I say I wasn't." He shakes his head and chuckles now. "My ex-wife used to sound like this when she was accusing me of cheating on her."

"Did you cheat on her with other women?"

"Should I plead the Fifth on that?"

It's almost as if he's enjoying this back-and-forth, I think. *As if he's the one cross-examining me.*

"I only want you to admit to an affair with Kathy Gates if it's the truth, Mr. Miller."

"Only it's not," Miller says, "no matter how much you want it to be."

He looks past me, seems to wink now at someone in the gallery. But I stay on him.

"I know I should have cleared this up the first time I was on the stand," Otis Miller continues, "but I thought that my private life ought to remain private. And that we, meaning you and I, both knew you were making shit up."

"Language, Mr. Miller," Judge Prentice says. "Even if it's Ms. Smith to whom you're speaking."

"I apologize, Your Honor."

"Your private life gets to stay private unless and until it's relevant to a murder trial," I tell Miller now. "At which point it becomes everybody's business."

"So you're saying that it's everybody's business that I'm gay?" Otis Miller says.

Boom.

It's like a hockey hit in that moment, the way I used to feel when I'd get slammed into the boards and the butt end of my stick would go into my midsection and I couldn't get my breath and would just sit there on the ice until I could.

Jimmy Cunniff told me one time that Mike Tyson used to say everybody had a plan until they got hit.

The best I can do to respond, all I got in a courtroom that has gone completely still, is this:

"Fuck."

It just comes out. I meant it to be under my breath.

Not even close.

"Ms. Smith!" Judge Jackson Prentice says, swinging his gavel to back that up.

Otis Miller has been playing me all along.

Gay.

I'd come here looking to establish plausible doubt and now there's no plausible doubt, none, about that. Unless we're all supposed to believe he's telling the world he's gay in open court just for laughs.

Miller, smiling now, says, "This isn't the way I wanted to make things official, but that good-looking blond guy in the second row is my partner. Has been for the past six months or so. We've been spending most of that time in the city, because he's directing a new play."

I can't stop him.

"I'd been alone for the past few years when Mitch and Kathy Gates rented their house, after a bad breakup. The truth is, Kathy Gates had been helping me get through it."

At this point, the good-looking blond guy offers a small, self-conscious wave as everybody in the room turns to him.

And then I am no longer speaking under my breath in Judge Jackson Prentice III's courtroom.

"Fuck...fuck...*fuck,*" I say before the judge is fining me for contempt of court.

I deserve it.

But not because I've got a dirty mouth.

Because I'm the one feeling as if I just got screwed.

FORTY-SEVEN

Jimmy

THE JUDGE CALLS A recess after he hits Jane with contempt for her language. When they're outside, Jimmy apologizes for not knowing about Otis Miller being gay. She says that it sounds like only his partner knows. And maybe Miller's ex-wife, and that neither one of them thought to ask her if her ex likes guys better.

Jimmy tries to lighten things up by telling her that Miller and Kevin make a cute couple. She tells him she's in no mood. Jimmy says he can see that.

"Oh," she says, "now you're a great detective."

They both know Jimmy never planned to spend the whole day in court; he's on his way to the city to meet up with his old partner, Mickey Dunne. As curious as Jimmy is to see how he can change the subject and make something out of what turned into a shit day for her, he calls for an Uber, then takes the 3:20 train to Penn Station out of Riverhead.

It's for the best, he knows. As much as Jane Smith hates being surprised in court, she hates looking bad. She knows Otis Miller made her look bad.

Worse, the guy played her. Had really been playing her all along.

"Call me with some good news" was the last thing she said to him. "Or else."

Jimmy has nothing more than his gut to go on that the guy stalking him is ex-NYPD. His gut and his ear. Jimmy is sure he heard Bronx in the guy's voice. People from out of town, Jimmy knows, think all New *Yawk* accents are the same. But Jimmy knows there is more than one. Brooklyn doesn't sound like Queens. Neither one of those boroughs has ever sounded like the Bronx to him. Or Staten Island.

Manhattan? Manhattan is all of them at once.

He's settled in a window seat by now. The seat next to him is empty, always a joy on the LIRR. He smiles. Still something about going to the city.

When he told Jane where he was going and who he was going to see, she said, "You still have friends in the department?"

"More than you, missy."

Mickey Dunne is still working out of the 19th, same as he did when he and Jimmy came out of the Academy together. They partnered up early, before the brass separated them, thinking two cowboys working together was one too many. Jimmy believes in his heart that if Mickey were still his partner in the aftermath of Jimmy shooting a big-time dealer of heroin and coke named Angel Reyes, Jimmy would have beaten the rap, at least internally.

But Jimmy's partner at the time—the one whose name must not be mentioned—sold him out. Internal Affairs believed his partner's account of the shooting, not Jimmy's. Jimmy got canned. He kept trying to tell himself that things worked out for the best, because he ended up with Jane.

Detective First Grade Michael (Mickey) Dunne wanted to meet at McSorley's, on 7th in the East Village. Just the thought of the joint makes Jimmy happy. He's always loved McSorley's, with the green sign over the door saying they'd been in business since 1854, with the best dark beer in the city, and with the one sign in particular inside that Jimmy loved:

BE GOOD OR BE GONE.

Damn straight.

Mickey still isn't close to putting in his papers. As much as he bitches, he still loves the life. The way Jimmy did. Mickey and Jimmy. In the day? They were some pair.

Mickey doesn't look much older than the last time the two of them were together. Maybe a little heavier. The hair more white than gray now. His nose a shade more of drinker's red. Mostly he is still Mickey. Foxhole loyal, the way Jimmy is. And every bit as tough.

They both order McSorley's Dark, a glass of Jameson on the side. Old times.

They drink to each other.

Mickey says, "I hear your boss got her ass handed to her by a witness today."

"Happens," Jimmy says. "But it never lasts for long."

"She's a bad girl, that one."

"Baddest girl on the planet."

They've scored a corner table near the front window. The whole place looks to Jimmy the way he imagines it looked a hundred years ago.

It takes being inside to make Jimmy remember just how much he has missed this place. And being a partner to Mickey Dunne, who grew up in the shadow of the old Yankee Stadium, Grand Concourse, Bronx, New York.

"I hear you've been talking to Organized Crime about the Garden City thing," Mickey says.

"You know I'm doing a lot more than making calls, right?"

"I'm old, partner. But not dead."

They both raise their Irish whiskey and clink glasses and drink to that.

"The mob piece turned out to be a dead *end*," Jimmy says. "The guy was in deep to Bobby Salvatore. But I don't think this is about that, necessarily."

"What, then?"

"Beats the hell out of me. But somebody wants me and Jane off this. Like, bad."

Jimmy tells him all of it now, everything that's happened, like he's reading out of an old murder book. Artie Shore. McCall. The guy getting the drop on him. The needle. Jane's dog. The fire.

"I heard about the fire," Mickey says. "That shit is messed up."

"Guy then informed me it was my last warning. *Our* last warning."

"You believe he wore the uniform?"

"I do."

"And you believe he wore it here?" Mickey says.

Jimmy says, yeah, he does.

"You think of anybody you ever knew or ever heard about capable of shit like this?" Jimmy says. "Being a killer or a fixer or both?"

Mickey finishes his beer, and his whiskey, and waves for more, pointing at Jimmy as he does.

"Funny you should ask. Just on account of the other thing you got going."

"The trial."

"No, your stamp collection. Of course your trial."

"What you got?" Jimmy says.

"There's this guy who kind of maybe might fit the profile

you just gave me," Mickey Dunne says. "Fixer and hitter for the rich and famous back in the day. There's just one small problem."

"Waiting."

"Guy's dead."

FORTY-EIGHT

RIP IS WAITING FOR me when I come through the door.

"What's that you're asking?" I say to him as I scratch him behind an ear. "How did my day go, dear?"

He looks at me expectantly, as if I have promised him a treat. "Don't ask."

I do give him a treat and let him out into the backyard and feed him dinner. I take a long, hot bath, then turn on the television to watch the Mets. Or they watch me once I hit the couch—hard to tell. I always like listening to the Mets announcers. As if they owe me a good performance, either way, you can never tell from them whether the team is winning or losing. They do their job.

I did some job today, didn't I?

A shit job.

Nice work, Janie.

Before I walked into the courtroom this morning, I'd told myself that I wasn't going to win my case today, not with this much trial left.

But I hadn't expected to walk out feeling as if I'd lost it.

"How could we have not known the guy was gay?" I'd said to Jimmy before he left for the city.

"I should've known," he said. "This is on me."

"We both should've," I said. "And you know why we didn't? Because we were dumb enough to think he didn't fit some kind of profile. War hero. Local tough guy. Divorced. As if a guy like that couldn't *possibly* be gay."

I'd made a faulty assumption. Jimmy and I both had. And then I'd walked right into it.

Or stepped into it—that was probably a better way of looking at it.

Otis Miller had known I was going to ask him again about the affair, or else I would never have called him back to the stand. And he had been lying in wait for me. The divorced, local hero, Army vet, ready to turn the tables and ambush *me*.

I'm gay.

That's my partner, sitting right there.

On top of everything else, I'm the lawyer who just outed a gay man.

It was right before my client threatened to fire me during the recess, calling me, among other things, an amateur.

Hard to disagree with him.

Just like that, I'm restless.

Need to be in motion.

I get up, grab my bag, the car keys still in it. Lock the house, tell Rip I'll be back, go outside, and get into the car, back it out of the driveway, pull up alongside Kenny Stanton's.

"I'm going out for a bit. I'd rather you watch the house than stay with me."

"Jimmy's my boss," Kenny says. "I'm supposed to take my orders from him."

"And I'm his. I thought you cops were bears for chain of command."

"You sure this'll be okay?"

"I'm sure. Get some rest. Don't think I'm not aware you pulled a double shift tonight."

As I drive up the street, I see him move his car closer to the house. Then I make my way back to Abraham's Path and head for the Springs. I haven't called ahead. I really haven't decided for sure that I am even going over there until I have the car in motion.

It has been a while, but I remember how to get there without using Waze.

The two-bedroom cottage, purchased twenty years ago before prices got jacked up in the Springs the way they did everywhere else in the Hamptons, is still sitting on a half acre that backs up to the bay. I'm willing to bet anything that the canoe is still at the same little dock, where the land ends and the water begins.

Lights on inside the house.

Car in the driveway.

First break I've caught all day.

I knock on the door and Dr. Ben Kalinsky opens it.

He smiles when he sees me standing there, almost as if telling me that everything is going to be all right before I even say a word.

"You lost?" he asks.

"There's something I need to tell you."

FORTY-NINE

Jimmy

JIMMY SHOWS UP AT Jane's house at seven the next morning, with coffee and her favorite donuts from the M and R Deli over by the East Hampton train station.

"Kenny says you went out and didn't come back till right before dawn," Jimmy says when they're in her kitchen.

"I went to see a friend."

"Male or female?"

"None of your business."

"That means male. You go see the vet?"

"What part of 'none of your business' is eluding you here?"

She is already dressed for court. And looks good, Jimmy thinks. Tired but good. Maybe tired from being out so late with Dr. Ben. Jimmy is fine with that, if that's where she was. Ben Kalinsky is good people. And she needs somebody in her life.

Anybody, Jimmy thinks sometimes.

Jane keeps telling him, when the subject comes up, that she doesn't need a man. Been there, done that, she says. Jimmy thinks she's wrong. Not to complete her or any of that antiquated bullshit. Just to have something in her life other than her work and a dying dog.

He knows enough not to bring up what happened in court yesterday. Nothing to say. They got clipped, and now they move on, like always. She'll find a way today to dig herself out of the hole. Jimmy has seen her do it plenty of times before on her way to the winner's circle.

But they did get clipped, no two ways about that.

They drink coffee and eat donuts and he tells her what he's learned about Joe Champi, ex-cop, everything Mickey Dunne told him at McSorley's.

Champi had been on his way out of the NYPD, at their request, at about the same time Jimmy and Mickey were still in uniform and first hitting the streets. Mickey says now he remembers hearing about him at the time. Jimmy does not. Joe Champi: Great cop. First in Vice, finally undercover. Until he went bad. Always with a reputation, all the way along, of operating well outside the margins.

Once he was out of the department, he graduated to doing body work, as a fixer and a cleaner—and hitter, or so legend had it—for some powerful people in the city. The real estate guy who reimagined Fifth Avenue. One of the guys who used to own the Islanders. The guy, dead now, who used to run one of the biggest limo companies in town. Big stuff and small. Whatever you needed.

"Sounds like a player," Jane says.

"Except he didn't play nice, even before he got with our friend Bobby Salvatore and ended up being one of your persons of interest in about half a dozen disappearances."

"Like Gregg McCall's."

"Bingo."

"What finally happened to him?"

"What happened is that he shocked the shit out of everybody by taking himself out. He goes to McSorley's one night, before they find his car later near the Verrazano Bridge on the Staten Island side. Buys drinks all around, tells everybody they're not going to see him again, he's through being a dirtbag, only one way to make things right. Leaves a note on the dashboard. Good-bye. His phone is on the front seat. Becomes a missing person, presumed dead. Eyewitnesses talk about what they heard at McSorley's. Note in his own hand."

Jane looks at her watch. "I need to get to court. I assume you're going to tell me why I should care about the dead dirtbag."

"Three reasons," Jimmy says. "One is that it's the way I would have set it up if I wanted everybody to think I took myself out. Two is that he happens to fit the profile of the dirtbag I'm looking for to a T."

"What's behind door number three?"

"Turns out there's one other person Champi did some work for once that I didn't mention yet."

FIFTY

I'M SITTING IN THE attorney room waiting for my client to be delivered, fifteen minutes before court, still thinking about Ben Kalinsky.

Why didn't I tell him last night?

It was a dream opportunity. Not just to tell him but to finally get him into bed, something I knew wasn't going to be much of a challenge at this point, certainly not for me.

I did neither.

We just talked, into the night.

I made up something about being torn up that I might be defending a guilty man. It's the truth. But not what I wanted to tell him, about cancer.

I hear the door open now. Rob Jacobson comes walking in. New day, another new suit for him. I'm wishing again I had his wardrobe budget. It occurs to me, also not for the first time, that an accused murderer dresses better than I do.

A lot better.

And his clothes fit him a lot better.

He sits down across the table from me.

"Good job yesterday, Jane, no kidding," he says. "Getting a gay guy to come out in open court. Wow. Didn't see that coming."

He's still pissed and has a right to be. But I'm not in the mood. And tell him so.

"Really?"

"Really," he says. "Guess what. You know who doesn't get to cop an attitude today? *You,* counselor."

"Fair enough."

He leans forward. Familiar snarky grin on his face. The longer I'm with him the easier it becomes for me to understand why so many people on the East End aren't sure which way to root. Or perhaps are.

"Listen, I need to ask you a question before we go inside."

"You want my help remembering how to be a good lawyer?"

"You done now?" I say.

"Pretty much."

"Who's Joe Champi?"

Stops him. But not for long. He's never at a loss for words. Just gathering himself before he starts up again.

"Joe *Champi*? Where did that come from? And what does he have to do with my case?"

"Not a thing."

"Then why are we talking about him?" Jacobson says.

"His name came up on something else Jimmy and I are working on."

"And I'm supposed to care about that?"

"How do you know him?"

"*Knew* him. Isn't he dead?"

"That seems to be the prevailing wisdom," I say. "But Jimmy's not so sure."

"I thought only good guys rose from the dead."

"Stop screwing around and tell me: how do you know him?"

"He got me out of a couple of jams when I was a kid," he says. "A friend of mine told me about this cop who was kind of a fixer and could make things go away, if you had the cash, and you didn't want your parents to find out. He made a DUI disappear for my friend. Did the same for me, even though it cost a shitload of money."

"And that was it?"

"Pretty much, other than a few odd jobs here and there," Jacobson says. "Until you brought him up just now, I haven't thought about him in years."

"Why do I think you're lying?"

"Your problem, counselor. Not mine."

"Aren't you interested in how his name came up?"

There's a knock on the door. The clerk pokes his head in, points at his watch.

"Does it help get me acquitted?"

"Unlikely."

"Then stop wasting my time with things that have nothing to do with me, or this case," he says. "And be the kind of goddamn fixer I'm paying *you* a lot of money to be."

He stands.

"At least Joe Champi got shit done."

FIFTY-ONE

Jimmy

JIMMY KEEPS TELLING HIMSELF that he's spending too much time and energy chasing a ghost, that he should get off Champi, that all he's going on with Champi is his gut.

But his gut, which has rarely failed him, won't allow it. Keeps telling him, shouting at him sometimes, that Champi is still alive, and that he's the one who made Gregg McCall go away.

And if he didn't have something to do with the murders of the Carsons of Garden City, he might know who did.

He's thinking about McCall and the Carsons again tonight, sitting in the front seat of his car, telling himself again that being overly cautious is never a waste of time, especially when the job is keeping Jane safe.

He knows what Jacobson told Jane about Champi before court today, how their paths crossed a few times in the past. And maybe, Jimmy thinks, that's all there is. Maybe coincidence isn't always the load of crap that he believes it is. Who knows what Jacobson, even as a kid, might have paid Champi to make problems go away? Or what his old man might have paid when he was still around? Mickey Dunne said Champi didn't come cheap, even when he was still on the job, that his prices just went up when he started freelancing. The guy sounds to Jimmy like that fixer on television, Ray Donovan, except Jimmy watched the show a few times and the character—he can't remember the name of the actor who plays him—does have some redeeming qualities.

By all accounts, Champi had absolutely none.

"Put it this way," Mickey said. "If Champi *is* still alive, I'm shocked he didn't kill her dog."

Jimmy is back in front of Jane's house, waiting for Kenny to come relieve him for the really late shift tonight. He has his laptop with him, using his phone as a hot spot rather than hijack some neighbor's Wi-Fi, trying to get back to work on the Jacobson case, refocus himself on that, reading back on the guy again, looking for something or anything that might help Jane out. Still searching for something or anything that will convince her and Jimmy both that the guy didn't do it.

The trial is starting to grind her down—Jimmy can see it. She even admitted to him today that she's tired, the first time she's *ever* admitted that.

Jane keeps saying that the evidence against Jacobson is *too* perfect. Jimmy doesn't want to debate the point with her, because he knows how much she wants him to be innocent, as much of a royal pain in the ass as he is. Maybe needs him to be innocent so she can live with herself. But maybe the evidence is perfect because it's real.

Because the guy did it. Killed those people—father, mother, daughter—in cold blood.

So he googles Rob Jacobson again, taking another trip down memory lane, and is about to switch search engines when the first bullet shatters the passenger window.

FIFTY-TWO

I'M WIDE-AWAKE AT three in the morning, unable to sleep again, still reading over today's testimony from my forensics expert, having just let Rip out and then back in again, when I hear the first shot.

I'm in sweatpants and a T-shirt, my sneakers still on from being in the yard, as I grab the gun from the table in the hall and head for the front door.

I hear the second shot then, from up the block, from where either Jimmy's car is or Kenny's—I don't know if Jimmy has been relieved yet.

I'm out the door, staying low as I move along the front of my house, cutting across Marty Getchel's front lawn, then sprinting for the street.

It's Jimmy's car.

I manage to exhale when I see him sitting next to the driver-side door, the window on the passenger side gone. He's holding his hand to his right shoulder. I see the blood on his white T-shirt starting to spread.

Shit.

At the same time I look to my right and see a figure running toward Abraham's Path.

"You're hit," I say.

"I'm all right. Through-and-through."

"Call 911."

"Already did."

"I'm going after him," I say.

He reaches up, grabs my arm with his left hand.

"No, you're not. I can't cover you."

I take his hand and press it against his shoulder.

"Yes. This might be our one shot at him. And the asshole just shot you."

Lights are coming on in the neighborhood as I start running hard after him, Glock pressed to my chest the way Jimmy taught me. Thinking this is a different kind of biathlon now. Just with real bullets this time.

Bigger stakes.

I can hear my father's voice, my father the Marine, telling me to attack now. *You back up in any kind of fight, you've already lost it.*

The guy—I assume it's a guy—makes a right onto Abraham's Path, heading for the railroad tracks. Still too far away for me to get off a good shot at him. I'm worried that if I do start shooting, somebody else who can't sleep might be out for a late-night stroll and walk right into the crossfire.

I'm running easily, though. And feeling as if I'm making up ground, the guy still visible up ahead.

No cancer tonight.

He makes a right when he gets to the other side of the tracks. I get a better look at him now, silhouetted against the night sky, running past the horse farm I know is to his left. Big guy.

Did Jimmy say Champi was big?

I'm ready if he stops and turns and takes a shot at me.

He does not.

Not yet, anyway.

He's starting to slow.

I'm not.

Both of us running on gravel now, me on one side of the tracks, him on the other.

I hear the blast of the train whistle.

Eastbound train in the night. I love the sound of that train, even when it wakes me up sometimes.

Just not tonight.

I see the headlights.

The lights distract me enough, briefly blind me enough, that I stumble on the gravel, putting my free hand down to keep myself from falling.

The train is getting closer.

I feel as if there is a spotlight on me now. On both of us. I look up the tracks. He has what looks to be a blue ball cap pulled down tight over his eyes.

I start to raise my gun.

Too late.

His is already up.

Two hands on it, classic shooting pose.

Clear shot.

I think: *Good Christ, is this the way I go out?*

Only he doesn't take the shot.

What the hell?

I fire the Glock now, miss.

Fire again.

Don't know if I've hit him or not because then the train is on both of us. At the last moment I realize I am too close to the tracks as the train roars past me, the force of the draft coming off it knocking me off the gravel and into grass.

I lie there out of breath, not because I'm out of shape, not because of the chase, but the air went out of me as the train's close pass knocked me down.

When I get back to my feet, the night clouds have parted and now it's a full moon lighting the tracks.

The bastard is gone.

FIFTY-THREE

Jimmy

IT IS MOVING UP on four in the morning now. Even less chance than usual of either Jimmy or Jane getting any good sleep, so Jane makes them coffee. The EMT who bandaged Jimmy told him he ought to head over to the new urgent care in Bridgehampton to have the wound looked at. Jimmy lied and told him he'd head over there first thing. The EMT told Jimmy he was lucky that it was a through-and-through shot.

"Years of practice," Jimmy said.

He's made Jane tell him everything that happened at the tracks. Twice. She wants to know how much pain he's in because of his shoulder. He says it only hurts when he laughs. She says he's not laughing.

"Then I don't want to find out how much it will hurt when I do," he says.

They sit at the kitchen table, the dog on the floor next to Jane.

"This time he tried to kill you."

He grins. "You don't miss anything."

"Whatever happened to both of you being cops? Isn't that what he told you at McCall's house?"

"We're assuming it's the same guy?" Jimmy says.

Jane tilts her head, an amused look on her face. "Come on, man."

"So the state of play has changed. Maybe because he knows I know who he is. And knows I'm coming for his ass."

"Has to be Champi."

"Yes, ma'am."

"I've told you before to never ma'am me."

"Withdrawn."

He drinks some of Jane's coffee.

"He had a clear kill shot at me," Jane says. "Didn't take it."

She looks at his shoulder. He refused the EMT's offer of a sling.

"Why are you suddenly expendable and I'm not?" Jane asks.

"Beats the shit out of me."

"Damn. I was afraid of that."

FIFTY-FOUR

SOMEHOW, EVEN AS JAZZED as I am on caffeine and adrenaline, I manage to get a couple of hours of sleep after Jimmy leaves.

Good thing, because I have a big morning coming up in court.

My surprise witness.

One I need, don't just want.

One I need at this point in the proceedings.

When I'm fully awake again, a few minutes before six, I take Rip in the car with me and drive to Indian Wells Beach and we go for a walk. Not a long one. He's not up to that yet, or running, even though he's getting stronger by the day. When we come back, I feed him, drink more coffee, then fix myself a huge plate of scrambled eggs and bacon. Joke of it all? My cholesterol levels are perfect. Dream numbers across the board.

What a lucky girl am I.

I wear a blue suit I haven't yet worn at this trial. A little looser on me than when I purchased it, but not so much that I need to have it taken in. Amazing how cancer can help you with those hard-to-lose five pounds.

I get a call from the clerk on my way to Riverhead, informing me that my client would like to meet with me before court is in session. I lie and tell the clerk to tell Rob Jacobson that unfortunately I'm running late and will be lucky to get there by nine o'clock.

So I linger in the car until it's five minutes till and act rushed when I sit down next to him.

"You okay?" he says.

"Never better."

"Who's leading off today?"

"You'll see."

"You sound mysterious," Jacobson says.

"Keeps our relationship fresh."

Then everybody in the room is being told to rise, as Judge Jackson Prentice III enters and takes his seat.

"Are you ready to call your first witness, Ms. Smith?"

"I am, Your Honor."

I rise again, just as the double doors at the back of the room open and my sister comes walking in.

FIFTY-FIVE

Jimmy

MICKEY DUNNE IS ALREADY on the Long Island Expressway, at Exit 50 he says, when he calls Jimmy and tells him he has a day off and, what the hell, he thought he'd come out and see how Jimmy and the rest of the fancy people live.

"You must have a reason," Jimmy says.

"I do. Something you should see."

"What?"

"Tell you when I see you. I'm getting as geeked about talking on the phone as you are."

"You better not be screwing with me, partner," Jimmy says.

"By making a trip all the way out to you I don't need to make? In what world?"

Jimmy tells Mickey to meet him at the Candy Kitchen in Bridgehampton, Jimmy's favorite diner in the area, good enough to be the kind of breakfast joint you see every couple of blocks in the city, one with homemade ice cream, too. Cash only. Old-school.

Jimmy is waiting in a booth in an otherwise empty back room, the place having thinned out the way it always does in the late morning. Mickey is wearing baggy blue jeans and a black short-sleeved polo shirt with a logo Jimmy doesn't recognize. A NEVER FORGET baseball hat. As usual, he orders like he's going to the chair: eggs and bacon and home fries and a stack of pancakes on the side.

Jimmy tells him about his night.

"When's the last time you took a bullet?" Mickey says.

"Been a while."

"Still feel the same?"

"What do you think?"

"Guy shoots you and not her. How does that figure?"

"I will make sure to ask him when I find him," Jimmy says.

Mickey reaches down into the ancient leather satchel he has with him, a gift from Jimmy about a thousand or so years ago, places a notebook on the table between them, Crime Scene Log written in Magic Marker on the cover.

The book is about six inches long, maybe four wide—that size so it can fit into the side pocket of police pants. Something else that's old-school. Nowadays, Jimmy knows, the notes from a crime scene are typed into an electronic copy of the report. Just not back in the day, when you wrote it all down in great detail by hand if you were doing your job, usually the junior officer on the scene, and then the most relevant pages would be torn out of the book and copied again into the detectives' case file.

Mickey tells it his way, at his own speed, like always.

"Charlie Culligan was the junior officer on the day in question," he says. "The senior guy was Ernie Gottlieb, now deceased. They're the ones who caught the case."

Jimmy opens the notebook. Mickey taps the page with a stubby finger, the name he wants Jimmy to see clearly written at the bottom.

"As luck would have it, I ran into Charlie the other day. He's about six months from putting in his papers. I told him I was with you, what you got going, not just the thing with the trial but the other thing. And he tells me about this."

The name at the bottom of the page is Joe Champi's.

"What was *he* doing there?"

"That's the part that jogged Charlie's memory," Mickey says. "The weird part of the piece. Champi was assigned to Queens that day. But then when they find the bodies, Champi is right behind them. Or maybe ahead of them, and just takes a walk around the block to make it look as if he's behind them."

Mickey taps the Crime Scene Log again.

"You don't have to read the rest of it. All the shit about the medical examiner and the 'need to know' from other people in the building and what the kid said."

He slathers the pancakes with syrup and cuts into them as he keeps talking.

"There's just the one mention of the guy. Charlie Culligan says Champi told him he was on his way over the Queensboro when he heard the call and turned his car around because he said it sounded like fun."

"Fun," Jimmy says.

"Just telling you what Charlie remembers him saying."

Jimmy quickly leafs through the rest of the book now, closes it finally, looks over at Mickey Dunne.

"So it must have slipped his mind that Champi showed up at his apartment the day his old man shot that girl and then shot himself," Jimmy says.

"Imagine that," Mickey Dunne says.

FIFTY-SIX

KEVIN AHEARN HAS FINALLY stopped objecting, both from his table and then in front of Judge Prentice, about having had no prior notice that I was calling Brigid. I tell him she didn't decide until this morning, which isn't entirely true; it was last night.

Close enough.

"And she's her *sister,* for God's sake," Ahearn says when we approach.

"And proud of it," I say.

"Ms. Smith," Prentice says.

"Sorry, Your Honor."

Prentice says, "Mr. Ahearn, if you need extra time to prepare for your cross after Ms. Smith has finished with her witness, we can then adjourn until tomorrow morning. But I see no reason not to have her testify at this time."

"Your *Honor,*" Ahearn says, sounding as if he's pleading now. "I'm not sure what the letter of the law is about being blind-sided by counsel's sister, but it seems to me as if it violates the spirit of the law."

He knows he's overplayed his hand when he sees the look on Judge Prentice's face.

"I am well aware, sir, about both the letter *and* the spirit of the law. Now you go back to your table and, Ms. Smith, you get your witness sworn in."

I go back to my own table and briefly sit down. As I do, Rob Jacobson leans over and whispers to me.

"I don't want you to do this."

"You've heard this from me before," I whisper back. "I. Don't. Give. A. Shit."

Then I get up and approach the witness stand. Even with the weight she continues to lose, somehow my sister still manages to look like a million damn dollars.

Kevin Ahearn has just told the judge that he's the one getting blindsided here. But I felt the exact same way when my sister informed me she'd decided to testify.

And why she'd decided to testify.

"I'd like to clear something up before we get started," I say to her. "Was it my idea that you be here today?"

"It was my own decision, no one else's."

"But you had previously resisted being a witness in this case, isn't that correct?"

"It is."

"And why is that?"

"Because I thought it would cause undue pain to my husband, whom I love, and who should not be a part of this," Brigid says.

"But you changed your mind because you felt it was your obligation to give the testimony you're about to give."

"Objection," Ahearn says. "Ms. Smith isn't questioning her sister. She's coaching her. The way she probably coached her to make the big entrance she just made."

"Wait," I say. "Now I object."

Prentice slams down his gavel.

"Stop. Both of you. Both objections are overruled. Now please continue, Ms. Smith."

I do. "Would you please tell us, in your own words, why you did change your mind?"

"Because I finally decided that telling the truth outweighed my desire to protect my family" is Brigid's answer. "And that my husband and I have a marriage strong enough to survive any embarrassment my appearance here today might cause us."

"And what is the truth, Brigid?"

It seems silly to call her by her married name.

"Rob and I were together that night."

I think about the story she told that day at Bostwick's, the opposite of the one she's just now told under oath.

"She's lying!" I hear from behind me.

Just not from the district attorney.

From my client.

FIFTY-SEVEN

THE ROOM IS GRIPPED by a brief, stunned silence.

Starting with me.

Only because I've just heard my client basically act as his own rebuttal witness against the witness who has maybe, just maybe, gift wrapped a credible alibi for him. Or at least given him one that the jury has to consider.

When I look over at Kevin Ahearn, even he appears speechless. When he catches my eye, he just shrugs and puts his hands out as if to say, *You want to object to what your own client just yelled, have at it.*

He seems perfectly content to sit this one out for the time being.

It is Judge Jackson Prentice III who shatters the silence in his courtroom by slamming his gavel onto its block, making even a couple of jurors jump.

"Sit down, Mr. Jacobson," Prentice snaps.

"But, Your Honor..."

Prentice points the gavel at him. *"Not...another...word."*

Up until now, the only place where Rob Jacobson, who truly does love the sound of his own voice, especially with me, has been able to keep his mouth shut is here.

He won't do it now, despite the way he has royally pissed off the judge.

"I have a right to defend myself," he says.

"It seems to me that you have Ms. Smith for that," Prentice says, then turns away from him to face the jury, telling them to ignore the defendant's outburst, before addressing Brigid, apologizing to her for the interruption, asking her to please continue.

Rob Jacobson, though, won't give it up. Or can't make himself give it up.

"But that's my lawyer's sister, Judge, and I don't see how she can allow her to lie like that when she's under oath."

Now Prentice bangs his gavel down much harder than before, the sound like a thunderclap in his courtroom.

"This is your last warning, Mr. Jacobson. I have muzzled defendants in my courtroom before, and I will quite happily do it with you."

Prentice's gavel remains hovering over its block, as if he's ready to swing away again.

"Don't speak," Prentice says, still glaring at him. "Just nod your head if you understand what I have just told you."

Finally, I'm thinking, *Judge Jackson Prentice and I are on the same side of something.*

I am looking across the room at Rob Jacobson, imagining how much of his adult life he's managed to live without somebody talking to him the way the judge is talking to him right now in open court.

Only now his circumstances have changed, rather dramatically. Now this judge is the boss of him.

Jacobson nods.

"Now, for the last time, sit your ass down," Prentice says.

Whoa.

Jacobson does. I ask the judge if I can have a brief word with my client.

"I encourage it."

So I walk over to Rob Jacobson, smiling at him as if what has just happened in court happens all the time. I lean down then and cup my hand around my mouth and quietly say, "If you open your mouth again while I am questioning this witness I will stick your elbow in it. Now nod if you understand *that*."

And he does.

Prentice says, "Ms. Smith, do you need more time?"

"How about a month?"

It actually gets a smile out of Judge Jackson Prentice. I even hear some muffled laughter from the jury, muffled because they don't want Prentice turning on them, too.

"Seriously, Your Honor, my client understands the possible consequences of another outburst, and I know he's sorry for this one."

"Then if it's just the same with him, because we certainly wouldn't want to upset him, would it be all right if we proceed?" Prentice says.

"Yes, Your Honor."

I walk back toward Brigid.

"As I was saying."

Now she smiles.

"Brigid, was my client aware you would be testifying here today?"

"Yes."

"Did you tell him any of the specifics of the testimony you are prepared to give?"

"In general terms, yes."

"And what was his reaction to it?"

"He told me that I didn't need to lie for him, because the truth is that he's innocent," Brigid says.

"So you must have been as surprised at his outburst as the rest of us."

"Yes," she says. "I can't imagine the stress he's under."

She offers a weak smile. Clears her throat. I start to ask another question, but she holds up a hand to stop me.

"By the way, I told him that at least we were in agreement about that. Not the lying part. That he's innocent."

"Objection!" Kevin Ahearn says. "Your Honor, this witness has made it abundantly clear that she is a longtime friend of the defendant. In addition, she is the sister of defense counsel. Is she now auditioning to be judge, too? Or should I say jury?"

"Sustained," the real judge says.

"Sorry," Brigid says to him.

Still the nice one.

"No need to apologize to the court."

"Sorry," my sister says again.

Then she shoots an embarrassed smile at the jury. I watch them watch her. They're clearly on her side. They *like* her. Of course they do. She's Brigid.

But do they believe her after she's just been accused of lying her ass off?

Or do they believe the guy I'm trying my ass off to defend here?

"You're my sister, and I believe you," I say to her. "But who should the jury believe here, you or my client?"

"On whether we were together that night? Me. Totally."

I make a quick pivot to see Rob Jacobson's reaction. He gives a couple of quick, exasperated shakes of his head. But manages to keep his mouth shut.

I hesitate, giving myself one last chance not to break the promise to my sister I'm about to break.

About to go where I swore up and down that I wouldn't.

Everybody lies.

"Brigid, are you in love with Rob Jacobson?"

She hesitates now, just long enough to shoot me a look I've been getting from her my whole life, all the way back to the dinner table, when I'd tell my parents something she thought had been a secret between us girls, about boys or school or anything.

She looks down at her hands and then back at me and says, "I love him as a friend."

"Isn't it more than that, Brigid? Isn't that why you're really here today?"

This jury does like her. And she might be as much of a character witness for my no-character client as he's going to get.

I have to take this all the way.

"No," she says in a small voice.

"Isn't it true that the real reason you have been reluctant to testify up until today isn't just because the two of you were together that night but the *way* you were together?"

In the next moment I hear the angry scrape of a chair behind me, right before the chair is crashing to the floor behind Rob Jacobson, who is jumping to his feet again.

It turns out Judge Jackson Prentice doesn't need to gavel him back down this time.

Because Prentice watches now, as everybody else does, as my client, red-faced, mouth opening and closing but no words coming out of it, grabs his chest with his right hand before he pitches forward onto the table in front of him, spins off it, and ends up facedown on the courtroom floor.

I look past him and see Claire Jacobson standing expressionless in front of the courtroom doors, making no move to come to her husband's aid.

As I do move toward him, Brigid is already out of her chair and brushing past me, slowing down just enough to get close to my ear and say, "I hate you."

FIFTY-EIGHT

Jimmy

THEY RUSHED JACOBSON TO Peconic Bay Medical Center by ambulance—alone with the EMTs, his wife nowhere to be found—for observation and to make sure he hadn't had a heart attack.

Apparently, the bastard suffered one five years earlier. So he ended up there, Jane telling Jimmy on the phone that he was going to spend the night. There would, she said, be a cop posted at his door, though for the life of him Jimmy Cunniff can't understand why.

Where is the guy going?

He doesn't want to run. Shit, it's like he's running *toward* the spotlight. Jacobson *wants* this trial. Seems to be almost reveling in the goddamn thing. He's done everything except hire a sky-writer to tell the whole world he didn't do it, that he's going to be vindicated in the end. Now today he called Jane's sister a liar before he did a face-plant in front of God and Judge Jackson Prentice, as if he doesn't even need her to give him an alibi for the night of the murders.

When Jane gets back home from the hospital, there will be a car from the East Hampton Police out in front of her house, the way there has been since the night Jimmy got shot there.

Ahearn actually arranged it. Jimmy was with Jane during a recess when Ahearn told her that he wanted to beat her straight up, be the one to pin her first loss on her, and couldn't have her up and dying on him.

"No," Jane said, "we certainly wouldn't want that."

"I mean it."

"Your lips, God's ears."

Jimmy knows Ahearn is a born-again. At that point he actually asked Jane if she'd accepted Jesus as her Lord and Savior.

"I keep telling myself I'll get around to it. But I've been a little jammed up lately."

Jimmy cautioned Ahearn that at least some of the members of the local constabulary, didn't matter which town, weren't too keen on Jane at the moment, without telling him about the other Jane-involved shooting over in the Springs that night. Ahearn told Jimmy he'd already made it crystal clear to all departments that if anything happened to Jane Smith on their watch, their next duty would be directing traffic at the corner of Main Street and Newtown Lane at the Fourth of July parade.

Jimmy is at the bar tonight. Kenny Stanton is working the stick. Good crowd. But then business has generally been better than ever since the fire, as if the town wants to let whoever did it know that shit won't stand.

The Yankees game is on television. They've won four or five in a row. But it's too early for Jimmy to get excited about them; they've burned him too many times before by showing him early speed.

Jimmy's been nursing a Johnnie Walker Blue, the good stuff, since he sat down. Jane just called to tell him she was still waiting to get with Jacobson at the hospital.

"The good news," she told Jimmy, "is that it appears to have been a false alarm on the heart attack, and that he's going to live."

"Bad news?"

"That he's going to live."

Kenny walks down to where Jimmy is sitting and asks if he wants his drink topped off. Jimmy says he's good. Kenny asks how Jimmy's shoulder feels. Jimmy says bad, but not bad enough to take the pain pills he had left over in his medicine chest at home.

Kenny says, "You know what you need to do with those pills, right?"

"Flush 'em."

"Good boy."

Kenny stands there, arms crossed, grinning at Jimmy.

"What?"

"I know that look by now, is all."

"What look?"

"The one where you act like you're watching the ball game but all's you're really doing is thinking about that Joe Champi."

Jimmy puts up his uninjured arm, half surrendering. "You got me."

"You'll catch up with the jag-off eventually," Kenny says.

"How do you figure?"

"Because you always have."

"Kiss ass."

"*Bet* your ass."

Jimmy drinks the last of his Johnnie Walker. The small house he bought about five years ago, in North Haven, right after the divorce, a mile or so from the Shelter Island Ferry, is five minutes away, tops.

Too early to head home, though. But if he sits here he's going to have to answer more questions about the goddamn trial. Or deal with regulars wanting to know if there're any new leads on whoever tried to torch the place.

He hears a burst of laughter from a cop table at the other side of the room, Mike Rousselle is there. When he sees Jimmy eyeballing him, he grins and gives him the finger.

"Yeah," Jimmy calls over to him, "we're number one."

Jimmy waves Kenny down and says he's going out for some air but might be back.

"Shouldn't that arm be in a sling?" Kenny says.

"Yes," Jimmy says.

He takes a right out of the bar, heads east on Bay Street, past the gym on his left at the end of Division. Dopo La Spiaggia, a pretty good Italian joint, is up ahead on his right. The water to his left is lit up like Yankee Stadium because of all the big boats docked here, with more on the way.

Quiet night in Sag Harbor, Jimmy thinks. Calm before the looming summer storm, when Jimmy knows he'll once again be asking himself if the extra business he gets from the Summer People is worth it.

Good for business, he thinks. Just bad for the soul.

Jimmy sticks his right hand into the pocket of his windbreaker, because letting the arm flop around hurts too much. Yeah, he thinks. Getting shot still hurts like a son of a bitch.

It's so quiet—no foot traffic on the sidewalk in either direction—it reminds him of winter, the time of year he likes the best out here, even if there are nights when the bar is almost empty and the antique cash register is so light on cash Jimmy worries it might float away.

Jimmy Cunniff is so lost in thought that he never hears the guy coming, never sees the punch that catches him flush on the right side of his face, spins him around and puts him down on the bad shoulder.

The pain of landing on it makes him feel as if he's gotten himself shot all over again.

Then the guy is on top of him, so much weight on Jimmy's chest that the air comes right out of him. Jimmy's thinking the guy must know about the shoulder somehow, because he grinds it into the sidewalk with one hand while he keeps punching Jimmy in the head with the other, nothing for Jimmy to do but take it until he feels himself about to go out.

Another feeling you don't forget.

Somebody trying to punch your lights out.

FIFTY-NINE

ROB JACOBSON HAS BEEN given a spectacular private room. It turns out he's an annual donor to just about every hospital from Manorville to Montauk. Who says crime, even alleged crime, doesn't pay?

Jacobson isn't cuffed to the bed, as I thought he might be. Just attached to a heart monitor instead. He told the EMTs that he knew from experience what a heart attack feels like and was sure he was having another one. It turned out, after a battery of tests, that he was not. They have him spending the night in the hospital as a precaution anyway. The judge has already called off further testimony until Monday.

"This'll be the best night's sleep I've had in months," he says. "Prison bed is the worst I've had since Duke. And, Jesus, the stuff you hear in jail all night long. It sounds like a zoo."

"That's fascinating, Rob, no kidding. Why am I here?"

I was halfway home when I got the call from his hospital bed that he needed to see me tonight, that it couldn't wait. I turned the car around and sat a couple of hours in the waiting room until the doctors were completely finished with him. Now here I am. Jimmy is constantly reminding me how much the man is paying us, and that means we have to eat some shit along the way.

"Just to be clear," he says. "Everything I say to you is protected by lawyer-client privilege, right? Even in the hospital?"

"It is."

"You can't repeat any of it, not even to your sister, correct?"

"Not if you don't want me to. You don't have a lot of rights at the present time. But that happens to be one of them."

"Okay, then," he says. "Everything I tell you in this room stays between the two of us."

"You know what they say. What happens in the Peconic Bay Medical Center..."

He smiles at me, then asks me to get up and make sure the door is closed. I get up and make sure. Then he motions me to bring my chair closer to him, which I do.

"I'm the one who's been lying. Like a champion."

"Even about the heart attack?"

"About all of it," Rob Jacobson says, "except that I didn't do it."

SIXTY

THE PAIN IN HIS shoulder is getting worse, pretty much by the second.

He wants to scream but doesn't. If this is Joe Champi on top of him, if the guy has been cocky enough to jump him in the street this way, Jimmy isn't going to give him the satisfaction.

Jimmy hasn't lost consciousness, as close as he was coming a couple of minutes ago. But now he wants the guy to think that he has. Lord knows he's had enough boxing trainers tell him to stay down in his life.

He stays down now.

It's dark enough at this end of Bay Street that Jimmy opens an eye, just barely. The guy hasn't moved; he's still on top of Jimmy but breathing hard now, like maybe he's punched himself. Jimmy sees that he's wearing some kind of dark-colored ski mask, slits for eyes, covering his face.

For the moment, he has stopped hitting Jimmy in the head.

Jimmy is still having trouble getting enough air into his lungs, just because of the weight of the guy on top of him. He tells himself to breathe through his nose and continue to play dead.

Enough, he thinks now.

Enough.

And even on his back like this, having just had the holy hell beat out of him, Jimmy Cunniff can still do something he has been able to do since the first day he walked into the Times Square Boxing Club when he was fourteen years old and Mr. Glenn, who owned the place, saw enough raw talent to tell him that he might be able to make a boxer out of him someday:

Jimmy Cunniff can still throw a left hook.

And throws one now.

Flat on his back the way he is, he braces himself on his bad right shoulder and puts everything he has into the kind of left hook that Mr. Glenn—Jimmy still thinks of him that way— told him one time you had to be born being able to throw.

You either have a left hand or you don't, Mr. Glenn said.

Jimmy Cunniff has one now.

SIXTY-ONE

ROB JACOBSON ACTS AS if we're sitting on his back deck, having drinks with umbrellas in them, looking out at the ocean, Jacobson acting as if it's still good—no, *great*—being him.

As if he's not actually in this hospital room, cop posted at the door, on his way back to what he calls the Riverhead Correctional Ramada, and then back to a murder trial after that.

"I faked the heart attack," he says. "And faked it pretty damn well if you ask me."

"And why did you feel it necessary to do something like that?"

"Because I needed Brigid to stop talking."

"Right after the part where you had just called her a liar," I say.

"Pretty convincing with that, too, if I do say so myself."

He jerks his chin at the cart carrying what looks like cranberry juice in a plastic cup, along with a pitcher of ice water. He can't reach it because he's attached to a heart monitor he's just informed me he doesn't need.

"Would you mind pushing the cart a little closer? I'm thirsty."

"I'm not your nurse. Or your waitress."

"You're joking, right?"

"Do I look like I'm joking, Rob? You're the one who continues to act as if being on trial for your goddamn life, the one you used to have, anyway, is some kind of joke."

"That's because you're going to make those charges go away."

"Am I?"

He actually winks at me. "Just keep being your best self."

"Sure. Go with that."

"So you know. Brigid was telling the truth." He smiles. "Being a good friend to the end."

He gives me a quick thumbs-up.

"Still lawyer-client privilege, right?"

"To the end."

"Just checking."

"Cut the shit," I say, "and tell me why you needed her to stop talking."

"Because I couldn't have her testify, under oath, that we were having an affair."

I'd been right. And about that, my sister *had* been lying all along.

Just not under oath.

At least not yet.

"How long?"

"The affair?"

"No, Rob, your membership at Maidstone. Of course the affair."

"How far back do you want to go?"

He's actually enjoying this.

Even here, even now.

I want to get out of my chair and give him a good smack. Not the first time I've had the urge. Surprised in the moment that my own heart rate isn't making *his* monitor jump.

When I have my breathing back under control, I say,

"Whatever the two of you were doing that night, she was still providing you with an alibi."

"I know that. But I couldn't let her testify that I was doing *her.*"

Now I am out of my chair before I even realize it, standing over him, nearly knocking down the little drink tray, my face close to his. And whatever he sees on my face in the moment, he tries to move as far as he can to the other side of the bed.

But I grab his free arm to hold him in place.

"You want to be a pig," I say quietly, "be one after I leave. And don't ever be one again when you're discussing my sister. Are we clear?"

"Yes. Now let go of me."

I let go of his arm and sit back down.

"Now tell me why you couldn't have her admit to the affair."

"Because of the prenup."

SIXTY-TWO

Jimmy

THE PUNCH, EVEN THROWN with his left hand, sends another hot current of pain all the way to his wounded shoulder.

But the punch connects, rocking the guy back, and the one Jimmy follows it with, another beauty, more of a short uppercut, causes a grunt of pain and puts the guy on *his* back now.

Just not for long.

He gets himself up, shaking his head. His bell rung now. They're both up. Still nobody else around at this end of Bay Street, for the feature bout of the night.

"Who *are* you?" Jimmy yells.

The guy doesn't answer. He's bigger than Jimmy, by about a head, maybe a little more. Big enough to be Champi, if it's him—Jimmy has seen pictures of Champi from the old days, towering above other cops.

Jimmy's right arm is hanging at his side, useless, still hurting like a bastard.

The guy, breathing hard, says, "You had this beating coming for a long time."

Then he's stepping in behind what turns out to be a wild right hand. No sucker punch this time. Jimmy snaps his head back and steps inside the guy's right hand and hits him with another left, this time to the body, like he's trying to drive it all the way through him.

It doubles the guy over.

If it is Champi, Jimmy thinks, *why the hell doesn't he just shoot me if there's nobody around?*

As he tries to come back at Jimmy again, Jimmy gives himself enough room, the slide step he learned in the Times Square club, moving away enough to throw another uppercut, this one connecting with the guy's chin.

It doesn't put him down but might as well have. Jimmy knows the look: the guy is done, his arms hanging now, head down.

Jimmy is tired and hurting and pissed off about being jumped this way. He's not an old cop now, he's an old fighter, and he wants to finish this guy, whoever he is, put him down, and out.

Jimmy steps in and pulls the mask off.

Not Joe Champi.

SIXTY-THREE

"THIS WAS ALL ABOUT a *prenup*? You have got to be kidding me."

Jacobson nods, as if somehow it's the most obvious thing in the world to him, as natural as screwing around on his wife in the first place.

"It's why I didn't want Brigid to testify. She thinks she's helping me. She thinks she's doing the right thing. For her, maybe. Not for me."

I just let him go. As always, he loves the sound of his own voice.

"If Claire can prove infidelity, it voids the prenup. And then the laws of the good old state of New York kick in. And you know what that means? Those laws kick me right in the balls."

"She gets half."

He snorts. "As she folds that prenup into a paper airplane."

"Rob. Help me out here. How the *fuck* do you plan on using the half that you'll get to keep when you're spending the rest of your life as a guest of the goddamn state?"

He smiles.

"Because I've got *you*, Jane," he says. "Because maybe now

you'll start believing me when I tell you that Claire is the one with the motive here, if she can pin this on me. She *wants* me in prison. It's not enough for her to get the money. She wants it all."

I look at the heart monitor for some reason and wonder idly how he'd do with a lie detector.

"You want to know the truth?"

"It would be a nice change of pace, you have to admit."

"I really always have believed she's behind this."

I say, "You've made that clear on more than one occasion."

"Think about it. You've said it yourself, even before you knew about the prenup. She gets rid of me, she replaces me with my pal Gus. Gus basically gets my business. Like a merger and goddamn acquisition. They win. I lose."

Then he says, "She called a little while ago, by the way. Claire."

"To check in on you?"

"To tell me she's leaving."

"And going where?"

"The way she described it, it's someplace where this trial can't find her."

He waggles a finger at me, and smiles.

"But I don't need her."

"Because you have me."

"Bingo."

I lean back in my chair now, put my head back, close my eyes. Wondering just how quickly I can get to Jimmy Cunniff's bar.

"Everything today was about a prenup," I say, really talking to myself.

"I couldn't let Brigid say what she was about to say."

I know he's still going to be in that bed when I open my eyes back up.

Unfortunately he is.

"There's a line I hear all the time in sports. When they say it's not about the money, it's *always* about the money. I don't care how much my wife hates me," he says. "She's not walking off into the sunset with mine."

"Just curious again, Rob. What do you think is going to happen when the trial resumes and Brigid is back on the stand?"

Biggest smile yet. All those amazing white teeth. His closer smile.

"Then she really is going to lie for me," Rob Jacobson says. "Like a champion."

"And you know this...how?"

"I spoke to her a little while ago. She's seeing the whole picture a lot better now."

"Really. And what picture is that?"

"There's an experimental treatment for her type of cancer at this cutting-edge clinic in Switzerland. There's no way she and her husband can afford it. But I can."

I stare at him, wondering all over again what my sister possibly could have seen in him, all the way back to college. What she still sees in him. And why she is protecting him, even now.

"You're bribing her with her *cancer*?"

"That's your interpretation. Mine is that I am offering much-needed, and potentially lifesaving, financial support to a dear friend."

"By buying her silence."

"I should have thought of this before she ever sat down in that chair and swore to tell the whole truth and nothing but," he says. "She gets something, I get something. You learn that in business. Always leave something on the table, so you *don't* look like a complete pig after the deal is done."

"But that's exactly what you are. And who you are."

He shrugs. "I am who I am."

"One last question, at least for now. What *haven't* you lied about to me?"

"Killing those people. That's always been the truth. And the truth is supposed to set you free, right?"

"The truth might not be able to set *you* free, Rob. But I can."

I stand up. My hand is on the doorknob when I hear him laugh from the bed.

"You know what you and I have, Jane? A marriage even worse than my real one."

"How do you figure?"

"Can't live with you, can't kill you."

I turn to look at him. He's not smiling now.

"*Yet,*" he says.

SIXTY-FOUR

Jimmy

IT'S A KID, the area around his right eye starting to color, blood coming out of his nose. He can't be much more than a teenager. But then everybody is starting to look younger and younger to Jimmy Cunniff.

He is sitting on the street now, beaten. Jimmy sits down across from him. When the kid's head starts to drop, chin to chest, Jimmy grabs his long blond hair and jerks it back up.

"I need a name."

"I'm not telling you shit."

"The next punch breaks your nose," Jimmy says.

"Do it," the kid says. *"Do. It."*

Then he says, "Pat Palmer."

A car rolls past them without stopping, heading back toward Main Street. Jimmy can feel his phone buzzing in his pocket. Jane, probably.

"I loved her!" the kid says.

"Loved who?"

"Laurel Gates," Palmer says.

"She was your girlfriend."

"She was my girlfriend."

He looks as if he might cry.

Jimmy looks down at his left hand, sees it already starting to swell. The one he used to break all the time when he was still fighting. The one that threw the best punches he ever threw but ended up being the reason he quit.

"So you decided to come after one of the people trying to save the guy you think killed her and her whole family."

"Don't think," Palmer says. "*Know.* The way everybody around here except you and the lawyer bitch knows. He did it, and now you and the lawyer have whored yourselves out trying to prove that he didn't."

Nothing to say to that. Nothing that is going to change his mind, now or ever.

Palmer leans forward a little. Jimmy is ready if he tries to throw another punch. But he doesn't.

"He didn't just kill her. Way before that, he'd already raped her. You didn't know that, did you, smart guy?"

Jimmy reaches over and backhands him across the face.

"What the hell was that for?" Palmer says.

"For not being the guy I was hoping you'd be," Jimmy says, before standing up and then helping the kid to his feet.

"Why didn't Laurel tell anybody what he did to her?"

"Because Laurel told me he made them all sign that piece of paper," Palmer says, "and then he paid them off."

SIXTY-FIVE

Jimmy

JIMMY HAS CALLED AHEAD and gotten a heads-up on when they're going to process Rob Jacobson out of the hospital. It's earlier than Jimmy thought it would be. Maybe the asshat forgot to pay for late checkout like he would at a Ritz.

Yeah, Jimmy thinks, *the rich are different from you and me.*

It always makes him want to laugh, just because that's the only part of the line everybody remembers from the F. Scott Fitzgerald story.

Jimmy, though, can quote the rest of it about the rich, how they possess and enjoy early. How they are soft where we are hard, and cynical where the rest of us are trustful.

Jacobson is still in his bed and surprised when Jimmy walks into the room.

"What do you want?" he says.

Jimmy doesn't answer him, just grabs the chair next to the bed, turns it around, tips it back, and leans it underneath the doorknob. He's only doing this for show. He knows the chair bracing the door won't keep the cop outside from getting inside if he wants to, not for ten seconds.

But Jimmy knows that Jacobson, the rich guy, is soft. And he wants to remind him Jimmy Cunniff isn't.

Now Jimmy sits down on the bed. Jacobson is already fumbling for the Call button. Jimmy gets his hand on it first and puts it out of reach.

"Hey," Jacobson says. *"Hey."* Then he says, "I could yell, you know."

Jimmy leans closer to him, smiling. "Yeah. But you won't."

Now Jacobson gives a little roll to his shoulders, straightens a little in the bed, like he thinks he can still take control of the meeting. Like he's still in charge. Something in this moment they both know is bullshit.

"What the hell do you want? First your boss shows up here to jam me up. Now you. I'm starting to think it's safer in prison."

"Shut up and listen," Jimmy says, and Jacobson does while Jimmy tells him about Pat Palmer jumping him and what he told Jimmy after he did, about Laurel Gates and the rest of it. "Did you rape that girl like he said?" Jimmy says when he finishes.

"He's lying."

Jimmy smiles at him again. What he thinks of as his best cop smile. Mickey Dunne always said it reminded him more of one of those fright masks people wear on Halloween.

"Amazing, when you think of it, everybody lying except you," Jimmy says to him now. "And you the only one locked up for a triple homicide."

"I keep trying to tell you. I didn't do the Gates family, even though somebody went to a lot of trouble to make it look like I did."

"Tell it to Jane. She's more trusting than me, even with a dirtbag like you."

This time when he smiles at Jacobson he reaches over and grabs a fistful of his hospital gown, hard enough to snap Jacobson's head back.

"Did you . . . rape that girl?"

Jimmy leans forward so that their faces are very close now.

"Did you?"

"For the last time . . . *no!*" Jacobson says. "Now let me go."

Jimmy does. Reluctantly. He feels the urge to get in a couple of punches on him the way he did with the kid.

"Why would the kid lie?"

Jacobson says, "Ask him."

Jimmy knows that Jane probably won't be happy when she finds out he came here without telling her, or before telling her about the Palmer kid. But even she has to know by now that Jimmy isn't much for chain of command.

Even with her.

"I think the one lying is you. Not the kid. There's a stink that comes off liars." Jimmy acts as if he's sniffing the air. "You just can't smell it because it's coming off you."

"Think whatever the hell you want about me," Jacobson says. "And then you explain it to Jane when I fire both of your asses."

"You're not going to do that. Especially not this deep into the game."

"You think Jane is my only shot to beat this thing?"

"Maybe your only shot."

Jimmy leans close again and enjoys watching the rich boy flinch.

"But she can't save your sorry ass if you continue to keep shit from her," Jimmy says. "And from me."

"I'm not."

"Well, at least not yet today."

Jimmy stands now, walks over to the door, grabs the chair, brings it back to the bed.

"One last question, for now. Did you pay them to keep them quiet?"

"Pay who?"

"The Gateses."

"Yes," Jacobson says.

SIXTY-SIX

MY SISTER ISN'T RETURNING my calls the morning after I've met with my son-of-a-bitch client in the hospital.

It's the way I think of him now, the words all running together, nothing I can do to stop them:

Mysonofabitchclient.

I know it's who he is and all he ever will be, whether he ends up getting found guilty or I can get him acquitted, whether he ends up a guest of the state of New York forever or eventually walks out of the Suffolk County Court a free man.

It's my sister I want to talk to this morning. Only she won't return my calls, or texts. There are several possible reasons for this, I'm aware. She's turned off her phone. Or she's at a doctor's appointment. Or she's at the gym. It's a fact that her body is more toned now than it ever was, even if she's lost as much weight as she has.

And there is, of course, one other possible reason why she's not returning my calls: she has the phone on, sees who keeps calling, and is simply ignoring me.

She's always graded high on that, too, when she's in the mood. Or in a mood.

But we really do need to talk, whether she's in the mood for *that* or not. She and Rob Jacobson have already provided me with enough surprises in the past few days. I can't afford to have any more once I get her back in the court.

If she's going to lie and say that she and Rob Jacobson hadn't been having an affair, I'm going to stand right there and let her. Why? Because I have no choice—that's why. I'll take what I've already gotten from her. She was with him that night, whether she can pinpoint when he left her or not. I knew from the time I decided to call Brigid as a witness the inherent risks of doing that, whether or not Ahearn would try to get her to admit in open court that she was sleeping with Rob Jacobson. But I've felt all along that there ultimately might be more reward than risk unless my sister says something really stupid, even though she hardly ever does that.

I just want her to talk, in a personal way, a little more about Rob Jacobson's state of mind on the night of the murders. If he ever mentioned any problem with any member of the Gates family. Was he angry when he left? Did he seem agitated? Any indication that he was a man on the brink. Like that.

And I know the jury will believe her. She's still Brigid. Everybody likes Brigid. In the end, even if the jury believes something more than friendship was going on between her and Rob Jacobson, they'll accept her version of things before they'll trust my SOB of a client on this one. They'll do that even knowing he called her out as a liar, right before lying his own ass off with that fake heart attack.

In the end, they'll take her side.

Mom and Dad always did, before Mom passed.

I'm confident that in the end I can handle Kevin Ahearn, who will have to be careful about going at her too hard, or risk losing the jury himself. If Brigid can handle me, I tell myself, she can handle him. And then once he's finished his cross, she can get up out of that chair and walk away from this trial for good.

While we were waiting in front of the courthouse for the ambulance, she said, "I never should have done this."

I didn't want to get into it with her but said, "Brigid, you *chose* to do this."

"You should have stopped me," she said.

There is something else I need to discuss with her this morning, even though I hate myself—acquired skill—for even considering it. As a way of making her even more credible than she already is, even more sympathetic than she already is, I want to ask her if I can put her cancer into play.

It's something we haven't yet discussed as it relates to the trial, and her testimony. I frankly didn't think I'd need it until my own client called his alibi witness a liar.

So am I willing to go there now?

Am I willing to out my own sister as a cancer patient the way I stepped in it with Otis Miller and outed him as gay?

I already know the answer to that one.

I call and leave one more message:

"Brigid, we need to have a talk."

But then she's always told me that when I put it to her like that, it means I talk and she listens. Which, she likes to point out, makes her like everyone else in my world, including two ex-husbands. Pointing out further, when we really get into it, that she believes it's one of the big reasons *why* they're ex-husbands.

Jimmy texts me now that he's leaving the hospital, and says we should meet later at Bobby Van's for lunch—there're things we need to talk about.

I text him back. why are u at hospital?

Of course he doesn't text me back. Jimmy Cunniff, for as long as I've known him, has never been one to believe that if you don't return texts immediately someone will come take your iPhone away. And maybe your driver's license along with it.

I decide to drive over to Brigid's house and make her talk to me if she's there. Or wait for her to come back if she's not there. She needs to know, from me, that the stakes of her testimony have been raised, exponentially, because of what happened before they carted Rob Jacobson off to the hospital.

She and her husband live at the east end of Amagansett, in a wooded area north of the highway, have been living a quiet life there, really, until I called my sister as a witness. And what had been a happy life there until she got sick.

Brigid's black Range Rover is in the driveway.

As I pull up behind the Range Rover, I see the front door open. But it's not Brigid who comes out, it's her next-door neighbor Maureen, keys in hand, locking the door behind her before she even notices me.

I get out of my car and ask her where Brigid is.

"The town car from East Wind picked her up a few hours ago," Maureen says. "She called me before it did, asking me to look after the house. Said she was going to be away for a while."

"Where's Chris?"

Brigid's husband.

"She said he'd gone to Maine, also for a while—took a leave of absence from the school," Maureen says. "I got the feeling it's because of what happened at the trial."

"She tell you where she was going?"

Maureen grins. "She told me you'd show up and ask that."

"Where's my sister?"

"She just said for me to tell you it's a place all smart lawyers like you know about. Out of your jurisdiction."

SIXTY-SEVEN

Jimmy

JIMMY GETS RIGHT TO IT, tells Jane about the fight with Pat Palmer, Palmer accusing Rob Jacobson of raping Laurel, the NDA he said the whole Gates family signed, the whole thing. When he's done, Jane tells him that Brigid is on her way to the Meier Clinic in Switzerland, on a full Rob Jacobson scholarship, as promised.

"Judge is going to be pissed," Jimmy says.

"Mostly at me," Jane says. "I can handle it."

"Not for nothing? Whole grand scheme of things? Her cancer is more important than our trial."

"Well, to her it's more important than the trial."

"What's that mean?"

"It means she's got her priorities and I've got mine," Jane says.

They're seated at a table in the middle of the room, close to the bar, near where the Steinway used to be when Bobby Van was still alive and playing the piano on Sunday nights. Jimmy likes the setup of the room just fine. He just liked the old room better. He likes a lot of old things better.

Hardly breaking news.

Jane circles back to Jacobson. "Let me get this straight. We're supposed to believe he did pay them off and did make them sign a nondisclosure even though he says he didn't rape that kid?"

"That's his story, and he's sticking to it."

"I must point out once again," Jane says, "that knowing him is truly a blessing."

She looks tired to Jimmy, more tired than she has at any point in the trial. But he knows better than to tell her that.

Now she says, "Why do you think it took the Palmer kid this long to come after you? It's not as if he didn't know where to find you before this."

"No idea. But it's not as if we had a bonding moment after we tried to beat the crap out of each other so's I could ask him." He reaches over and forks the other half of the cheeseburger he knows she's not going to finish. "You want to know what I really think? That our guy Rob might have paid the kid off, too."

"If he's talking to you," Jane says, "what's to stop him from talking to Ahearn, whether he has a nondisclosure or not? Because let's face it, the story he told you doesn't help us at all. But for Ahearn, it's pure gold."

"Say our client is passing around NDAs like business cards," Jimmy says. "And say the Gates family did sign one. Why go to all that trouble and then turn around and kill them anyway?"

The place is crowded at lunch. Jimmy always wonders how many of these people have jobs to get back to. Or whether they're just here living the life, even before summer has started.

Jane and him, they have jobs to get back to, even if this is one of those days when Jimmy feels as if they're the ones who are really out to freaking lunch.

He says, "The kid stood down a long time. I'm thinking that if Jacobson did pay him off, it was enough to make him think twice about coming forward, no matter how much he might have loved that girl."

"But he came after you," Jane says. She grins. "And looks like he got some good licks in."

"You know what they say. You should see the other guy."

"Have another chat with him, first thing. Just play nice this time."

"Maybe if Jacobson did rape her, maybe somebody else besides the Palmer kid knows," Jimmy says. "Like Nick Morelli maybe knew more than he was telling, which is why somebody wanted to shut *him* up with a more permanent kind of NDA."

Jimmy waves for the check.

"Weird that the kid came after you."

"It's called transferal," Jimmy says. "He couldn't get in any swings against Jacobson. I was the next best thing in his mind."

"'Transferal.' You do have a lot of fancy words for a tough guy."

"Fuckin' a," Jimmy says.

After Jane leaves, he walks up Main Street to where he parked his car, realizing he left his phone in it while he and Jane were having lunch.

There's a text from Mickey Dunne.

Just one word of text, actually.

Champi

SIXTY-EIGHT

Jimmy

IT TAKES JIMMY ONLY a few phone calls to get an address for Pat Palmer in the Springs. And the name of the body shop where he works on Springs Fireplace Road. The body shop is on the way to the Springs. Jimmy stops there, and Palmer's boss, whose name tag reads STAVROS, tells him he's out of luck, Pat Palmer isn't around.

"He called in sick."

"He do that a lot?" Jimmy asks.

"Is never a lot?"

Jimmy thanks him, gives him a card, tells Stavros to tell Pat he's looking for him if he checks in. Then he continues on his way to the Springs, what turns out to be a small ranch house set back from the street on Sand Lot Road.

No car out front.

Shit.

He is thinking again about Nick Morelli disappearing after he put Rob Jacobson with Laurel Gates that night across the street from the Stephen Talkhouse. His mind has gone back there because where else would it go until he locates Palmer, and finds out he's gone without a trace, too?

It doesn't take much effort for Jimmy to pick the lock

on the front door with the kit he still carries around in his glove compartment, just in case the opportunity for B&E presents itself.

The place is practically military neat inside. Two bedrooms, across from each other down a short hallway. Two bathrooms. Decent-sized kitchen. Pictures of the kid on the walls leading down to the bedrooms, of him and Laurel Gates, most of them beach shots, one on top of the lighthouse in Montauk.

The bed in the master bedroom is made.

Huge flat-screen television above the fireplace in the living room, practically a necessity for all young guys everywhere.

But nobody home.

Jimmy finally lets himself out, goes back to the car, calls the number Stavros gave him for Pat Palmer.

Gets his message: *"This is Pat Palmer. You know what to do when you hear the beep."*

Jimmy thinks about calling the East Hampton Police, but for what, the guy taking a sick day and not answering his phone? Because Nick Morelli went over the side of his boat since he knew something about Rob Jacobson and Laurel Gates?

Pat Palmer doesn't call him back. Mickey Dunne doesn't call him. Jimmy drives home, knowing what he's really doing is driving himself crazy waiting for the damn phone to ring, or chirp, or whatever it's doing these days.

A couple of hours later he's at his bar, watching the Yankees, thinking he might make another run over to Palmer's house.

Maybe the kid didn't want to show up for work looking like he *did* lose a fight, and it's as simple as that, and Jimmy needs to stop making himself crazy. Tells himself he'll just take one more ride over to the Springs to ease his mind, then call it a night.

He's just walked out of the bar, fumbling for his keys, wondering once again why he doesn't just leave them in the same pocket every time, when he gets the call.

SIXTY-NINE

I AM HAVING DINNER with Dr. Ben Kalinsky and Rip the dog. The dining room table is set for two, with candles. The candles are for Dr. Ben and me. Rip doesn't care, one way or the other. He is parked in his usual spot, to the immediate left of my chair.

I have prepared pasta primavera with fresh vegetables purchased that afternoon from the Balsam Farms stand a couple of miles from my house. The salad includes avocados and cucumbers and tomatoes and radishes. We have made the decision to go with red wine, a Cabernet I love called Train Wreck.

I have managed to get another annoying coughing fit—my mouth is dry all the time, something Sam Wylie told me to expect—under control by the time Dr. Ben arrives, so as not to sound like the patient I'm going to be before much longer. A good thing. Ben Kalinsky may work on animals and not humans, but it has been my experience that he misses very little, medical or otherwise.

"You know," he says, "that if you continue to feed the dog from the table he will continue to beg."

"Veggies are good for him. Balance his diet right out."

"Not the point, counselor."

"And just so we're clear," I say, "I've discussed this with Rip. He doesn't consider what he's doing begging. He thinks of it as us sharing."

Ben smiles. I think the only person in the entire world who smiles at me like this—who smiles at me at all these days—is him. In addition to being a world-class smile, it even makes me feel pretty at a time in my life when hardly anything does.

He does.

Before we put the sharing thing to rest, he says, "Let me ask you a question. Does the dog ever share his food with you?"

"Oh, dear God. You're starting to sound like a lawyer."

"Don't be mean," he says.

Before getting sidetracked on me feeding my own damn dog from the table and not considering it a capital crime, we are talking about the trial. His choice, not mine. He is genuinely interested in it. And me. Perhaps not in that order. Hopefully not in that order. I once again ask him if he really wants to see how the sausage is made.

It makes him laugh.

"You're asking that of a *surgeon*?"

I sip some wine. My second glass.

Look at me. Living it up.

"I'm curious. Do you ever operate on an animal knowing you have no chance to save it?"

"Now, there's an odd question."

"Not from an odd duck like me."

"Well, the answer to your question happens to be yes. Sometimes saving a life simply means prolonging one. Or improving its quality until you can't."

Now he grins. You hear about crooked grins. He actually has one. Lower on the left side than the right.

Works for me.

But then not much about him doesn't.

"I think of myself as an optimistic fatalist," Dr. Ben says.

"Is that really a thing?"

"With me it is. Or maybe I'm just a realist." He grins again. "I always think about a line I heard one time when I was watching *SportsCenter* on ESPN."

"I know what *SportsCenter* is, Doc."

"Sorry. I forget occasionally that I'm sitting with a former enforcer for Boston College hockey."

"I considered myself more of a finesse player."

"Sure. Go with that."

He sips some of his wine. I watch him do it. Our eyes meet. Now we're both smiling at each other. Sometimes when I'm with him I feel normal. Happy almost. Not healthy—I know better than that. Just not sick for a little while.

"Anyway, one of the anchors was talking about some injured player being day-to-day. At which point he paused, looked into the camera, and said, 'But aren't we all?'"

I stare at him over my glass, maybe for a beat too long, and finally say, "Some of us more than others."

"You mean like Brigid."

"Sure," I say, winking at him. "Go with that."

"When do you think you'll hear from her?"

"She's kind of day-to-day," I say, and we both laugh.

It's when we're clearing the table of the dessert plates and about to move to the living room with coffee that I hear the knock on the front door.

When I open it, Jimmy Cunniff is standing there.

"Somebody killed him," he says.

"The Palmer kid?"

"Mickey Dunne."

SEVENTY

Jimmy

DR. BEN KALINKSY EXCUSES himself after Jimmy shows up. Jimmy practically walks him to his car, apologizing for screwing up his dinner date. Ben Kalinsky tells Jimmy, "I would have screwed it up myself eventually, just off my track record." Then he puts a hand on Jimmy's shoulder and tells him how sorry he is for his loss. "He sounds like he was a good friend," the vet says.

"More than a friend," Jimmy says. "He was my partner."

Jane pours Jimmy coffee that she was supposed to have been drinking with Dr. Ben, she says. Jimmy tells her he's leaving for the city from here. He tells Jane how they found Mickey, two shots to the forehead, close range, in an alley a few blocks from Yankee Stadium, between two buildings, 158th and Gerard.

"So mob style," Jane says. "You think this might have something to do with the mob?"

"Not a chance in hell."

He has already told Jane about Mickey Dunne's text. Now he shows it to her on his phone.

Champi

The last thing Mickey Dunne ever said to him.

"You know what I think?" Jimmy says. "Mickey must have

thought he had a lead on Champi. Only Champi found him first."

"Was his phone still with him when they found him?" Jane says.

She points at his coffee. Jimmy shakes his head, tells her he doesn't want to hit every other rest stop on the LIE on his way to the city.

"No phone."

"His was NYPD issue, right?"

That actually gets a smile out of Jimmy Cunniff.

"Mickey always insisted on using his own," Jimmy tells her. "He never wanted the bosses to know who he was talking to. Or where he was at any particular time. Just because it was generally somewhere they didn't want him to be."

He tells Jane then that he may be in the city for a couple of days, that he is making it his goddamn mission to find out where Mickey Dunne was on the last day and night of his life. To find anything Mickey might have left behind for Jimmy to find, before everything went sideways for him. Because something had to have gone sideways, and got him killed. If Mickey Dunne thought he was in real trouble with Joe Champi, he would have called Jimmy after the text. On account of them always having each other's backs, long after they officially stopped working together.

"You don't think there's any possibility that this might be OCC related?"

Organized Crime Control.

"No, Jane, I do not. *Okay?*"

He put some snap into it.

Jimmy gets up from the table. "How's the judge going to take Brigid taking a flyer?" he asks her.

"How do you think?"

"What about you? You didn't seem to be taking it too good at lunch."

"I was angry more at myself than at her," Jane says. "For being more worried about our goddamn case than I was about my own sister."

As Jane is walking Jimmy to his car, she waves to the East Hampton cop sitting behind the wheel of his own car, halfway up the block, as always. The guy blinks his lights.

"We still don't know where the Palmer kid is," Jane says to Jimmy.

"He'll turn up."

He does the next morning.

SEVENTY-ONE

WE ARE IN THE chambers of Judge Jackson Prentice III. Him. Kevin Ahearn. Me. We're all here because Kevin Ahearn has announced that he wants to call Pat Palmer as a witness. In the middle of my case.

"I'm sorry," I tell Ahearn in front of the judge. "Did the defense rest without somebody telling me?" Then I slap my forehead. "Oh, wait, that couldn't possibly have happened because I *am* the defense."

"Ms. Smith happens to be right about this, Mr. Ahearn," Judge Prentice says. "If you want to call this young man, you're going to have to wait until the defense does rest."

Ahearn has to have known better. But it's as if he had to try. "If I had been aware of the information Mr. Palmer has, information that is essential to the state's case, I would already have called him. But he just came forward."

"I am going to restate the obvious," Prentice says. "You're still not allowed to bring forward a rebuttal witness until the defense does rest."

It turns out that the reason Jimmy wasn't able to locate Pat Palmer was because he was with the district attorney for most of the day, telling the story Ahearn says the jury needs to hear.

Palmer is currently down the hall in an empty jury room while we're all thrashing this out. Rob Jacobson is in a separate room of his own.

"You can't let that guy violate an NDA," my client said to me before being escorted out of the room.

Jacobson was gripping my forearm, much too hard. I looked down at his hand, then back up at him. "Let go of me and let me go do my job."

"I'm trying to help you do that," Jacobson said.

I looked him in the eyes. "Rob? You hardly *ever* help me."

I got close to his ear before he stood up.

"If you get bored," I whispered, "go fake another heart attack."

The first subject once we were in chambers actually wasn't Pat Palmer. It was the sudden absence of my sister, Brigid. But as soon as I explained where she was, and why she was there, and that I honestly couldn't tell a cancer patient not to try to get better, Brigid quickly became a sidebar.

At which point Pat Palmer, and what he's told Kevin Ahearn, and the NDA with Rob Jacobson that he signed, became the main event.

"Here's the deal, Kevin," I tell Ahearn. "You know and I know and people in outer space know that you are going to have to wait to call this guy as a rebuttal witness, because we all know that's the law. And you have to know that when you do call him, he can't violate the sanctity of a nondisclosure agreement."

Judge Prentice is nodding in agreement. Today he likes me. It probably won't last. But in the moment, I want to give him a big kiss.

"Mr. Palmer has had a change of heart about the NDA," Kevin Ahearn says.

Now I can't contain myself. And we *are* in chambers. No need to keep my voice down.

So I'm shouting, just like that.

"It doesn't work that way and you know it!" I take a great big deep breath. "You don't get to keep the money *and* tell your story in open court. Unless we're talking about a *non*-nondisclosure agreement."

Ahearn isn't going down without a fight, I have to give him that.

"The NDA shouldn't apply here," he says stubbornly.

Ahearn turns away from me now and toward the judge.

"Your Honor, I understand how unusual these circumstances are, and how unusual my request is," Ahearn says. "But not only does the jury have the right to hear what Mr. Palmer has to say, they *need* to hear. The way they need to know that Ms. Smith's client tried to buy the young man's silence."

I try to remain calm this time. Ladylike, almost.

"Whether we like the circumstances, or motivation, or not, my client *did* buy Mr. Palmer's silence."

"Except that Mr. Palmer is prepared to say that your client raped the teenage victim in this case," Ahearn says. "The *underage* teenage victim. And he deserves to be heard on this in open court."

"Come on, Kevin," I say, purposely using his first name, like I want us to be buddies. "Even you know that the laws of this state aren't a buffet table where you can pick and choose the ones you want to enforce. You can't break the law trying to uphold it."

Ahearn ignores me again, goes back to working the judge.

"Your Honor, whether Ms. Smith will acknowledge it or not, everyone still in this room knows that it would go against the public interest, in an almost profound way, for Mr. Palmer not to get to tell his story, whether he signed that piece of paper or not."

"In your opinion," I say calmly.

"If you had any decency, especially as a woman, it would be your opinion, too!"

"*Enough,*" Judge Prentice says. "*From both of you.*"

If we were in his courtroom, he would have gaveled us into silence. Instead he places his hands on the desk in front of him, as if trying to calm himself now.

"Here is my determination," the judge says, "one that might not satisfy either one of you but is the only practical and fair solution. When the time comes, Mr. Palmer will be compelled to testify, even if he's had a change of heart. And he will say on the witness stand what he has already said to Mr. Ahearn, and his nondisclosure agreement be damned."

I open my mouth, but know enough to close it, telling myself I'll deal with Palmer when the time comes.

"Mr. Ahearn," Judge Prentice says, "you can go down the hall and inform Mr. Palmer that I'm sorry he wasted a trip here today, but we'll see him soon."

I'm sitting with Rob Jacobson ten minutes later when there's a knock on the door, and Kevin Ahearn comes walking in.

"No need to worry about what Pat Palmer does or doesn't have to say," Ahearn says. "He's gone."

SEVENTY-TWO

I SEE THAT KEVIN AHEARN is red-faced and breathing hard. And is quickly standing near Rob Jacobson's chair, looking down at him.

"You happy?" Ahearn snaps at him.

"About what? Sitting here minding my own business? Yeah, I'm thrilled."

"Kevin," I say. "You know you shouldn't be in here."

I move around the table with a pretty quick move of my own and situate myself between the district attorney and Jacobson, sensing that things will spiral out of control if my client says anything stupid.

"Kevin," I say quietly, "you need to move away from him before you do or say something you'll regret."

Ahearn isn't moving.

"Did you get to Palmer somehow while we were in chambers, you prick?" he asks.

"Can he talk to me like that?" Jacobson asks me.

"He just did."

"Well, you might think you have to listen to him," Jacobson says, "but I don't."

He starts to get up. I turn and put a hand on his shoulder.

"Sit."

It occurs to me, the thought there and gone, that this is the tone of voice I use with Rip.

"What did you do," Ahearn says, "offer him more money?"

"And how exactly am I supposed to have done that?" Jacobson says. "I was here the whole time. The first I heard that the punk was gone was when you just came in here and told us."

"*Punk,*" I say softly. "Nice, Rob. No shit."

"Sorry, Jane, but I had a deal with him. He was about to break that deal. That makes him a punk in my book."

"You've been buying your way out of trouble your whole entitled life, so why wouldn't I think you didn't just do it again?" Ahearn says to Jacobson. "You think anybody's forgotten how Nick Morelli conveniently disappeared when he was the one with bad shit on you?" Ahearn turns to me. "Wherever your sister is, I'd post a guard outside her door."

"Is there anything else you want to accuse me of today, Mr. Ahearn?" Jacobson says. "Maybe causing COVID?"

I walk over so I'm standing next to Ahearn, a few feet from the door.

"Kevin," I say, "you've gotten some things off your chest. But you really need to not be here now."

I can see he doesn't want to leave. Finally he does. I walk out into the hallway with him. He's still clenching and unclenching his fists.

"What happened with Palmer?" I say softly.

"We had a bailiff posted at the door, just to keep him away from everybody," Ahearn says. "And he says that all of a sudden the door bursts open and the kid's staring at his phone like he's seen a ghost."

"And the bailiff didn't stop him?"

"Like you stopped your sister?" He squeezes his eyes shut

and shakes his head. "He had no authority to stop him," Ahearn continues. "We couldn't hold him here against his will. He came here today wanting to testify. I never even got the chance to tell him that he was going to have to wait."

"Did he say anything to anybody before he was outside?"

"He was talking to somebody on his phone by then. As he's on his way out the door the cop hears the kid say that no, he *didn't* think this trial was worth dying over."

SEVENTY-THREE

Jimmy

JIMMY NEVER CAME RIGHT OUT and asked Mickey Dunne, in all the years they knew each other, how Mickey always managed to live as well as he did, even the way he'd gotten tagged in his divorces.

One time when he was about to get tagged again—Jimmy can't remember whether it was by the second or third ex-wife—Mickey said, "I ought to write a book about being married."

"Like a how-to manual?" Jimmy said.

"How-not-to."

Jimmy laughs now, thinking about that one, having gone through the morning not knowing whether to laugh or cry thinking about him.

Somehow, despite the divorces, Mickey *had* always managed to live well. Did that mean he'd had some side action going, even on the job? Some side income? Probably. Did that mean he'd taken payoffs from some of the bad guys he was working along the way? Without having any proof, other than the rent Mickey was always paying, and the alimony, Jimmy suspected that he probably had, because the financials couldn't possibly line up otherwise. Mickey always ate at the best restaurants, and they all couldn't have been comping him. He drove a

Mercedes for a while, and then a sporty BMW convertible that he'd bought used. He was enough of a cop character that he always had a regular table at Elaine's, when Elaine's was still around, and the place to be seen. He was Mickey. A force of nature.

Until now.

Champi, the text had said.

Mickey had been trying to track down Joe Champi for his old partner, do his old partner one last solid, and it had gotten him dead.

Can Jimmy prove that it was Champi who took out Mickey Dunne? He cannot.

Yet.

Yet.

Jimmy gets off the FDR and makes his way down to the Village, the narrow streets down there even more narrow now that so many of the restaurants are keeping the outdoor tables they started using during COVID as a way of staying in business. Jimmy has spent most of the ride calling in favors all over the place, in the city and back in the Hamptons, trying to locate Claire Jacobson. No luck yet, but he's always been an optimistic bastard.

Mickey's latest—and last—apartment is in the West Village, on Perry Street. Another ancient building that's been gutted inside and turned into a high-end downtown address, a short walk from one of Jimmy's favorite restaurants down here, Extra Virgin, and not just because of the name. It was their go-to when he'd come in from Sag Harbor to have dinner with Mickey. Just not lately. They kept saying they needed to get together more often. Next week or next month and now never.

Jimmy tells the super that Mickey is dead, flashing his counterfeit NYPD badge, Jimmy talking quickly, telling the guy that he and Mickey had been partners, and he's here on official business, working the murder, and he needs to get inside the apartment.

Jimmy shoots him a fifty then, smiling again as he hands the guy the money and watches it disappear, knowing it's exactly what Mickey Dunne would have done, Mickey having always tipped people, all over town, like he was a Rockefeller.

But Mickey hadn't called it tipping.

He'd always called it "whip-out" and told Jimmy that it was the real coin of the realm in New York City, what made the world of the city go round.

As Eduardo unlocks the door, he says to Jimmy, "I was waiting to tell you that I already know about Mr. Mickey."

"Some cops beat me here?"

"Just one."

Jimmy knows without knowing.

"Big guy?"

"Yes," Eduardo says. "How do you know?"

"I know all kinds of interesting things," Jimmy says.

SEVENTY-FOUR

NOON AT DR. SAM WYLIE'S office. She wants to talk about the new oncologist she says I need to see, right now, and one she assures me I'll like. I ask her what's wrong with the old oncologist she suggested, and she says she found a better one, so sue her.

"What is this, Tinder for cancer specialists?"

"Please don't make this any harder on yourself," she says. Sighs. "Or on me."

"I hate oncologists."

"You already know some?"

"No."

"Just on general principle, then."

"More as a practical matter."

"You need to see this woman ASAP," Sam Wylie says. "You saying no is not an option."

"Lawyers always have options."

"Jane. The longer you put off treatment, the greater the chance you're shortening your life."

"And that would be so unfair, my life being shortened this way, don't you think? Why can't you just treat me?"

"Because you need a cancer specialist, for fuck's sake!" she shouts at me, just like that. "I can't treat this. They can."

"With treatments that would do everything except cure me," I say.

It is still only midday, and I suddenly feel exhausted.

"Which would likely slow the progress of the disease, hopefully for a long, long time."

"Or not."

"Come on," she says. "I'm speaking to you as your doctor *and* as your friend. The sooner you attack this thing, the better chance you might give yourself of living past the prognosis I gave you at the start."

"Not to get stuck on this one point," I say, "but the cancer could still kill me anyway, whatever I do."

"But perhaps later rather than sooner."

"So I might live longer than a year? No, wait. I forgot I plea-bargained with you for fourteen months."

"You're being an idiot," she says. "And I say that with love."

"Not sure I'm feeling the love right now."

"Jane. The sooner you get treatment the sooner we can see how you're *responding* to the treatment."

"And if I respond well?"

"Then your life gets extended."

"And if I don't?"

She takes another deep breath. "Then it's a question of how fast the horse is going and how close it is to the cliff."

"Horse imagery?"

She smiles. "I save it for horse's asses."

It occurs to me in the moment how much she loves me and how much I love her, and how we have been friends so much longer than our relationship as doctor and pissy patient.

"Your bedside manner sucks—you know that, right?"

"Only with you," she says. "Most of my patients find me quite welcoming."

I wonder if I look as tired to Sam right now as I feel. I've started to lose weight, if only incrementally. And the soreness in my throat is slowly getting worse, as Sam Wylie told me it would, like low-grade strep that just won't go away.

I can't lose my voice.

Not yet.

"The pictures you're going to take today, what do you want them to show?"

"No growth of the biggest tumor on your neck," she says.

"And this will please you."

"To no end."

"Hey," I say, "maybe I can be the one to kick cancer's ass."

"This isn't a game," Sam says.

"You sure about that?"

An hour later, I am out of my hospital gown and in my suit and on my way back to Riverhead when the clerk of the court, Johnny Angelini, the man I call Johnny Angel, calls.

"It's about your witness," he says. "The one we found for you and served like you asked."

It had taken some doing, by the court and by Jimmy Cunniff. But we had, as Jimmy likes to say, got 'er done.

"What about her?"

"She has just informed Mr. Ahearn and Judge Prentice that upon further review, like the football refs say, she has decided to ignore your subpoena."

"I assume that you have all pointed out to her that subpoenas aren't like Evites to which you can RSVP no."

"Where are you right now?" he says.

"Water Mill."

"Then you can tell her yourself when you get here."

"It will be my pleasure."

If I couldn't kick cancer's ass today, I could at least kick somebody's.

"You sound almost happy," the clerk of the court says.

"What can I tell you? Life is good."

SEVENTY-FIVE

Jimmy

HE KNEW THE BIG cop was Champi before he showed the super the picture. Two detectives would have shown up here if the investigation was legit, not one.

Champi probably kept his own badge when he faked his death. Or had a replica made that looked real enough. Who knows? What Jimmy does know is that if Champi came here, he was looking for something. Maybe something that would help Jimmy tie him to Mickey's death.

Something else that makes Jimmy smile today: a cop who's supposed to be dead looking for something that will connect him to the cop he might've just killed. Jimmy tells Jane the same thing, all the time, about almost everything:

You can't make this shit up.

Jimmy's shocked to see a treadmill in a corner of the living room once he's inside, wondering how many miles Mickey actually put on it. Mickey kept talking about getting a gym membership, all the years Jimmy knew him, but never did. Maybe the treadmill is as close as he ever came.

What fits the room much better is the half full bottle of Jameson on the coffee table. Empty glass next to it. Yesterday's *Daily News* next to that. A pizza box on the counter in the kitchen. Jimmy makes a quick tour—it's actually smaller than he expected. Not that big an apartment for what Mickey was probably paying for the address. Bed not made. Jeans slung over a chair in the bedroom.

There is no laptop anywhere in the apartment. If there was one, Champi took it for sure.

No cell phone.

No landline.

There is a small desk against the same wall as the treadmill. Some bills on top of it, including his most recent Amex bill. A couple of notebooks, new, in the middle drawer. Nothing written in them. If there'd been one with notes on Joe Champi, Champi surely took that, too. Or took it off Mickey Dunne after he shot him.

Yeah, Jimmy thinks. *Just like a mob hit.* By the gangster Joe Champi had become. Or maybe always had been, even when he was on the job, before and after he apparently faked his own death.

All of a sudden, just like that, the realization of what's happened takes all the air out of Jimmy Cunniff at once. He walks over and sits down in Mickey's recliner, facing the big flat-screen on the wall.

He's gone.

The guy who was so much more than a brother, and not just in blue. The guy he stood up for at his weddings. Chased women with when Mickey was between marriages, and sometimes during. Went to Yankees games with. Got shit-faced with, constantly. Laughed with and even cried with sometimes, at that time of the night when even tough guys, with enough of a load on, get too weepy.

Gone.

He'd been here yesterday and then got some kind of lead

on Champi and texted Jimmy. Then he went off and found Joe Champi or Champi found him.

Nothing else made sense.

Jimmy gets up and takes a couple of steps to the coffee table, uncaps the Jameson and raises the bottle.

"To you, partner."

He drinks.

First of the day, Mickey always said, was the best one.

Just not today.

Jimmy goes back into the bedroom. Just a couple of framed pictures on the wall, small ones. Mickey was never one for decorating. One of Mickey with a woman Jimmy doesn't recognize, outside the new Yankee Stadium, in front of the BABE RUTH PLAZA sign. One, much older, of Jimmy and Mickey on the beach at Rockaway, from some long-lost summer when they were both a lot skinnier, and had a lot more hair.

But looking happy as hell, both of them, as if they were going to live forever.

Next to the pictures are a couple of commendations, framed.

Jimmy goes back through the drawers of the nightstand. A bottle of Xanax in the top one. Mickey must have needed more than Jameson to sleep sometimes. An old Dunhill lighter, engraved, that Jimmy had given Mickey for his first marriage. Or maybe his second. When Mickey was still a smoker.

"Gimme something, Mick," Jimmy says out loud. "Gimme *anything.*"

His voice echoes in the empty bedroom.

Mickey's bedroom.

Maybe from here Jimmy can go to the precinct, ask if he can go through Mickey's desk, if somebody would do him a solid there. Somebody who went back far enough to know what Jimmy and Mickey had meant to each other.

Jimmy goes back to the desk. There is a Con Ed bill, past due, underneath the Amex. A cable bill. Also past due. Jimmy smiles again and thinks: *Late paying bills to the end.* He'd always suspected that Mickey Dunne had a credit rating you could fit inside a shot glass.

Just to make sure he's not missing anything, Jimmy takes the drawers out of the nightstand and tosses them onto the bed.

The false bottom slides halfway out of the middle one.

Jimmy slides it all the way out.

There is an envelope.

A photograph inside.

Important enough to Mickey Dunne that he hid it.

Kids, looking like teenage kids, posing for the camera.

Boy and three girls.

The boy has what Mickey Dunne always called hippie hair, even now, and is wearing a bathing suit a lot smaller than young guys wear nowadays.

They happen to be standing next to the ATLANTIC AVENUE BEACH signs in Amagansett, in front of a beach Jimmy Cunniff has walked with Jane plenty of times.

The beach doesn't interest Jimmy so much.

It's the kids in the picture.

The boy has his arms around all three girls at once, all the girls in bikinis, one of the girls with an old blue-and-orange Mets cap pulled down low over her eyes, so Jimmy can't make out much of her face.

But the boy—no doubt in Jimmy's mind whatsoever, none— is a much younger version of Rob Jacobson.

He stares at him.

Then at the girl closest to him on his left.

Takes out his phone just to make sure that he's certain about her, *her* face not covered by a hat, a lot of red hair and some body on her, smiling and squinting into the sun.

Looking so much like her daughter would look later, before they got shot to death in Garden City.

"Nice to finally meet you, Mrs. Carson," Jimmy says. "Wish it was under better circumstances."

SEVENTY-SIX

I SIT ACROSS THE small table from her in the downstairs coffee shop at the Suffolk County Court.

She looks as beautiful as she always does, even as steamed at me as she so clearly is. I'm no fashionista, and have the clothes closet to prove it, but I know it's an expensive black dress. Chanel maybe, but I'd only be guessing. A single strand of pearls.

No wedding ring.

That's new.

"Why won't you leave me alone?" Claire Jacobson says.

She is about as happy with me as my sister would be if I'd hauled her back here from Switzerland to testify. A contact of Jimmy's from the FBI helped them track down Rob Jacobson's wife, and serve her, before she boarded a private jet at Teterboro Airport in Jersey, trying to get to their place in Cabo.

"I hardly think that calling you as a witness in your husband's murder trial is a form of harassment. Were you heading to Cabo alone when you were served? I'm just curious."

"None of your business."

I sip some coffee. There is some fresh fruit on a plate in front of me. I'd promised Sam Wylie before I left the hospital that I would try to start eating better. That may have fallen under the category of lie, because presently the fruit remains untouched.

"Claire," I tell her, "we can do this the easy way or we can do it the hard way. And the hard way only begins with Judge Prentice holding you in contempt if you refuse to testify. And we both know you're not going to get on the stand and invoke your Fifth Amendment rights and look as if you're the one who has something to hide. Imagine the cocktail party chatter that would generate out east."

She smiles thinly. "Don't be so sure. And by the way? I thought contempt was my husband's thing."

She leans forward slightly, points a finger at me.

"I am not allowing the likes of you to drag *my* good name through the muck."

"Why do you assume that's what I intend to do?"

"Because you're *you*," she says. "If you'd sell out your own sister, you'd sell me out in a heartbeat. Which, I might add, is why your sister got even farther away from this trial than I had planned to be."

"You're his wife."

"She was his mistress, even if she never got around to admitting that in open court."

"Alleged mistress. To be fair."

"Screw you. Like my husband was screwing sweet little Brigid and everybody else."

"Claire, in about fifteen minutes you're going to be in that chair, whether you like it or not."

"My lawyer is of the opinion that I can ignore the subpoena, citing spousal privilege."

"Your lawyer is about to walk you right into a jail cell."

I know it will never come to that, even if Prentice cites her for contempt. But she doesn't know that, especially without her lawyer here to hold her hand.

For now it's just us girls.

"I don't see how I can possibly help his case," she says, "especially since the longer this trial goes, the more I am convinced that he did it. How would you like it if I shared that heartwarming sentiment from the stand?"

"Not so much. And we both know you're not going to do that."

She smiles.

Her own killer smile.

Maybe she and her husband used to practice it on each other.

"And why, pray tell, is that?"

"Because you don't really want to be known as the wife of a murderer," I say. "It will get you uninvited from all the best parties."

"Ex. Ex-wife. First chance I get. And then I will end up somewhere where even you and your friend Mr. Cunniff can't find me."

"You can go on one of those space missions with some of your rich friends for all I care. But before you do, you and I are going to talk to each other upstairs."

Her eyes turn to slits now. They remind me in the moment of cat eyes. I remember a friend, a cat person, telling me once that the only reason that cats scratch your wrist is because they're not big enough to rip your throat out.

What do you want from me?" she says, the words coming out hot.

I tell her.

"Not a chance in hell," she says.

SEVENTY-SEVEN

Jimmy

JIMMY CUNNIFF SITS AT Mickey Dunne's desk and stares at the girl he is sure Lily Carson used to be, then back at the images he has on his phone of the woman she became.

And now it's like every other time he came up with a clue in a case he and Mickey were working, all the way back, even when they were rookies together.

He wants to talk it through *with* Mickey.

So he does.

"Where'd you find this, partner?"

Knowing that's not even the question he really wants to ask him.

So now he asks that one.

"Why did you hide it?"

No matter how many times he looks at the photograph, nothing changes. It's her. The younger version of her. The spitting image of her daughter. He goes back to his phone now and finds the picture of the Carsons that *Newsday* ran on its front page the day after the murders, a picture to break your goddamn heart, the Carsons posing in front of their Christmas tree.

The mother looking like an older sister to the daughter she

would have later. Same red hair, though Jimmy figures the mother was needing help to keep it colored that way by the time that particular photo was taken.

I got so fixed on the husband's gambling, and all the bad guys he got hooked up with, Jimmy thinks, *I never looked at the wife.*

Schmuck, he hears Mickey saying to him.

Champi has done everything possible, at least so far, to run Jimmy and Jane off the Carson case, starting with making Gregg McCall disappear. Coming for Jane at the house. And torching Jimmy's bar—Jimmy knew it was him behind that, because it was way too late in Jimmy's life to start believing in coincidence.

Now Mickey Dunne was dead in the Bronx.

Was it because Mickey had found out there was a prior relationship between Rob Jacobson and Lily Carson?

Had he come here today wanting to see what kind of proof Mickey had?

Rob Jacobson tied to another triple homicide?

What the hell? Jimmy thinks.

There's no reason to rush back to Long Island. Jane is in court, and will be in court for the rest of the day. So he sits himself back down in Mickey's recliner and imagines himself being a flatfoot again, just not knocking on doors but making his way across social media.

Jacobson and Lily Carson. The former Lily Biondi.

Jacobson suddenly a nexus that Jimmy wasn't looking for, not for one minute, between the murder of the Carson family and the murder of the Gates family in the Hamptons.

But how much of a nexus?

An hour later Jimmy still hasn't left the apartment. He is back to sitting at Mickey's desk, hoping it will make him smarter, wandering around the internet, banging around from

Google to Bing to DuckDuckGo, looking anywhere and everywhere for some further connection between Jacobson and Lily Biondi. Or Jacobson and Hank Carson. There is more to read on Jacobson, even before the murders, because of the way his old man died and how the tabloids went batshit crazy with that at the time. Hardly anything on Hank Carson because of the way he and his family died.

Jimmy remembers the days when to do this kind of work he ended up at the New York Public Library on Fifth Avenue, going through microfilm of the New York papers, as far back as he needed to go.

He was about to give up when another old picture popped up on his screen.

"Well, I'll be a son of a bitch," Jimmy says.

SEVENTY-EIGHT

KNOWING MY CLIENT IS already in his seat at our table, I am still in the ladies' room at five minutes before court will finally be called back into session. My throat is even more raw than usual today, so I polish off one of the two bottles of water I keep in my bag. Then I run a brush through my hair. Quickly apply some makeup under my eyes and then blush to my cheeks.

Not enough time for an extreme makeover.

I stare in the mirror and at my face and see how tired I still look.

Do I just look tired to everybody else?

When will I start to look sick?

When will they know?

No time to worry about that now.

"Showtime," I say, patting my cheeks again.

Still my go-to move, even when I feel the way I feel right now.

I slap my cheeks with a little extra vigor this time, enough to put more color in them without more makeup.

I walk out of there having decided, and not for the first time, that whoever it was that said what doesn't kill you makes you stronger was full of it.

SEVENTY-NINE

"THE DEFENSE CALLS CLAIRE JACOBSON to the stand, Your Honor," I say five minutes later.

She is back in the front row, her old seat, behind her husband and me. She ignores her husband as she makes her way past our table, slowing just barely enough to shoot a look at me that makes me want to check to see if she's the one who's drawn blood.

Rob Jacobson sees the look, leans over, and whispers to me, "Now you know how I feel."

Claire Jacobson is sworn in. As I approach the stand, I ask her, for the record, to state her relationship with my client.

"I'm his wife."

There is no heavy lifting after that for either one of us; it's all strictly boilerplate stuff as I ask her how long they've been married, what kind of father Rob Jacobson has been to their children, her role in the community along with his. All bullshit legal foreplay.

"Would it be fair to say, Mrs. Jacobson, that until your husband was charged with these crimes, both of you were regarded as pillars of the community?"

"I believe that's fair."

"And wouldn't it be equally fair to say that you, more than anybody else, were shocked when he was charged with this hideous crime?"

"I was."

"Because you know him."

I am afraid, in the moment, that she might say that she thought she knew him.

But she does not.

"Yes," she says.

"So I can only imagine what this experience has been like for you. Not just you but your children, their father locked up for a crime he didn't commit."

"Objection," Kevin Ahearn says, almost wearily. "Counsel sounds as if she's putting a fact into the record, as opposed to her opinion."

"Sustained," Judge Prentice says. "Save it for your summation, Ms. Smith."

"I apologize, Your Honor. It's just that I believe so passionately in my client's innocence."

"Objection," Ahearn says again. "Still editorializing, Your Honor."

"Sustained. Ms. Smith, how about we focus on your witness and not any and all of your deeply held beliefs."

"Noted."

I turn back to Claire Jacobson.

"Mrs. Jacobson. We were talking about how difficult these charges against your husband, this entire process, has been for you and your children."

"Not as hard as it's been on Rob, of course."

His first name. Nice touch. As if she's actually on his side. And mine.

"Of course."

"At least the children and I are able to live our normal lives," she says.

"I think any husband or wife in this room can empathize with that."

I ask her if she ever heard her husband express any animosity toward Mitch Gates.

"Never. I know what Gus Hennessy has testified to, that argument he says he heard on the beach. But Rob still disputes that the argument ever occurred. The truth is, I never heard him mention Mr. Gates, or his family. They were in their world, we were in ours."

And what rarefied air it is.

Yours, Claire.

Not theirs.

"But then," I continue, "those two worlds collided, at least in the view of the state, on the night of the murders, correct?"

"Obviously, yes," she says.

I look at her admiringly, the role she's playing of supportive and caring wife. She really does look sensational. The whole package. Clothes. Hair. Makeup. Jewelry. Her entire regal bearing.

"Now, you told police that you weren't aware what time your husband came home the night of the murders. Isn't that right?"

"That's right."

"When originally interviewed, you told the police that you'd been at a meeting of the East Hampton Historical Society."

"I'm a board member," she says.

"And you further informed the police that when you returned home, your husband was still out."

"Yes."

I am leaning against my table, my tone relaxed and conversational. Jimmy has said in those moments I'm trying to sound like the solicitous solicitor. Almost as if Claire Jacobson and I are gal pals.

"You told police that when you did arrive back home, straight from the meeting, you took a sleeping pill and were then, in your words, 'completely zonked.' Correct?"

I'm smiling again. Good neighbor Jane.

"I'm not proud of the fact that I occasionally need to medicate to get a good night's sleep," she says. Then adds, "Now more than ever."

"Completely understood."

I pause just slightly. "I don't need to remind you, do I, that you're still under oath?" I ask.

"Of course not."

"But again, you told police that you came straight home from the Historical Society meeting, which ended at eleven o'clock, according to the minutes."

I see a little something in the cat eyes. Not fear, exactly. Wariness. I'd asked her downstairs how quickly she could produce the prenup she'd signed with her husband. She'd said no way in hell.

But I didn't need it.

At least not in the way she thought, the language in it about how a murder conviction would cause the "moral turpitude" clause to kick in.

And enable her to walk away with everything.

"Yes," she says. "I came straight home."

"But you didn't come straight home, did you, Mrs. Jacobson?" I ask.

Now she pauses.

"I'm not sure I'm following you."

She clears her throat. As if she's the one who needs a good drink of water.

Shifts just slightly in her seat.

"Isn't it true, Mrs. Jacobson, that your husband might very well have been asleep in the guest room in which he's been sleeping for some time when you arrived home that night, and before you completely zonked out?"

She stares at me now, knowing I have walked her into a trap. And what might be a perjury trap depending on what she says next.

But before she can answer, I say, "Isn't it true, Mrs. Jacobson, that you neglected to mention to police that while you did return home after the Historical Society meeting that night, you made a side trip to Montauk, and Gurney's Inn, one of the deluxe oceanfront suites, to meet Gus Hennessy?"

Best hotel in the Hamptons. By a lot. Jimmy checked. Those suites have spectacular views of the Atlantic.

"*How dare you!*" she says.

She turns to Judge Prentice. But he's not going to save her.

"Do I even have to dignify an insulting question like that?"

"I'm afraid you do," he says.

She turns to stare at me again. Then at her husband. Then back at me.

"At this time," Claire Jacobson says, "I'd like to invoke my Fifth Amendment right and decline to answer."

Well, I think, *I didn't see* that *coming*.

"But Mrs. Jacobson, why would you need to protect yourself from self-incrimination on something that is hardly a crime?"

"Yeah, sweetie," Rob Jacobson says from behind me. "Why don't you tell everybody what you're afraid of?"

"*Order in the court!*" Judge Jackson Prentice shouts.

But that ship has sailed.

EIGHTY

Jimmy

IT VARIES FROM DAY to day what time the judge has them break for lunch in Riverhead. So Jimmy doesn't know if Jane has already seen the text he sent her before he started to head back east.

But he sent it anyway: call when u can.

She'll know it's important. He never wastes her time the way she never wastes his. Part of their deal, from the beginning.

What Jimmy Cunniff also doesn't know yet is just how important it is that their client in Riverhead, on trial for killing three people, has a connection to three other people who were previously murdered up-island.

It's not a recent connection between Rob Jacobson and Lily Biondi Carson; it's one from at least twenty-five years ago. But they're still connected, and not just because they had their picture taken at the beach one day a long time ago but because Jacobson took her to the prom at Dalton when he was a senior and Lily Biondi was a sophomore.

What are the odds?

Jimmy keeps wondering what the odds are on that, and on Jacobson walking right out of one case and into another this way. What he doesn't know, and what he wants to talk out with Jane because he can't do that with Mickey Dunne, is what it all might mean.

If it means anything.

For some reason Mickey hid the picture of Rob Jacobson from around the time in his life when his father shot his girlfriend and himself, on the day when Joe Champi magically appeared at the Jacobsons' town house. And established *that* connection.

Jimmy is thinking about all of this, head spinning, as he makes his way up the FDR and over the RFK Bridge, on his way to the Long Island Expressway, when he gets the call about the East Hampton cops finding the Palmer kid's Subaru in Montauk, at the bottom of the Shadmoor cliffs.

EIGHTY-ONE

Jimmy

THE CLIFFS IN SHADMOOR STATE PARK, Jimmy knows full well, are among the most spectacular landmarks in Montauk, and maybe Jimmy's favorite, even if he's never considered himself much of a nature lover. You live out here long enough and the water is the water, from no matter how many different angles you look at it. But this walk along the cliffs is different, stretching from the town beach all the way to an area called Ditch Plains, the cliffs part of a long line of coastal bluffs that runs all the way out to Montauk Point, the only bluffs like them from here to the Caribbean.

It doesn't take long for Jimmy to determine the view is much better from up here, and up high, than where they found Pat Palmer's car on the rocky sand at the water's edge.

There are police boats in the water, Jimmy can see, bobbing in the waves, being thrown around more than a little by the wind.

"But we don't know if the kid was in the car when it crashlanded," Jimmy says to the chief, Larry Calabrese.

"What are you saying?" Calabrese asks. "He got the car rolling and then jumped out instead of trading it in?"

Jimmy notices a pinch of tobacco under Larry Calabrese's lip. The chief turns and spits, with the wind, fortunately.

"It now appears that we got two witnesses who have ended up in the water, and apparently not by choice," Calabrese says.

"Technically," Jimmy says, "it's only one actual witness, because the Palmer kid did a runner before they got a chance to swear him in."

"Why'd the kid run?"

"He got a call right before he was about to testify that our client raped the Gates girl and then talk about all the payouts to keep everybody quiet."

"Then Jacobson killed them anyway?" Calabrese says. "How does that work?"

"The thought has occurred."

They both go back to staring out at the boats in the water— big waves today, wind from the east now becoming a gale. Truly one of the most beautiful places in the whole country, Jimmy thinks.

Unless you look down.

"You know about the rape part and the payoff how?" Calabrese asks.

"Palmer told me after he jumped me one night outside my joint."

"Interesting way you've got of getting a guy to open up."

Jimmy says, "Before Palmer bolted from the courthouse that day, somebody heard him on the phone saying that none of this shit was worth dying over."

"Empty boat for Nick Morelli. Empty car today," Calabrese says. "The boat and car owned by two guys talking very bad shit against the defendant. Now they're both gone and who benefits? Your client does."

"Another thought that has occurred."

They turn and start walking back to where they've both left their cars.

"Let me ask you something," Jimmy says. "How many people do you have to kill to be considered a serial killer?"

Chief Larry Calabrese spits again.

"Three or more," he says.

EIGHTY-TWO

"THINK OUR CLIENT WILL BE the one trying to plead the Fifth?" I ask Jimmy.

"Don't worry, he'll talk to us," Jimmy says. "Matter of fact, we might not be able to shut him up."

"You sound pretty sure of that."

"The guard, Tommy Murray, drinks at my bar. As soon as he drops off Mr. Wonderful, he's going to take a walk." Jimmy grins. "Give us our privacy."

It had been Jimmy's idea to wait to talk to Jacobson at the jail, saying that jumpsuits and cuffs always take the swag right out of prisoners, no matter how hot shit they think they are.

Rob Jacobson still tries his best to act like he's in charge of the room when he sits down, not even noticing that Tommy, the guard, has quietly disappeared.

"I'll talk to you," Jacobson says to me, "but not this asshole."

He nods at Jimmy.

"Mr. Cunniff and I said everything we needed to say to each other at the hospital," he says. "So he goes, or I head off to my fashionably late dinner reservation in the mess hall."

I watch as Jimmy casually reaches across the table and grabs the front of Jacobson's jumpsuit and jerks him forward before Jacobson even knows it's happening.

"*Hey,*" Rob Jacobson yells. "*Hey!*" He manages to turn his head and yell, "*Guard!*"

Only now does he become aware that the guard is gone.

"I felt we could speak more openly this way," Jimmy says. "Get in touch with our feelings."

"Let go of me," Jacobson says.

Jimmy jerks him a bit closer, their faces very close now. "Only if you promise to be nice."

"When you let go of me."

Jimmy shoves him back.

"Does this guy work for you, or is it the other way around?" Jacobson asks me.

"Boy," I say, "how many times have I asked myself *that* question?"

Jacobson manages to smooth out the front of his jumpsuit with his cuffed hands. "Does this have something to do with what my wife did today?" he says to us.

Jimmy doesn't answer him, just takes the photograph out of the inside pocket of his blazer and places it on the table in front of Jacobson. "Explain," Jimmy says.

"My Speedo?" Jacobson says. "It was the style back then."

I look at him, fascinated. Even here, even now with Jimmy Cunniff up in his face this way, Jacobson can't help himself from *being* himself.

Jimmy pokes Lily Carson's face with an index finger.

"You know Jane and me are looking into Lily Carson's death," Jimmy asks. "How is it that you never mentioned you knew Lily Carson when you were both kids?"

"Because the fact that I took a picture with her twenty-five years ago, or whatever, does absolutely nothing for me now—that's why."

"You didn't just take a picture with her at the beach one time," Jimmy says. "You took her to the prom."

Jacobson smiles. Still trying to be the cocky bastard he's always been.

"Cunniff, do you have any idea how many girls I had when I was in high school? Including more than one the night of that prom to which you're referring?"

Jimmy gets up and walks around the table, and now he sits next to Jacobson.

"Rob," he says, still in the soft voice, "my old partner has just been shot to death, point-blank range, in the Bronx. It is my strongly held belief that Joe Champi, an old acquaintance of yours, is the one who did the shooting. Nod if you're following."

Jacobson does. They are very close to each other.

"And when I went to my old partner's apartment this morning," Jimmy continues, "I discovered he had hidden this picture of you and Lily Carson and two other girls. So now I am here asking you why in the world my ex-partner thought a picture of this was worth hiding, most likely from your old friend Joe Champi."

"Joe is dead," Jacobson says.

"He was at Mickey Dunne's apartment this morning."

"Somebody might have been there. But I'm telling you it wasn't Champi."

"How can you possibly know that?"

"Because I had it done," Jacobson says.

"You expect us to believe you had Joe Champi killed," I say.

"Said the client to the lawyer," Jacobson says.

"Let's say you did, despite the history you have with the guy," Jimmy says. "*Why* did you?"

"Because he had something on me, something I thought I'd settled with him a long time ago," Jacobson says. "But he came back wanting more, even after he faked his own goddamn death, and told me that if I didn't pay, he was going to take it to the DA." Jacobson shrugs. "And you can understand how in my present circumstances I couldn't have done that."

Still just the three of us in the room.

I say, "What did he have on you?"

"Things got out of hand one night with one of those girls I told you I had," Jacobson says. "And then she died."

EIGHTY-THREE

I'M DRINKING MONTAUK SUMMER ALE at Jimmy's bar. He's sipping on Pappy Van Winkle bourbon, from the one bottle he keeps, seventy-five dollars a glass for the customers who know he has it behind the bar and are willing to pay for it.

"He wouldn't even admit whether it was him who killed the girl he told us about or Champi," Jimmy says.

"After bragging about how his uncle Joe had been making problems go away since he was in college."

"Makes you wonder exactly how many problems there were. Or how man dead girls."

"Until even Champi couldn't make a triple homicide go away."

It's a slow night here. Ball games on both sets, at each end of the bar. Maybe three tables full.

Before they left the jail, Jimmy asked Jacobson who he thought had killed Mickey Dunne if Joe Champi hadn't.

"Not my problem," Jacobson said.

"I thought I might have to pull you off him at that point."

"You would've had to if Tommy hadn't come back," Jimmy says.

I finish my beer. Jimmy finishes his drink. Jimmy walks me

out to the parking lot behind the bar. I ask him if he really believes Joe Champi is gone.

"Jacobson acted pretty proud of the fact that he'd taken him out," Jimmy says. "After Uncle Joe had become *his* problem."

"Even though it was supposed to look like a suicide."

Jimmy leans against the hood of my car.

"But if all this is true, then we might have ourselves a new problem."

"Such as?"

"Maybe Champi had a partner."

EIGHTY-FOUR

Jimmy

MICKEY WOULD ALWAYS SAY, every single time they thought they had a case rolled up, "Anything?"

Meaning, was anything still bothering Jimmy?

Maybe saying that it had been too easy. Or that they were still missing something.

That maybe they had the wrong guy.

That they hadn't finished the job.

On the drive home after he says good night to Jane, Jimmy keeps asking himself the same question about what Jacobson told them tonight, about Jacobson's history with Champi, pretty much since Jacobson's old man had taken himself out:

What is still bothering him?

A lot, is what.

Say Champi *is* dead, this time for real. That can only mean there has to be a second hitter out there, unless Nick Morelli and Pat Palmer made themselves disappear, and Jacobson, even from jail, has somebody new making problems go away.

Jimmy had been so sure that it was Champi after Gregg McCall got gone without a trace. But what if there *is* somebody else?

I need another drink, Jimmy thinks, *with Mickey Dunne sitting next to me, listening while I talk things through, and seeing if he thinks I missed anything.*

Jimmy doesn't want to turn around and go back to the bar. But he doesn't need to, either, because he's brought the bottle of Pappy Van Winkle; it's sitting right there on the seat next to him.

He doesn't know if any bottle of bourbon should be worth so much.

"But I am," he says as he pulls into his driveway.

The bullet hits him before he's all the way out of the car.

EIGHTY-FIVE

I AM SITTING IN the living room with Rip the dog, who, to be fair, seems to be in better shape than I am these days.

There is still a police car stationed in front of my house each night. I keep telling Jimmy that I don't need it, and he keeps telling me to leave it right where it is.

I know I should be tired, but I'm not. Maybe too much stimulation today, way too much going on, Palmer's car ending up at the bottom of the cliffs, the trial, our jailhouse meeting with Rob Jacobson, with Jacobson telling us he had Champi taken out.

All prefaced the night before by Jimmy's former partner being shot to death.

"Rip," I say, "what a challenging and exciting life I lead. I am truly blessed."

He looks at me expectantly the way he always does when I address him directly, as if I've just offered to go find him a bone, or a piece of meat.

I know myself well enough to know I'm not sleeping anytime soon. So I make myself a cup of an English decaf tea from Fortnum & Mason that Brigid gifted me last Christmas—my sister being a major tea nerd—back when she still liked me.

Brigid.

Still no word from her. I hope she's getting better. I *pray* she's getting better.

While I'm in the kitchen, I do get some treats for Rip, who really does look to be feeling better than he did when I took him in. But the last time Dr. Ben Kalinsky was over, he was the one giving Rip some treats, and pointed out that the dog's eyes showed the early stages of cataracts.

"What can I do about that?" I asked.

"Don't let him drive at night," he said, cracking himself up. "I never get tired of that one. Kills me every time."

So far Dr. Ben hasn't gotten tired of me, either. I keep asking myself where we're going with this, whatever *this* is. But being such a hotshot lawyer, I already know the answer to that one.

We're heading right into a dead end.

Literally.

I know I should end it before we go much further, but I also know why I'm not doing that, at least not yet.

He makes me happy.

Or as happy as I can be. Neither one of us has talked about love. If he turns out to be the first one of us to do it, I'll probably feel the urge to pull a gun on him. But I think he might already be about halfway in love with me.

And me with him.

Good timing, Jane.

I want to tell him about my condition. Tell Jimmy first, then him. But for now, my condition—it sounds far more benign when I call it that—remains a secret between Dr. Sam Wylie and me, until I start to get sicker or start treatment and can no longer keep it a secret.

I have spread out a lot of my case notes on the kitchen table and go back to them now with my mug of hot tea.

The BC fight song blares from my phone.

The screen says: "Bridgehampton Trauma Center."

It's the new, small hospital they've built behind the mall in Bridgehampton, the one with the only operating room east of Southampton Hospital, the place having opened about six months ago.

The voice, male, on the other end of the call identifies himself as Dr. Williams and tells me that Jimmy has been shot.

"I should say he's been shot again, because I couldn't help but notice what looks like a very recent wound not terribly far from tonight's."

Jimmy.

Shot.

Again.

Twice in the same week.

He'd done so little complaining—really, no complaining at all—about getting hit in the shoulder the first time that I'd almost forgotten about it.

I remember it now. And feel as if I've stopped breathing.

Or being.

"Is he alive?"

"Yes," Dr. Williams says. "We were told that you are his closest contact." There's a brief pause. "Are you his next of kin?" he asks.

"Even closer than that," I say. "How bad is it?"

"You should get over here," he says.

EIGHTY-SIX

THERE ARE ACTUALLY A lot of thoughts floating around inside my brain as I blow through more than one red light on my way to Bridgehampton on 27. But I keep going back to the big one:

He can't die on *me*.

I know he was shot as a cop. Never since he started working for me. Now this. I am putting him more in the line of fire than the NYPD ever did.

When I get to the trauma center, I can't talk to Dr. Raymond Williams because he's in the OR, attending to Jimmy.

I ask an emergency room nurse how long the surgery might take, knowing I sound like a complete idiot as soon as the words are out of my mouth.

As if she has any idea.

"There's just no way of knowing that," she says patiently. "The EMTs said that your friend had lost a lot of blood."

"Do you know where he was shot?" I ask.

"Somewhere in the midsection is all I really know. They wheeled him past me pretty quickly, as you might imagine."

She smiles at me.

"I'm sorry, were you asking about the wound or about where

they picked him up?"

"Both."

"It was North Haven," she says.

"Was he conscious?"

"I really didn't have eyes on him long enough to notice whether he was or wasn't. I've really told you all I know."

"I'm sorry to be bothering you."

"You're not bothering me. Are the two of you close?"

"More than I could ever properly describe."

I feel like I'm in some sort of fever dream, talking to this woman just to talk, preferring that to taking a seat in the waiting room and being back inside my own head worrying that something might go wrong and Jimmy might not make it through the night.

I do take a seat now, but then I'm right back up and walking back to where the ER nurse is on the other side of a clear plastic partition.

"Do you have any idea who found him and called it in?"

"I found him," a man's voice behind me says.

EIGHTY-SEVEN

Jimmy

THE FIRST FACE HE sees is Jane's.

"Well," Jimmy says to her. "I can't be dead."

"Why is that?"

"Because if you're here, this can't be heaven."

"Don't make me laugh."

"That's supposed to be my line."

Jane pulls a chair up next to the bed.

"They find the bullet," Jimmy asks, "or was it another through-and-through?"

"Dr. Williams has it," Jane says. "The bullet. He found the little sucker after establishing that no major organs had been damaged."

"Where's the bullet now?"

"In the able hands of Chief Larry Calabrese. He sent one of his guys to collect it—he wants to run it through the system right away."

Jimmy tries to sit up a little in the bed, turn more toward Jane, but then realizes his good arm is attached to an IV.

"Good thing it missed my heart," Jimmy says.

"What heart?"

She manages a smile, Jimmy sees. Just not much of one. He's

afraid she might start crying on him. It would be the first time she's ever done it. Not cried. Cried in front of him.

"I was so scared," she says in a small voice.

"Get out of here. Nothing scares you."

"Don't believe everything you hear."

Jimmy doesn't know what kind of medication they're giving him. But for now, it must be working like a dream, because he's feeling no pain. Like he's floating.

There were two other times on the job when he took a bullet. One time in the shoulder when he saw the shooter before Mickey did and jumped in front of Mickey and knocked him out of the way in the same motion and probably saved his life.

The other time was when Jimmy was alone, chasing down a gang kid in Hell's Kitchen, not knowing the kid was carrying until it was too late. The kid wasn't much of a shot once he turned around and fired on Jimmy. That one was also a through-and-through, flesh wound to his left hip.

This was different.

This time he got ambushed.

What he can't understand is why the shooter didn't finish the job.

Jimmy tells Jane that all he remembers is stepping out of the car and getting hit.

"How did I even get here?"

"Because Pat Palmer brought you. Right before he told them to call me."

"Wait. The kid isn't dead?"

Jane shakes her head.

"It's why you're not."

EIGHTY-EIGHT

DR. BEN KALINSKY AND I are having dinner at Sam's, our favorite Italian restaurant in East Hampton. I've been telling him about Pat Palmer's life being threatened, about him faking his own death, about him hiding out on the North Fork until he thought somebody traced him there. The kid finally decided that the only person he could trust was Jimmy, so he followed him home from the bar, and he was close enough behind him when Jimmy got to his house that he heard the shot.

"He was driving a car he borrowed from a friend, but he had his own gun with him," I say. "He didn't have much of a plan once he saw Jimmy go down, so he leaned on the horn and started firing his gun into the sky, and spooked the shooter. Then he called 911."

"Then he came to the hospital?" Ben says.

"To make sure Jimmy hadn't died on him," I say.

"Where is he now?"

"Gone again."

I see him smiling at me. "But you know where he is, right?"

I smile back at him. "No comment."

In the aftermath of Jimmy's shooting, Judge Prentice granted me a continuance, until the next afternoon. I did not tell Kevin

Ahearn about Pat Palmer, because I promised Palmer I wouldn't. All Ahearn knows is that an anonymous neighbor of Jimmy's was the one to call 911. Pat Palmer still doesn't want to testify and I don't want him to, because Laurel Gates and the rape and the NDA and the money will do my client no good whatsoever.

"You keep telling me you're going to win this case," he says.

Now I smile at him over my wineglass. "If I'm lyin', I'm dyin'."

When we finish our dinner, he drives me home. The squad car is where it's supposed to be.

"Very romantic," Dr. Ben says, "having a cop as a chaperone."

"It won't always be this way. This thing is winding down."

Like me.

"I'm going to hold you to that," he says.

I lean over and kiss him, not caring whether we're being watched by the East Hampton Town Police or not.

Dr. Ben says, "I promise not to break any laws if you invite me in."

"One of these days you're going to get lucky," I tell him. "Just not tonight, dear." I kiss him again. "And not because I'm not in the mood."

I go inside and collect Rip and walk him up and down the street, and then lock up for the night and set the alarm and get ready for bed. I think Rip might be picking up some speed on these walks. Or maybe it's that I'm losing a step.

I think about calling Jimmy at the hospital, but I don't want to wake him if he's asleep.

Before I shut off the lights, I open up my laptop and check my email one last time.

The last one came in about fifteen minutes ago.

"Well, I'll be damned," I say to Rip.

Dr. Ben Kalinsky didn't get lucky tonight.

But I just did.

EIGHTY-NINE

MY FIRST WITNESS THE next afternoon is Chief Mort Laggos of the Southampton Police. He is dressed in full uniform today, maybe to make himself look as official as possible. I don't know him. Jimmy likes him. And respects him.

"Good morning, Chief," I say.

"Good morning to you, counselor. Heard what happened to your partner. Glad he's going to make it."

"Not nearly as glad as I am, Chief."

I walk to my table now, reach into the small cardboard box that has been sitting in front of Rob Jacobson and me, come out with a ziplock plastic evidence bag, one that is already labeled.

I walk back over to Chief Laggos.

"Chief, do you recognize the contents of this bag I'm holding?"

"I do. It's a bullet." He grins. "As anybody could plainly see."

"Objection, Your Honor," Kevin Ahearn says. "If Ms. Smith is going to introduce anything into evidence, I have a right to inspect it first. If not, it's nothing more than a prop."

"Hardly," I say to him. I walk over and place the baggie in

front of Judge Prentice. He looks at it and nods as he reads the label.

"I'll allow this," Prentice says. "And when Ms. Smith finishes questioning the chief here, and this item *is* officially introduced into evidence, you can inspect it all you want, Mr. Ahearn. Objection overruled. Proceed, Ms. Smith."

I hand the evidence bag to Chief Laggos and ask him, "When did you first set eyes on this bullet?"

"When Chief Calabrese of the East Hampton force drove it over to us the other night after Mr. Cunniff was shot."

"And what did you then do with the bullet?"

"I handed it over to our forensics specialist and had him look at it first thing this morning," Laggos says. "You always want to know if it's a possible match for other bullets in our system."

"And how do you determine if there is a match?" I ask.

"When a bullet is fired from a firearm, and goes through the barrel, the barrel leaves markings on the bullet that are unique to a specific firearm."

"So what you're doing, if I understand you, is cross-checking that a particular bullet might have been fired by a gun used in a previous crime. Isn't that right?" I ask. "Whether you have the weapon in your possession or not."

"Yes, that's exactly right."

I walk back to the table next to ours where one of the clerks is seated, and the clerk hands me another envelope, introduced into evidence during that first week of the trial by Kevin Ahearn. This one contains the three bullets collected by Laggos's cops from the Gateses' home after the murders, even though the gun that fired them was never found. I hold the envelope up for the jury and tell them what's inside.

Now I ask Laggos to come down from the stand, as I remove those three bullets and carefully place them on the table next to the bullet Dr. Raymond Williams removed from Jimmy Cunniff.

"Now, Chief, would you care to inspect the grooves and what are known as the lands on these bullets?"

"I don't have to," he says. "I already have because you asked me to before we came into the courtroom this morning."

"So I did. But would you please tell the *jury* your expert conclusion regarding the three bullets found at the Gateses' home after the tragic murder of that family and the bullet fired into my associate Jimmy Cunniff last night."

"They were all fired from the same gun," he says.

"Your Honor!" Kevin Ahearn bellows. "With all due respect, Chief Laggos isn't a forensics expert."

"With all due respect, I'm just telling the court what the forensics expert you already called reiterated to me before I came over here today," Mort Laggos says.

Ahearn sits back down. He's got nowhere to go in the moment, and he knows it. This is, after all, a cop from Suffolk County. They're on the same team.

Gotcha.

"So just to be clear, Chief, you are saying that the bullet the doctor removed from Mr. Cunniff was fired by the same gun used to kill Mitch and Kathy and Laurel Gates."

Mort Laggos nods. "That's exactly what I'm saying."

The murder weapon had never turned up, as all the cops who worked the case know, and I know, and so does Kevin Ahearn. When the cops first questioned Rob Jacobson, they asked if he owned a gun. He said he did. They asked what kind. He said a .22 that he kept in a lockbox and had never fired—his wife felt safer having one in the house. They asked if they could see the lockbox. When he opened it, there was no gun inside. He acted shocked and said somebody must have taken it. Or stolen it. The cops wanted to know who that might have been. "Maybe somebody trying to make me look guilty," Jacobson said. At the time, the cops knew the missing gun didn't rise to the level of probable cause, even if the Gateses had been shot dead with a .22. But what they call "articulable suspicion" was just one more brick in the wall they finally built around my client.

Laggos, a big, wide-body guy, walks back to the witness stand and sits himself down. I walk back over to him. But I'm not really talking to him now.

I'm addressing the jury.

"We're all here because the state says that my client shot and killed all three members of the Gates family."

I pause now.

"So let me ask you one last question, Chief: how is it that somebody else managed to use our murder weapon to shoot Jimmy Cunniff?"

"Objection," Ahearn says. "Calling for a conclusion."

"Sustained," the judge says.

"Withdrawn," I say. But then as I pass the jury, "Unless it was the real killer doing the shooting at my partner."

NINETY

AHEARN DOES HIS BEST to repair the damage on cross, exploring with Mort Laggos all the possible ways that the murder weapon could have ended up in the hands of Jimmy's shooter.

"Have there been times in your experience when either a bullet or a gun from another crime shows up in another case on which you're working?" Ahearn asks.

"It's never happened to me personally," Laggos says. "But I've read about it happening."

"And isn't it possible, Chief, that after shooting Mitch and Kathy and Laurel Gates, the defendant didn't dispose of the gun and instead gave it to a friend or associate?" Ahearn says.

"Objection," I say. "Mr. Ahearn doesn't know if Rob Jacobson disposed of the murder weapon because he can't prove my client ever had it in the first place."

"Sustained," Judge Prentice says.

"Let me rephrase," Ahearn says. "Isn't it possible that the gun used on the Gates family and on Mr. Cunniff could have had several owners over the past year or so?"

I can see that my new best friend Chief Laggos isn't buying it, but he at least tries to be a good soldier.

"I suppose that is possible, yes."

When Ahearn is finished, I stand. "Redirect, Your Honor?"

Prentice waves me forward.

"I'd like a moment to respond to Mr. Ahearn's fabulism," I say.

"Objection," Ahearn says in a blink. "And look who's talking about fabulism."

"Sustained."

"Let me rephrase," I say.

"I would," Prentice says.

"Just for the sake of conversation, Chief, let's say that it was Mr. Jacobson's gun and he did give it to someone after that tragic night at the Gateses' house. As a veteran police-man, does it make *any* sense that this imaginary friend would think attempting to kill an essential member of the defense team trying to acquit him would somehow be helpful to Mr. Jacobson's cause?"

"Objection," Ahearn says. "Calls for speculation."

Before Prentice can say anything, I say, "Withdrawn."

I've brought back Marge Florio, my forensics expert from John Jay, and I tee her up after Laggos steps down. She explains about markings on bullets, and both the statistical and scientific improbability of Jimmy's bullet being fired by any gun other than the murder weapon. It is tedious stuff, but I just want to lock in my alternate theory about another killer for the jury. A couple of weeks ago I made fun of Rob Jacobson for using the expression "real killer." Now I just did everything except set it to music. Girl's gotta do.

When court adjourns, and before the guards come to collect my client, Rob Jacobson asks who I plan to call to the stand tomorrow.

"To be determined," I tell him.

"How close to the end are we?"

"Very."

He starts to get up. I put a hand on his arm. It's just the two of us left in the courtroom.

"Do you have someone new cleaning up messes for you the way Champi always did?"

He smiles. "I'm innocent."

"So you swear to me that you didn't send somebody after Jimmy after we came to the jail?"

"It's like you yourself just said," Jacobson says. "Why would I put out a hit on somebody I need to get me the hell out of this?"

Before I realize what he's doing, he leans over and kisses me softly on the cheek.

"Even if the only one I really need is you, sweetheart."

NINETY-ONE

THE SQUAD CAR IS gone when I get home. I stopped at the hospital in Bridgehampton on my way from court, and I finally won the fight with Jimmy about who needs protection more at this point, him or me.

This was after he informed me that he'd won his own fight with Dr. Raymond Williams and was about to be released.

"Nobody's coming back for me," Jimmy said.

"You don't know that."

"And you're not suddenly safe because somebody shot me." He sighs. "If you don't want a car out front, at least promise you'll set the alarm."

He'd had an electrician put in a new one for me.

"I've been doing it every night. Scout's honor."

"You would have made a shit Girl Scout."

"But one hell of a Boy Scout."

I get home knowing I need a hot bath, and a drink, in no particular order. I told Jacobson that we're near the end of the trial, for the simple fact that we are. But I know that will mean the beginning of my treatments. Chemo. Or radiation. Or both. Probably both. Something else to be determined.

I can only imagine how romantic all that will be for Dr. Ben Kalinsky.

I know, on a fundamental level, how risky it's been putting off treatment even for a few weeks. But starting it when I got the diagnosis would have meant someone else finishing the trial. And that was never going to happen, especially if this is the last case I'm ever going to try. Worst-case scenario. Sometimes I think that's the only scenario there is.

I remember being at Jimmy's bar with him one night, and the Yankees were on the television because they always seem to be, and a friend of Jimmy's sitting next to us told Jimmy he was way too obsessed with the Yankees.

"Baseball's not a matter of life or death," the guy said.

"You're right," Jimmy said that night. "It's way more serious than that."

And now I'm the one treating my defense—*our* defense—of a shitheel like Rob Jacobson as a matter of life or death. For both of us.

While I've got a life-or-death situation of my own going on.

I never lose, I tell Jimmy all the time.

But what am I winning here in the end, really, whatever happens at the end of the trial?

I take my bath, a glass of vodka with ice and an orange peel placed carefully on a corner of the tub. I feel below my ear. Is the lump back there getting any bigger? Hard to tell. But it's not getting any smaller, either.

I hope not to have to wear a scarf to court before the trial is over and have people thinking that I'm making a fashion statement, at long last. Dr. Sam has told me that it's not a given that I'll lose my hair because of chemo. But then she added that me keeping my hair isn't the way to bet.

I put on one of my favorite BC T-shirts, and sweatpants,

and start to think about whether I want to cook something myself or do Uber Eats, when I hear the faint click of the front doorknob being turned.

I have not yet set my fancy new alarm tonight. I don't do it until I've walked Rip for the last time.

I quietly move into the front hall and take the Glock from the top drawer of the antique table there.

Behind me I can hear a low growl from Rip, who's still in the kitchen. But no barking from him. I gently close the kitchen door behind me.

I see the front door begin to open.

I stand there in the middle of the front hall, both hands on the gun.

"Don't shoot," my sister says as she steps into the house. "I'm unarmed."

NINETY-TWO

Jimmy

DR. WILLIAMS TELLS JIMMY he has to take it easy for a couple of days. Jimmy promises him that he will. Dr. Williams tells him that if he wants to exercise while the wound is fully healing, he can walk around his neighborhood, upping the distance every day as he sees fit.

Jimmy promises him he'll do that, too.

It reminds Jimmy of the old days, when one of his superiors would call him in and tell him to back off a particular suspect or perp or case. Jimmy would nod them and yes-sir them to death, and then ignore all of it.

"If you somehow see me out and about for the next few days," Jimmy tells the doctor, "I give you permission to shoot me again."

Dr. Williams, a nice enough guy, seems to buy it.

But Jimmy is out and about the next morning, in his car, on his way to Little Neck, Queens, to the address on Knollwood Avenue, where Lily Carson's father, Paul Biondi, lives.

The night before, he searched the internet like a demon and made some calls and found out that Biondi had owned a service station and repair shop in Little Neck before retiring a few years earlier. And that he had raised Lily by himself after the girl's mother ran off to Santa Fe to find herself and never came back.

"Thank you for seeing me," Jimmy says when Biondi opens the door.

"My experience always was that you decline to talk to a cop, you look guilty," Biondi says.

"I'm an ex-cop."

"Wouldn't make me look any less guilty if I'd told you to buzz off."

He is short and wide but solid-looking, big hands and muscled forearms, the left one featuring a Marine Corps insignia. White hair buzzed into a crew cut. Eyes the color of coal. He looks nothing like his daughter.

There is, Jimmy notices, some faint scar tissue around the eyes.

"You box?"

"How'd you know?"

Jimmy taps a finger next to his right eye. "Dead giveaway."

Biondi says, "Golden Gloves until I quit." He shrugs. "You either got a good left hand or you don't. I didn't. They can teach you a lot. Not that."

He asks Jimmy if he wants coffee or water or something. Jimmy says he's fine, he doesn't want to take up too much of his time.

"Tell me about Rob Jacobson," Jimmy says.

"Tell you what?"

"It's like I told you on the phone, Mr. Biondi, I'm just looking for anything that might help me find out what really happened to your daughter and her family," Jimmy says.

"What's Jacobson got to do with any of that?" Biondi asks. "He's on trial for the other thing out east."

"I discovered a connection between him and Lily," Jimmy says. "And once I did, I found out he took her to a prom."

Biondi's big hands are on his knees. He clenches them now and blows some air out through his nose.

"You want to know what I really know about that son of a bitch?" Biondi says. "I should have killed him when I had the chance."

NINETY-THREE

MY SISTER IS BACK on the stand the next morning.

The night before, she asked to finish her testimony, saying she "misremembered" some things the first time around.

"Like what?" I asked.

"Like things that are important, and that I believe can help you," she said. "And help Rob in the process."

"Great. Will they by any chance be true?"

"Of course. You know I don't lie."

"Do I?"

Now I've had no choice but to tell the jury about her condition, the real reason for her absence, knowing as I did that it would elicit for her even more sympathy. And make her more believable in the process. Which right now is the whole ball game, at least as far as her kid sister is concerned.

"How are you feeling now?" I ask.

"Much better, thank you. And strong enough to be back."

"We all thank you for that," I say.

"You're all very welcome."

She smiles at the jury. I see some of the jury members smile back at her.

"Now, the last time you were here, you told the court that

you weren't sure of the exact time Rob Jacobson left your home the night of the murders. Isn't that correct?"

"That's what I said."

"And I had just asked you to describe in just what way you were together that night. That was right before Mr. Jacobson fell ill. Do you recall that sequence of events?"

"Hard to forget."

I shoot a quick look at Jacobson.

For some reason, he's smiling.

"So let's start over. Having had some time to reflect, do you now remember when Rob Jacobson left you that night?"

"As a matter of fact, I do."

"When *did* he leave?"

My sister has a sheepish look on her face, as if somehow she's been caught being a very bad girl.

"He didn't leave."

I look back over at my client. He doesn't call Brigid a liar this time. He doesn't fall over the table, faking a heart attack to protect his precious prenup.

But he's still smiling, even more brilliantly than before.

NINETY-FOUR

Jimmy

"IT WAS THE NIGHT of that stinking prom," Paul Biondi is telling Jimmy. "Some fancy spot in Manhattan. We were still living over by Little Neck Parkway at the time."

"The Midtown Loft and Terrace," Jimmy says. "Where the prom was. I checked."

"Whatever you say."

"How'd they meet? Lily being from Little Neck Parkway and him from Central Park West?"

"Some party they ended up at together," Biondi says. "She's still only sixteen, but she decides he's her Prince Charming."

Jimmy and Paul Biondi haven't moved from the living room. Somehow Biondi, taking up as much of the couch as he does, makes the room look even smaller than it really is.

He is clenching his fists again. Old boxer's hands, looking as if they got run over by a car.

"So she tells me before she leaves for the prom, in the limo he shows up in, that she's going to spend the night with one of her friends whose parents booked her a hotel room," Biondi says. "But in the morning, she's in her bed."

He stares down at the big hands now, then up at Jimmy.

"There's bruises on her face and neck. One eye starting to

314

color. When I ask her about it, she tells me she had too much to drink and fell in the ladies' room."

"But you didn't believe her?"

"You're a cop. Who bruises their neck slipping and falling in the ladies' room?"

Jimmy just nods.

"I felt like I'd done a pretty damn good job raising this girl on my own," Biondi says. "But at that point I knew as much about teenage girls as I did about brain surgery."

It is very quiet in the house. His eyes are suddenly very red.

"I promised myself I'd be a better grandfather to her daughter than I had been a father to her. But now they're both gone."

"How'd she get home?" Jimmy says.

"That's the best part. The asshole sent her home in the limo. Just alone this time."

He's telling it at his own speed and Jimmy knows enough to let him.

"She breaks down finally and tells me what happened, pleading with me not to do anything about it," he says. "He took her back to his place. His old man was dead by then. The mother, as far as I could tell, was long gone. Just the two of them. She says she begged him to stop. But the more she told him that, the rougher it got. And no one there to hear them until it was done."

He shakes his head.

"I never should've let her go," Biondi says. "It didn't feel right. But she was so goddamn desperate to be breathing that air. To be something more than the daughter of a guy who owned a goddamn gas station."

"Did you go looking for him?"

"Yeah. When I get to the apartment or town house or whatever the hell you call it, it's like he's waiting for me. Him and this big guy he introduces as his uncle Joe."

Champi.

Of course.

"The kid starts crying, not even denying it, begging me to forgive him," Biondi says. "Says he doesn't even remember all of it, he was blackout drunk. When he woke up he called for the car and sent her home. Swears on his dead father he'll never go near her again."

Biondi isn't crying. But Jimmy thinks he's close.

"That turns out to be BS, of course," he says. "Before long he's calling her, but at least my Lily is smart enough at that point not to have anything to do with him."

"Is that all of it?" Jimmy says.

"No," he says. Voice not more than a whisper.

Now he does start to cry. Talking and crying at the same time.

"The uncle tells me he knows my business isn't too far from going under," Biondi says. "Then he reaches into his jacket and comes out with a check for more money than I've ever seen in my life, enough to keep the shop going, and enough to send Lily to whatever college she wants, which turns out to be Princeton, by the way, something I never could have afforded. And along with the check is one of those nondisclosure things."

Biondi is fighting to get some air into him.

"I took the money," he says, almost sounding as if he's choking.

Jimmy thinks: *Who the hell in this thing hasn't?*

NINETY-FIVE

I AM STANDING ON Atlantic Avenue Beach with my sister in the early evening.

"How much?" I ask her again.

We're both in jeans and vests. She's wearing a baseball cap that has one word written on the front: SIMPLE.

I wish.

"How much what?" Brigid says.

"How much did he pay you to come back to lie for him? After he initially paid you off to get you to leave."

"How about this? How about you thank me and leave it at that?"

"You're a liar," I say. "And under oath."

"And you're a bitch."

I'm breathing very hard all of a sudden.

"The jury may have believed that you were talking and drinking until you both passed out. But I know you never have gotten that drunk in your life."

We've made our way down to the water's edge. I look out now and think about all the times in my life, at least since I moved out here, when I've come here to find peace, if not

317

quiet. The walk from Indian Wells Beach to here has always been happy-making for me.

Just not tonight.

"How much?" I say again.

"He didn't pay me."

"Liar."

"Bitch," she says again.

I keep feeling as if we should retreat to neutral corners. Except there aren't any out here.

"It doesn't even matter whether you came up with that fairy tale," I say, "or he did. Neither one of you has to cop to being unfaithful. You give him an all-night alibi and, on top of that, he doesn't watch his prenup get shot out of a cannon. Now I know why he was smiling his ass off while you were up there. I'm surprised he didn't give you a standing O when you were done."

"You don't know him the way I do," she says.

"At this point, I actually might know him better."

A gust of wind comes off the water and nearly blows the hat off her head.

"How convenient that this new treatment for you didn't keep you from returning in the nick of time," I say.

"It doesn't matter what I say. You're going to believe what you want to believe anyway."

"Finally, my sister speaks the truth."

"He didn't kill those people."

"Says him. And says you."

"I'm not his lawyer."

"When did he really leave that night? It's not something I can use. Just something I need to know."

Somehow the cold out here is making my neck stiffen up. Or maybe it's simply the tension of the moment. I move my head from side to side to loosen it. Then do it again.

"What's wrong?" she says.

"My sister is a pain in my neck. When did he leave?"

"When I said he did."

"You know Kevin Ahearn isn't nearly done with you, right?" I say. "He's going to come back at you again tomorrow, and keep coming, and keep making you tell him why it took this long for you to come up with your latest alibi."

"You should have worried about Kevin Ahearn coming after me when you were the one who wanted to put me on the stand in the first place."

I tell her we're done, then. I've got nothing more to say to her, start walking toward the road, the beginning of my walk home.

But then I turn around and come back, straight into the wind. A feeling becoming more and more familiar to me.

"You know that you might be helping get a murderer off, right?" I say to my sister.

"Well, then, Miss High and Mighty," Brigid says, "that would make two of us, wouldn't it?"

Jimmy's waiting for me on my front porch when I finally make it back to the house.

"What?" I ask.

"I had a crazy thought about our client."

I grin at him. "You've come to the right place, then. I'm the mayor of Crazytown."

Jimmy says, "What if he did them all?"

NINETY-SIX

"YOU'RE BLEEDING," I SAY to Jimmy when we're inside.

He's wearing his old leather jacket, his favorite article of clothing, a white T-shirt underneath. His midsection is still bandaged—I can see the bulge from under the shirt—and now there is a small red stain seeping through.

"So I am," Jimmy says casually, looking down. "No thing. I was always a bit of a bleeder when I was still boxing."

"Maybe you overdid it today. Have you considered that, tough guy?" I ask. "Your shoulder wound has barely healed from the first time you got shot."

"I'm starting to lose track, I get shot so often."

"You want me to change your bandage?" I ask.

"You're a lawyer, not a doctor. If I popped a stitch, I'd feel it. I'm fine."

"Don't lie to me. I can see you're in pain."

"And you're being one," Jimmy says.

I grin. "I just told my sister the same thing a little while ago."

"You wanna play doctor or you wanna talk about our client?" He leans back a little in his chair, as if to make himself slightly more comfortable.

"You honestly think he might have had something to do with what happened to the Carsons?"

Jimmy asks me for a small whiskey and fills me in on where he's been and what he's heard from Paul Biondi as I go into the kitchen and pour him one and pour one for myself and come back with the two glasses. I ask if it's all right to mix whiskey with pain pills and he says that he's saving the pain pills for a rainy day.

He takes a small sip of whiskey and sighs contentedly.

"Lily Biondi Carson signed the same nondisclosure that her old man did," he says. "I asked him."

"NDAs," I say. "Kind of Rob's thing."

"And apparently from an early age," Jimmy says. "But what if—and I'm just spitballing here—Lily went to Rob wanting more money to help with her husband's gambling debts, all that time after prom night?"

"And threatened to tell everybody that he raped her when she was a minor," I say, "whether or not she signed that piece of paper and already got paid off."

Jimmy takes another sip of whiskey. I take a sip of my own. I watch him absently rub the area where he's been bleeding. He was lucky this time too, without question, with where the bullet had entered and where it had ended up and all the good things it had missed along the way. Very, *very* lucky. But as much of a tough guy as he is and always has been, he *was* shot, gunned down in front of his own house. And if he hadn't also gotten lucky with Pat Palmer being there and calling it in, he could have died. And the body count in the two cases the two of us are working could have gone up again.

I've told him that my defense of Jacobson will likely rest soon, and that closing arguments from Kevin Ahearn and me could begin early next week.

Then the only arguments that will matter will be the ones in the jury room, as they decide whether or not Rob Jacobson is one more sociopath with a big bank account and a famous name.

Jimmy Cunniff and I are having that same conversation right now, times two, knowing it sounds bananas to even suggest he might have had something to do with killing six people instead of the three for whom he's on trial.

"I do feel like the mayor of Crazytown even thinking that, as you have so eloquently put it, he might have done them all," I say.

"And yet here we are," Jimmy says.

"Hey, you started it."

"Damn straight."

He looks tired to me. But I probably look just as tired to him. I tell him he needs to go home and get himself about twelve hours of uninterrupted sleep, then rinse and repeat all the way through the weekend.

He'll leave in a minute, he says; he hasn't even finished his drink.

"Say I'm right about the guy," Jimmy says. "Say he did it or had it done with the Carsons even though we're the only people in the world who can connect him to them. Other than Lily's old man, of course. You know what that could mean?"

"I'll bite."

"It would mean that maybe Champi, along with somebody else Jacobson has maybe called in from the bullpen to replace Champi, has been running around removing loose ends from both our cases. The way he's maybe been removing loose ends for our client for a long time."

"You certainly are full of interesting theories tonight," I say, and finish my whiskey.

Jimmy starts to say something else, but then he looks at me, almost curious, or maybe confused, as his eyes suddenly close and he slides out of his chair, unconscious by the time he hits the floor.

NINETY-SEVEN

I RIDE WITH JIMMY in the ambulance that transports him back to the Bridgehampton Trauma Center, sirens and lights blazing on Route 27 in the night.

The primary emergency room for the area is still at Southampton Hospital. But Dr. Williams identified Jimmy as a legit emergency not long after I called the center to tell him that one of his patients was on his way, perhaps because of the aftershocks of his most recent gunshot wound.

In the ambulance I say to Jimmy, "Your idea of taking it easy worked like a charm, by the way."

Jimmy, who's regained consciousness, turns to one of the EMTs and says, "Who is this woman and what is she doing in this ambulance with me?"

"Who doesn't love 911 humor?" I say to one of the young guys monitoring Jimmy's vitals.

I watch him as the EMT watches his vitals. I know there is nothing I could have done to stop Jimmy Cunniff from doing whatever the hell he wanted to do, because there never has been. He's always been just as pigheaded as I am. Which one of us is the more stubborn is too close to call at this point in our relationship.

At the hospital, he is taken inside to Dr. Williams, and I wait for more than an hour. I find a vending machine and get a cup of coffee, not knowing just how long a night it is going to be. I'm not going anywhere until I know that Jimmy is all right.

Ms. Jane Smith: always much better at looking out for somebody else than for herself.

I was second-guessing myself all the way over here for not calling somebody as soon as I saw the blood. But it's Jimmy. Of course he checked himself out of the hospital early after taking another bullet like it was just one more punch, then hit the ground running, driving all the way into Queens to chase down a lead and driving all the way back. I'd convinced myself he was already as good as new, even knowing he couldn't be, because I wanted him to be as good as new. Like I could wish away his physical issues.

If only.

Finally Dr. Williams comes out to the waiting area. He is a compact Black man, solidly built. Good-looking. I manage to restrain myself from telling him he reminds me a little bit of Kevin Hart, just taller.

"You were with him when he collapsed?" Dr. Williams asks, skipping any small talk.

"At my house. I called it in right away."

"Good that you did," Williams says. "It turns out he's developed a post-op infection that escalated pretty quickly."

"They told me in the ambulance his blood pressure wasn't good," I say.

"You could say that. It plunged is what it did. I would bet before he passed out he was displaying some warning signs. Confusion, disorientation? He's lucky the infection hasn't yet developed into sepsis."

"What happens then?"

"Then it can kill the patient if we don't get there in time."

"Stop sugarcoating it, Doc," I say.

"I don't know you all that well, Ms. Smith," he says, "but you don't strike me as someone who wants things sugarcoated."

"You have no idea."

He tilts his head. "Have you had any serious health challenges as an adult?"

For some idiotic reason, his question makes me smile.

"Here and there," I say, "along the dusty old trail."

"And did you follow your doctor's advice?"

I still feel myself smiling even though none of this, not one part, is funny for either Jimmy or me.

"Here and there."

"Your friend might be clear out of good fortune after this," Dr. Williams says. "I'm hoping that this latest episode has gotten his attention. He couldn't do anything about being shot. That wasn't his fault. But he can do something to take care of himself."

"So you want me to drop the hammer on him."

"Very much so. If he had been alone when he passed out..." He shrugs and shakes his head before finishing his thought. "It would have been the same as if he'd bled out after being shot."

"Hearing you loud and clear," I say.

Now he smiles. "I know how persuasive you are as a lawyer. So I want you to get him to understand."

"Can I see him now?"

"Follow me. But don't stay too long. He needs the rest. He's spending a few nights here whether he wants to or not. Then you can pick him up if there are no further setbacks and drive him home and do your best to put him under house arrest."

It's the same room he had before. Antibiotics are being

pumped into him via an IV line. I pull up a chair next to the bed. At this point my partner and I have the hospital drill down pat, like we've choreographed it.

"Your doctor," I say, "told me before I came in that a couple of the warning signs for infection are confusion and disorientation. I told him no way either one of us would have picked up on that, since confusion and disorientation are pretty much your normal state."

"Oh, look," Jimmy says, "they've sent Florence Nightingale to check on me."

"You have scared me twice in the same week. *Stop it.*"

"You know I'm like a shark. If I don't keep swimming, I sink to the bottom."

I was the only person in the waiting room tonight. The last thing Dr. Williams told me before I came in here was to not be in here too long, what Jimmy needed most right now other than the antibiotics was sleep.

"I can get along without you for a few days," I say.

"Care to take a polygraph on that?"

"Come on, the trial is about to be over. Nothing more for you to do. Good time to catch your breath, big boy."

"As soon as I do, I am going to find out who killed the Carsons," he says. "Or had them killed. And who killed Gregg McCall. Or I *am* gonna die trying."

Suddenly I feel my throat closing up like a fist.

I swallow hard.

"You always say that. *Stop saying that!*"

He raises the hand not attached to the IV and says in a soft voice, "Okay, Janie. Okay. Relax."

I try to answer him but feel my throat closing up again, like a door being slammed shut.

I see him staring at me.

"Janie," Jimmy says. "I'm not going anywhere, I promise."

"Okay," I say in a small voice.

He smiles at me.

And then it happens, that fast, something I've been trying to contain for weeks. I start to cry, softly at first, but not softly for very long. Then it's like a seawall being breached, and I'm sobbing, hugging myself as if to keep myself from flying completely apart, struggling for breath.

I try to get some air into me, but for the life of me I can't.

"Janie?" Jimmy says. "What's wrong?"

Everything, I want to tell him.

But I don't say *anything.* I'm rocking back and forth in the chair now, somehow crying even harder than before, still gasping for air, wondering if they can hear me outside.

"Janie? *What's the matter?*"

"I'm the one who's dying," I say.

NINETY-EIGHT

Jimmy

HE LIES THERE IN the dark and the quiet, or at least as much darkness and quiet as you can ever have in a hospital room at night, after Jane has finally left.

Thinking: *She might have needed to be sedated more than I do.*

He asked how she planned to get back to Amagansett—he could call somebody at the bar to come get her. She said she was going to Uber. Jimmy told her that maybe it was not the best idea for her to be alone right now.

"Kind of my thing," Jane said to him. "Being alone."

By then she had taken him through all of it, from the time her friend Dr. Wylie gave her the original diagnosis.

"How'd she come up with fourteen months?" Jimmy asked.

"She didn't. I did. At which point I became the first lawyer in history to plea-bargain a sentence *up*."

And she explained to Jimmy why she had decided to delay treatment, telling him what kind of treatment would be involved.

"Finally," Jimmy said, "a way to shut you up."

At least she smiled.

"You need to tell Ben."

"When the trial is over."

"Because . . . ?"

"Just because."

They sat there in silence after that. All their history in the room with them, all that they feel for each other.

All that they mean to each other.

Jimmy thinking: *Even love doesn't properly describe it.*

Even love doesn't seem to do the job when it comes to what we have.

"Get some sleep," Jimmy said.

"That's supposed to be my line," Jane said.

He waved her to come closer then, and she did, leaning in, tilting her head down. Jimmy kissed her on the forehead, neither one of them moving for what felt like a minute. Or more. As if neither one of them wanted to pull back.

When Jane finally pulled back, Jimmy said, "Like everything else, we fight this together now. Understood?"

"Yes, boss."

"And in the end we kick cancer's ass together."

Jane managed to build another small smile, but somehow Jimmy thought she might start crying again.

In a voice that Jimmy could barely hear, Jane said, "Who's better than us?"

After that, he was alone.

But as tired as he is, he doesn't sleep right away. Thinking about her. And them. The two of them. He had Mickey as his partner, and then Jane.

Now Mickey is gone.

Jane has just told him she's dying.

The girl he's always thought of, with total love, as much as he has in him, as Jane Effing Smith.

Suddenly Jimmy Cunniff is the one who can't stop crying.

NINETY-NINE

THEY RELEASE JIMMY FROM the hospital on Sunday. I'm there to drive him home. He says that when I give my closing argument in the courtroom, he wants to be there.

"To be determined," I say.

"By what?"

"By whom. *Me*. And my associate, Dr. Williams."

On Monday, when court adjourns for the day, I have one last conference with my client, one that he has requested, in our usual room down the hall from the courtroom.

He told me beforehand that it's important. But then he thinks everything related to him is.

"I've changed my mind," he says when we're seated across the table from each other. "I want to testify."

"Yeah . . . *no*."

"I think the jury needs to hear from me. Nobody can convince them of my innocence better than I can."

"No."

"I think I can put us over the top. With some things about me I haven't even told you."

"Tell me now."

"Tomorrow," he says. "You have to trust me. This will be a game changer."

"On what planet?"

"You've said all along that we'd revisit the idea of me testifying before the trial was over."

"I was hoping you'd forgotten, actually."

"Well, we're revisiting it now," he says.

"Some defendants are able to help themselves on the stand. But you wouldn't be one of them."

He shakes his head, his smirk-face very much in place. "You really are a bitch."

"It's almost shocking how many people are telling me the same thing these days," I say.

"Not shocking to anyone who's taken the time to get to know you."

"Good line, Rob. You're still not testifying."

"This is where I remind you one last time that you work for me."

I'm tired. And my neck is starting to ache again, as it usually does now late in the day. I just want to get home and prepare my closing argument and get some rest so I'm as close as I can be to the top of my game tomorrow, when I will take my last best shot at getting an acquittal for the smug bastard sitting across from me.

One who may very well have killed those people.

"And is this where you expect me to tell you, one last time, to fire me?"

"Aren't you going to?"

I stand now and turn my back to him, before turning back around as if addressing a jury of one.

"You've got it wrong, Rob, the way you have from the start. *You* work for *me*. You want the whole truth and nothing but?

There it is. When we're in that room down the hall, you work for me. Which means that one last time tomorrow, when we're back in there together, I talk and you listen."

He grins at me. "Then before we do make it down the hall, I'm going to talk, and you're going to listen."

He talks for quite a long time and has my complete attention.

When he finishes, I get up and leave without even saying good-bye. I take the back roads to Amagansett, and when I get home I feed Rip and take him to the beach, Indian Wells tonight, and search around until I find a good piece of driftwood to throw. Then this is one of the nights when he actually fetches it a few times before I'm the one doing the fetching and he's staring at me from the sand as if to say, *What are you looking at?*

I go back home with my dog and panfry a burger and drink a beer as I eat it, and then begin a first draft of my closing argument, writing it in pencil, one of my trusty No. 2s.

In the morning, I will call Rob Jacobson to the stand.

ONE HUNDRED

AT A QUARTER TO NINE I'm in Judge Prentice's chambers along with Kevin Ahearn, informing them that there has been a last-minute change of plans and that my client is going to be my last witness.

"You're sure about this, Ms. Smith?" Judge Prentice says.

"My client and I are both sure, Your Honor."

Prentice turns to Ahearn. "I assume you have no objection," he says, not even making it sound like a question.

"*Objection?*" Kevin Ahearn says. "I feel like it's my birthday."

"So you're saying you won't request additional time to prepare for your cross?" the judge says.

"With all due respect, Your Honor," Ahearn says, "I've been prepared to do this since we arrested the son of a bitch."

As we walk out of the room, Ahearn says to me, "I'm not trying to talk you out of anything. But *are* you sure you want to do this?"

"Hundred percent," I lie.

We're in the courtroom, on our way to our respective tables, when Ahearn leans over and whispers one last thing to me.

"I actually misspoke inside. This doesn't feel like my birthday, Jane. It feels like I just won the goddamn lottery."

ONE HUNDRED ONE

ROB JACOBSON HAS ASSURED me that he will behave himself, and not make things easier for the district attorney from Suffolk County, who is fully expecting to fillet him as soon as he gets the chance.

Jacobson doesn't even make it until I've gotten the chance to ask my first question.

"Before we begin," he says after being sworn in, "I'd just like to state for the record that I am innocent of these charges."

"Objection," Ahearn says, sounding almost amused. "If it would please the court, could Your Honor please remind the defendant that this isn't an infomercial for his real estate company?"

"Mr. Jacobson, here's how we like to roll in my court. First you get asked a question. Then you answer it."

"I apologize, Your Honor," Jacobson says.

"Proceed, Ms. Smith," Prentice says.

I get up from behind the table and walk toward my client. Even having just been admonished by the judge, he looks as happy and excited as if it's *his* birthday, as if this is where he wanted to be all along, maybe even expected to be:

Ready for his close-up.

"Good morning, Mr. Jacobson."

"Good morning, Jane. And also to you, Mr. Ahearn."

I begin by taking him back to when he was a teenager and discovered the bodies of his father and his father's mistress.

"Is there any way, even after all this time, for you to properly describe a moment like that?"

"Horrifying. Traumatizing. And obviously life changing. Because I saw with my own eyes, in my own family and in my own house, what gun violence looks like. It's why my wife, Claire, and I have been making quite substantial, and annual, contributions to Moms Demand Action for years."

Before Ahearn is out of his seat to object, I introduce into evidence the parts of Jacobson's tax returns that prove he has been doing exactly that.

"So when it comes to gun violence," I say to Jacobson when I continue, "you have literally put your money where your mouth is."

"I have," he says. He stares at the jury now. "I hate guns."

I let that settle. I don't believe for a second that my client cares about gun violence or global warming or saving the whales, but even I have to admit how sincere he sounds.

Jimmy Cunniff told me earlier in the trial nobody fakes sincerity better than Rob Jacobson does.

"Let's fast-forward now to the night of the gun violence against the Gates family," I say. "Mr. Jacobson, you're aware that my sister, Brigid, has previously testified that the two of you spent the night of the murders together."

Now Jacobson offers the jury a sheepish grin.

"Most of it with me passed out, I'm embarrassed to say," he says. "We were talking, and drinking. And talking. And drinking. Until finally we were just drinking. Me, mostly." He shrugs, almost helplessly. "Brigid was being the awesome friend she always has been. I was being a drunk."

I watch as a few of the jurors nod in recognition.

"But you are also aware that a neighbor of the Gates family, Otis Miller, has testified that he saw you speeding away from the Gateses' house earlier that evening," I say. "Isn't that correct?"

"It's correct that he says he saw me," Jacobson says. "But I wasn't speeding. I was simply driving away."

"But you were there that night?"

"Yes. That's never been in dispute."

Not in dispute. But until now, only Otis Miller has put Jacobson at the house that night.

"And why were you there?"

"I was invited," he says. "We didn't know each other very well, but our daughters had become tennis friends."

"Who invited you?"

"Mitch Gates did."

"Could you please tell the jury *why* he invited you?"

Jacobson again turns to face the jurors. "He needed money."

A murmur runs through the courtroom now.

"A lot of money," Jacobson adds.

"And he was asking for it from the father of one of his daughter's tennis friends?"

"It wasn't like that."

"Could you please tell us what it *was* like, Mr. Jacobson?"

"I owed his wife a favor. *She* was *my* old friend."

The old friend who was the other girl in the picture Mickey Dunne left behind, as my client had informed me the night before.

"She saved my life once," Rob Jacobson says.

ONE HUNDRED TWO

Jimmy

HE'S LYING HIS ASS OFF, Jimmy knows.

Doesn't think he's lying. *Knows.*

Jimmy's seen it in courtrooms his whole life, every time he's watched a defendant take the stand. The really smart ones, and often the guilty ones, they know what's verifiable and what's not. They know what they can get away with, what they think they can sell to a jury, just how much shit they can make up.

Jimmy had a bad day yesterday, so he's watching it on the live feed, feet up, laptop open on the table next to him. He knows all the things Jacobson finally decided to tell Jane the night before. That Kathy Gates, the former Kathy Fuller, *is* the other girl in the picture, even if you can't see her face. That they were friends in high school, Jacobson from Dalton, Kathy Fuller from Spence.

That isn't all of the story, just the part Jimmy is watching Jacobson sell to the jury at the moment like a goddamn champ.

Jimmy remembers watching some big-shot woman from one of the big-shot drug companies take the stand in her own defense one time in a fraud trial about some miracle drug that wasn't, talking about years of physical and mental and emotional abuse from her partner, saying that she hadn't intentionally misled the public; it was because of her partner,

338

and his controlling and abusive ways. In the blink of an eye, she went from being one of those billionaire masters of the universe to a victim.

And ended up getting away with it.

Now Jane is saying to Jacobson, "Why is this the first we're hearing of your prior relationship with one of the victims?"

"Because this is the first chance I've had to speak on my own behalf."

"Except when you were calling opposing counsel's sister a liar," Ahearn says.

"Is that an objection, Mr. Ahearn?" Judge Prentice says.

"More of an observation, Your Honor."

"Keep those to yourself," the judge says, "at least until your cross."

Now Jimmy watches Jane ask, "Could you please tell us how Kathy Gates once saved your life?"

The feed switches to a camera that is close on Jacobson. Jimmy sees him look over at the jury with big, moist eyes. Charlie Sincere.

"It was depression," he says. "Not something guys my age talked about in those days. But something as real then as it is now. Severe depression."

"No one talked about it nearly enough in those days," Jane says. "Please go on."

Jimmy watches Jacobson take a deep breath now. Then another one. The catch in his throat is actually audible enough that Jimmy can hear it on the live feed.

"It was when I nearly OD'ed," Jacobson says.

"When?" Jane says, barely audible herself.

"When I tried to kill myself after my father killed *himself*," Rob Jacobson says.

ONE HUNDRED THREE

I KNEW COMING INTO the trial just how good Kevin Ahearn is as a prosecutor. And how ambitious he is. Knew full well he'd never lost a case, either.

But now, right here in front of me, I see, in full and in the moment, that he has saved his best for last. And has me thinking, really for the first time, that his best might be better than mine.

Bottom line is that the Suffolk County district attorney scares the hell out of me in the process.

He is theatrical, and in total command of the room, has the complete attention of the jury as he artfully deconstructs the case that Rob Jacobson has just tried to make for himself. Deconstructs it or simply unpacks it.

"Depression is something quite real and quite powerful. We put a bigger light on it all the time," Ahearn says. "But there are millions of depressed people in this country, a *majority* of the depressed people in fact, who don't pick up a gun and murder an entire family, including a teenage girl, in cold blood."

"Objection," I say. "Is Mr. Ahearn getting to a question anytime soon?"

"Sustained," Judge Prentice says. "She makes a good point, counselor."

"Here's my question, Mr. Jacobson," Ahearn says. "Were you ever treated for depression?"

"Yes. Sure."

"By whom?"

"A couple of therapists in the city," Jacobson says.

"Do you recall their names?"

I watch Jacobson's face now. And then see the hesitation that everybody else in the room sees.

"I can't remember their names. But what I do remember is that they got me through it at the time."

"So a couple of the therapists who pulled you back from the abyss, who may be the ones who really saved your life—you can't recall their names?" Ahearn says. "Interesting."

"I suppose I could get them if you need them."

"From where, Fantasy Island?" Ahearn says under his breath.

"Excuse me?" Judge Prentice says.

"I was just saying getting the names of the therapists isn't necessary," Ahearn says.

He isn't so much moving around the room as pacing it, I think.

Working it just the way I do.

"Let's switch gears," Ahearn says. "Do you find it interesting, Mr. Jacobson, that you only remember the things that seem to help make you appear more sympathetic?"

"Objection," I say, just because I need to do something, or anything, to stop his roll. "Argumentative."

"Sustained," Prentice says. "Jury will disregard."

"But I *do* continue to be fascinated by your memories," Ahearn says. "I mean, wouldn't you say that it's awfully convenient that you just now have remembered a prior relationship with the late Kathy Gates?"

Jacobson seems to squirm slightly in his chair.

In this moment, I know the feeling. I'm feeling a little squirmy myself.

"I guess you could call it an inconvenient truth," he says to Ahearn. "But it *is* the truth."

Ahearn nods. "At the same time, I'm wondering if you also find it interesting that a team of forensic accountants hired by my office to go through Mitch Gates's finances could find absolutely no evidence of him being in the dire financial straits about which you've just spoken?"

"People hide money," Jacobson says.

"Wait, they hide money they don't actually have?" Ahearn says. "Where does someone learn how to do that, Mr. Jacobson? The Bernie Madoff school of accounting?"

"You don't have to be sarcastic," Jacobson says to Ahearn.

"I'm not being sarcastic. I'm actually just pointing out how full of shit I think you are."

I don't get the chance to object before Judge Prentice interjects. "This is your first and last warning about language, Mr. Ahearn."

"Noted, Your Honor. I just lose my filter sometimes when I've found the perfect word to describe something."

I put a hand to my face, so neither my client, nor the judge, nor the jury, can see me smiling.

"Enough," Judge Prentice snaps.

"I honestly do apologize, Your Honor," Ahearn says. He turns to face Jacobson. "So to be clear, you're saying that Mitch Gates might have hidden money that didn't exist?"

"I can only tell you what *he* told me that night," Jacobson says. "Mitch said that things had gotten so bad that he didn't know if he was going to be able to send Laurel to college."

"Despite renting a Hamptons home for the summer?" Ahearn says.

"Maybe things cratered for him *after* he rented the house," Jacobson says.

Jacobson is trying to remain calm, but Ahearn has clearly knocked him off-balance. Or at least spun him around a little bit.

Makes two of us, I think.

Jimmy once said that a really good cross-examination is boxing without blood. I suddenly feel the urge to see if I'm the one who might be bleeding.

Ahearn is seated casually on the end of his table.

"High school depression really has nothing to do with this case, or the charges against you, does it, Mr. Jacobson?" Ahearn says.

"I didn't say it did."

"More of an implied-type thing," Ahearn says.

"Objection, Your Honor," I say. "It sounds as if Mr. Ahearn has jumped the gun here on his summation."

"Overruled," Judge Prentice says. "I'll allow it."

Just like that, Ahearn's voice is rising, to preacher level, and even though he is in the middle of the room, it's still as if he's managed to crowd Rob Jacobson.

"There was no suicide attempt, was there, Mr. Jacobson?" Ahearn says. "You're just putting an issue as serious as suicide into play in the same cynical way you tried to put depression. Isn't that right?"

"It's not like that."

"*It's exactly like that!*" Ahearn snaps at him. "*You've spent your whole life just lying to stay in practice. Isn't that right, Mr. Jacobson?*"

"Objection!" I say.

"Sustained," Prentice says. "You're all the way to the line, Mr. Ahearn."

"I'm telling the truth," Rob Jacobson says.

"Of course you are," Ahearn says.

I'm hopeful that he might be done.

Just not quite yet, unfortunately.

"Just one last question," Ahearn says, almost as if it's an afterthought.

He walks over to his table, moves some papers around, picks the top page up, studies it, nods. It might be something important, or it might be a grocery list. What he wants to do is heighten the drama, before whatever is coming next.

He puts the paper back down and turns back to the witness stand.

"Isn't it true that not long before the murders you entered into a nondisclosure agreement with Mitch Gates?"

"Objection!" I shout, once more before I'm out of my chair.

"I guess what we'd all like to know is just what you needed Mitch Gates to keep silent *about*." Ahearn shouts over me, and over the sound of Judge Jackson Prentice III's gavel, *"Or is that something else you've conveniently forgotten, you son of a bitch?"*

Now Kevin Ahearn crosses the line.

Happily.

ONE HUNDRED FOUR

I AM SITTING ON my back deck with Dr. Ben Kalinsky, the two of us sipping red wine, Rip stationed between Ben's chair and mine, snoring.

The rest of the world, the world of cancer and the trial winding down and dead bodies and Jimmy Cunniff still not fully recovered from his gunshot wounds—*and* me speculating all over again about whether my client is lying out his ass—is all still out there, somewhere beyond the perimeter.

But for tonight, it's just Ben and Rip and me.

I've got Diana Krall on the sound system. And am feeling almost normal tonight and almost happy. Like I'm falling for this sweet, gentle man that I know I'm going to lose eventually.

Maybe sooner than later.

Whatever "later" even means to me anymore.

I finished writing out my closing argument about an hour ago, got to where I was completely happy with that, knowing I'll change things when I'm actually in front of the jury, because I always do. But pretty much ready to go to the floor with it.

On the spur of the moment, I called Ben and asked him to come over for a civilized glass of wine and was delighted when he accepted.

"Only if you promise not to try anything," he said on the phone.

"I think you'll be safe."

"*Damn*. I was afraid of that."

When he arrived and we cracked open a new bottle of Train Wreck, still the perfect name for my favorite red even on a pleasant night like this, he wanted to know about everything that had happened at the trial.

"You're sure you wouldn't rather talk about something else?"

"No. I would not. And neither would you."

"Like you know me so well."

"Better than *you* know."

"Well, the bad news is that I got my hat handed to me by a great lawyer," I say.

"Better than you?"

I lean forward, and lower my voice to a whisper and say, "This has to stay between us. But yes. And if he's not better, we're both hitting the tape at the same time."

We both laugh. It has gotten easier and easier for me to laugh when I'm around Ben Kalinsky. Easier and easier to *be* with him. Easier to think when I'm around him. And just talk to him. But laugh most of all.

"You don't really believe he's better than you," Ben says.

"We're about to find out, one way or the other."

I drink some wine.

Then it just comes out of me, startling even Dr. Ben.

"*I hate to lose!*"

"But you never have. Lost, I mean."

"I'm pretty good at visualization, from having played hockey," I say. "And today I visualized being in that room in a few days and hearing the jury come back with three guilty verdicts."

Ben says, "If he did pay off the Gates family to keep them quiet, why go ahead and kill them?"

"Maybe he didn't."

"But maybe he did."

"Hey, whose side are you on?"

He grins. "Whose side are *you* on?"

We both drink then, and listen to the night sounds in the backyard, dominated by the tree owl who's been annoying Rip lately. In the distance, as always, I can hear the ocean, always there for me.

And suddenly I don't feel happy. I feel overwhelmingly sad. Not at the prospect of losing this trial.

At the prospect of losing this man, up and dying just when I'm getting to know this man and he's getting to know me.

"What a day," I say, and rub my eyes, as if trying to rub fatigue out of them. But it has nothing to do with fatigue. I just don't want him to see the tears forming. "What a damn day."

And maybe in the moment Ben Kalinsky senses a change in the night air between us. He puts down his glass now and gets up and covers the short distance between us, and leans down, and kisses me.

When the kiss finally ends, what feels like an hour or so later, I say, "There's a lot you don't know about me, Doc. Some of which might make you want to run in the other direction."

"Impossible."

"I'm being serious."

"So am I."

Tell him.

Tell him right now and get it over with.

Better or worse.

"You look as if you've got something on your mind," he says.

My answer to that is to smile, and stand, and put my arms

347

around him, and then we're kissing again, with even more follow-through than before.

"There's something I've been meaning to tell you," I say.

"And what is that?"

I take a deep breath. "Kind of a matter of life or death."

"I can handle it," he says. "I'm a doctor."

"I love you," I say.

ONE HUNDRED FIVE

I AM BACK ON the courthouse steps the next morning, doing my morning scrum with the media, one of only a few I have left.

Win or lose.

"So what can we expect today, Jane?" MSNBC's Jacob Soboroff asks. "Long summation or a short one?"

"With Kevin Ahearn? Pack a lunch."

"I meant yours."

"Bet the under. You all saw what happened yesterday, despite all the trickeration from opposing counsel. My client did most of the heavy lifting for me. You all saw, and you heard, everything the jury did. Did he sound like a guilty person to you?"

"*Oh, hell yes,*" I hear from behind Soboroff, and then Otis Miller, whom I've not seen in court since he testified, is stepping to the front of the crowd. The witness who saw Rob Jacobson's car leaving the Gateses' house on the night in question.

The witness I'd managed to out as a gay man, as I'd tried, in vain, to float the he-could-have-done-it defense.

"I'm sorry, Mr. Miller," I say, trying not to act rattled. "Are you properly credentialed?"

"Are you?"

349

"The people behind you are trying to do their jobs. We should probably both let them."

"I'm more interested in *your* job, Ms. Smith. What's it like trying to exonerate a murderer?"

"My *job,* Mr. Miller, is to give my client the best possible defense. And then leave it to the jury to exonerate him or not."

"By smearing people like me?" Otis Miller says. "What course in law school taught you how to do something as pathetic as that?"

I'm aware of the cameras. I'm aware this is all being recorded and will be going viral even faster than the speed of social media. But there's no place to run, no place to hide.

"If you were my client," I say to Miller, "I'd give you the best defense, too. But now I really have to get inside and continue to offer my current client my best effort."

I pull up the sleeve of my sincerity suit as if checking my watch, before realizing that I'm not wearing one today.

Otis Miller, though, isn't about to let me fade him.

He's suddenly standing right in front of me, perhaps hoping the cameras will show me backing up. Backing away from him.

If that's what he's hoping for, he doesn't know anything about me.

"What you're doing is sick," he says. "*You're* sick."

I smile brightly. "Well, Mr. Miller, you've got me there."

ONE HUNDRED SIX

I BET JIMMY CUNNIFF that Ahearn's closing would go for at least two hours.

It nearly does.

But along the way I lose track of time, because Ahearn's performance happens to be brilliant, and mesmerizing, as if he was just warming up the day before when he went at Rob Jacobson as relentlessly as he did.

It turns out he's an even better showman today than he was yesterday. I want to hate him for the way he's shooting one hole after another in my case. But what he's doing, even watching it from the other side, even knowing I'm being hurt here, is why I wanted to be a criminal attorney in the first place. For this kind of theater, with stakes as high as they can be, my client about to go free or die in prison.

Ahearn is being completely dismissive of any possible killer other than Rob Jacobson, or even the possibility that somebody could have set him up, planted as much evidence as there is in this case, and done all of it quickly enough to stay ahead of the police.

"There aren't even master criminals like this in the movies," Ahearn says. He pauses and grins and says, "Even good movies."

He covers a lot of the ground he covered the day before, acting as if the idea that depression and suicide have anything to do with these murders, this trial, is like some sort of fever dream on the part of Rob Jacobson.

And me.

I occasionally scribble some notes on the legal pad in front of me. But never for very long, because I can't take my eyes off Ahearn as I breathe his air, feeling my own heart begin to race, as if I'm the one out there on the floor and beginning my rebuttal already.

With my own A game.

At the finish he comes right back to the question I've asked myself from the beginning, even when I was convinced that the evidence against my client was simply too perfect:

If Rob Jacobson didn't do it, who did?

Who could have hated him enough to set him up in such a meticulous way, all the way to the blood from Mitch Gates found in Jacobson's Mercedes?

"Who did it?" Ahearn says.

He turns and points at Jacobson and says, "*He* did."

He walks over to our table, then turns to face the jury.

"This *isn't* the O.J. trial," he says. "There are no real killers wandering around out there, because the real killer is the sociopath sitting right behind me."

He jerks a thumb over his shoulder without even looking at Rob Jacobson.

I feel some movement next to me and am afraid Jacobson might stand and say something stupid after hearing "sociopath." So I put my hand firmly on his arm as I stand.

Then I'm on my way out there.

And as I'm the one taking the room now, for the last time in this trial, I feel an even bigger rush of adrenaline than I had at the start of the trial, all the way back to jury selection. I know how to do this. I know *what* I have to do. Know exactly what I want to say and how I plan to say it.

I walk to the middle of the room and am smiling as I turn to face the jury.

Otis Miller is only partially right, as it turns out.

I *am* sick.

Just not the way he meant.

And not today.

I walk slowly up and down in front of the jurors now, looking each one of them in the eyes as I do.

"Are you a murderer?" I say to the red-haired insurance agent from Manorville.

"Are you?" I say to the chef from Quogue.

"How about you?" I say to the foreperson, the retired English teacher from Riverhead whom I think of as Dame Maggie Smith. "Are you capable of murder?"

One after another, I ask them all the same question.

"Not one of you is a murderer, of course. It's why you simply cannot give an innocent man what is the equivalent of the death penalty."

I already feel like I'm back on my trail now, running and shooting, as I turn to face Rob Jacobson.

"Mr. Ahearn called my client a son of a bitch yesterday," I say. "And you know something? He was absolutely right. This man *is* a son of a bitch."

I smile.

"But if we're going to start giving out life sentences for that particular crime," I say, "we're going to need more lawyers."

I turn and nod at Ahearn, and think:

You're not as good as me today after all.

Nobody is.

ONE HUNDRED SEVEN

WE ARE AT A round table in a corner of Jimmy Cunniff's corner bar.

Just Jimmy and me.

Like it's us against the world one more time.

"I gotta say," Jimmy says to me, "that the real killer today was you, killer."

Jimmy, allowing himself to get out of the house for a couple of hours, has suggested ordering a bottle of his best Champagne. I tell him there is nothing to celebrate yet. And remind him that neither one of us really likes Champagne.

So instead of Champagne, there's his bottle of Pappy Van Winkle on the table in front of us. The very good stuff. And very expensive.

We clink glasses and drink.

I've never been a bourbon girl but have to admit it goes down easy. A little too easy. And I'm driving.

"I'm not bullshitting," Jimmy says. "I never heard you better than you were today."

"All I've got to show for it now is waiting for the jury to come back."

"Not your best quality."

"Wow, you picked up on that?"

"To impatience," Jimmy says.

He drinks. I sip.

"They always teach you to save your best fighting for the end of the round," Jimmy says to me now. "That's what the judges remember the best, and that's what you did today, kid."

Jimmy picks up his glass again but then puts it right back down.

"You have to tell him," Jimmy says. "Ben."

"I know who you meant."

"Janie, you're in love with the guy. You just told him you're in love with him. But he needs to know the rest of the story. For Chrissakes, you're starting treatment in a few days. He has the right to know before that. You think you can keep something like that from him?"

We sit there in silence for the next couple of minutes. He asks if I want more bourbon. I tell him I'm good.

Ten minutes later the call comes in.

Just not the one from the courthouse telling us the jury is back.

And not for me.

ONE HUNDRED EIGHT

Jimmy

JIMMY STEPS OUTSIDE TO take the call, from Detective Aaron McGrath, an old friend from the 111th Precinct, Queens, New York, telling him that Paul Biondi has been found dead in his garage.

Apparent suicide. Doors closed. Motor running. Adios.

Father of Lily Biondi Carson, whom he says Rob Jacobson raped when she was in high school. Paul Biondi: a man Jimmy questioned a few days before, because while the jury is about to come back on Jacobson's murder trial, it is very much still out on the shooting deaths of the Carsons of Garden City.

"Tell me again what the note said," Jimmy says.

"'The pain was just finally too much,'" McGrath says.

"He signed it."

"Yes."

"His handwriting?"

"Yes."

"So they find the guy in the garage," Jimmy says. "With the motor running."

"Cleaning woman," McGrath tells Jimmy. "She'd gotten jammed that day, showed up late in the afternoon. Yolanda Marquez. Smells the gas when she gets to the kitchen, which is attached to the garage. Freaks when she finds him in there, behind the wheel. Dead as fuck. Calls 911."

"Then you find my card in the pocket of his windbreaker," Jimmy says.

"I didn't have your new cell number," Aaron McGrath says. "But the dead guy apparently did."

The dead guy.

Paul Biondi.

Lily's dad.

The one who said Jacobson bought him off because of what happened on prom night.

Very much still alive when Jimmy went to see him in Little Neck.

"Sounds like he never got over his daughter and granddaughter dying the way they did," McGrath says.

"He might not have ever gotten over it. But he wasn't suicidal about it."

"You know this . . . *how*?"

"Because I was just with him a week ago," Jimmy says. "I looked him in the eye."

He is leaning against the front window. He turns and sees Jane staring at him from inside. The bottle of bourbon is still in front of her.

"Why were you with him?" McGrath says.

"Jane and me, we've been looking into what happened to Biondi's daughter, the whole family, in Garden City, favor to a friend. Biondi was helping me out on it."

"And you don't think it's possible he could have offed himself now that he knew the great Jimmy Cunniff was on the case?" Aaron McGrath says.

"Maybe not great," Jimmy says. "But still very, very good."

"You think somebody staged this?"

"Yes, sir."

Jimmy still finds himself getting tired if he stands too long, even though nobody shot him in the legs. He's not there yet. But he feels himself starting to sag.

Sagging in Sag Harbor.

Good one, Cunniff. No shit, you're some wit.

"Heard you took a bullet," McGrath says.

"Zigged," Jimmy says, "when I should have zagged."

He hears his old friend chuckle.

"Don't you hate when that happens?"

Jimmy looks down and sees he's put a hand to his midsection without even thinking about it. It's been happening a lot that day, almost as if he's trying to hold himself together.

"You still there?" Aaron McGrath says.

"He didn't kill himself," Jimmy says to him. "Somebody just wants it to look that way."

"Who?" Detective Aaron McGrath says.

"A monster, maybe."

ONE HUNDRED NINE

THE JURY COMES BACK late Thursday afternoon, after being out for a day.

Seven women. Five men.

I am seated in an attorney room with Rob Jacobson when the bailiff raps sharply on the door. Jacobson jumps at the sound, like a gun has gone off.

The bailiff pokes his head in and says, "They're back."

Just like that, the color drains from my client's face, nothing he can do to stop it. He's not cocky in this moment, or smug, or some kind of smart-ass. He's not slick and acting as if he's smarter than everybody, including me. He's just scared to death. I haven't been able to shut him up since we both sat down. It's as if it's finally sunk in that this is no game, that he can't bullshit his way out of a conviction, that his life is in the hands of those twelve people, more powerful on his day in court than the Supreme Court.

A jury now back.

Jacobson just finished asking me again what it means that they've been out this long.

"It's the same answer I gave you yesterday. You never know.

This isn't an exact science. I've had juries stay out for a couple of hours, or a couple of weeks."

"But then you've always gotten acquittals," he says.

"That doesn't matter now. Not even a little bit. And not to put too fine a point on things, but the district attorney has never lost, either."

"I can't spend another day in that cell," he says.

And he sounds as honest, and human, as he's ever been. With reality waiting down the hall. His old life, or life without parole. Those are the stakes, and now all the money in the world can't buy him out of the walk we're both about to take.

"I thought I was ready for this," he says. "I'm not."

"Hardly anybody ever is."

Before we leave the room Jacobson says, "You really don't like me very much, do you?"

The way he's asked it, as if he's somehow still curious about where I weigh in, actually gets a smile out of me, even if I'm as jumpy as he is, not that I'm going to let him see that.

"I'm sorry to say that the verdict on that one came in a while ago, Rob."

He holds the door for me, as if he's suddenly decided to be courtly, this late in the game. Somehow he's gathered himself by now, as if getting back into character, and doesn't want to walk in there looking scared. Or weak. Or both.

"Once and for all," he says, "don't you want to know if I did it?"

"No."

He leans in then, and once more puts his lips near my ear. I don't know if he's going to whisper something or kiss me.

I frankly don't care, either way.

I step back and slap him across the face. I slap him and snap his head back in the process, feeling the sting in my hand.

It feels good.

Very good.

Every part of it.

I can't believe it's taken me this long to do it.

Something changes in his eyes then.

And then, just like that, no hesitation, he slaps me back, as hard as I slapped him, knocking me back into the table, and nearly knocking me down.

I start to go back at him, gulping air, the old hockey fighter in me, but then stop myself, even as I feel the heat on my cheek, wondering what I'm going to look like when we're back in the courtroom.

"Showtime," I say.

ONE HUNDRED TEN

THERE IS A SLIGHT delay before Judge Prentice enters his courtroom. Maybe he's trying to milk the big moment for himself. I'm aware he's presided over a lot of big trials in his career. Never one as high-profile as this one.

So this is his moment, too. His, mine, Jacobson's, Ahearn's. The jury's.

Showtime.

"All rise," we all hear, and then he's walking slowly toward his chair.

Rob Jacobson and I watch as Dame Maggie and her fellow jurors file into the jury box. Nothing to tell from their faces. There really never is. None of them make eye contact with me, or my client, as they get themselves seated.

Jacobson does whisper something now.

"You see anything?" he says.

"Relief," I say.

"That it's over?"

"For them, it is."

And for me.

Win or lose.

As we sit down again, I suddenly find it difficult to swallow.

Or breathe normally. Watching as the bailiff takes what I know are three pieces of paper, for the three counts, from Dame Maggie, and walks them over to Judge Jackson Prentice. The sound of the bailiff's shoes seems quite loud. Other than that, Prentice's courtroom is completely silent.

All the cases are different, I think. But this moment is always the same. Something changing in the air, the way the air changes before a lightning strike.

I turn to look at Jacobson, his breaths moving in and out quickly, as if he's hyperventilating. Maybe because he is. He must have thought he had the whole world by the balls once. Only now everything has shrunk to the size of this room. And maybe the cell waiting for him upstate somewhere.

"Will the defendant please rise?" Judge Prentice says, and it's as if he's slapped Rob Jacobson now, knocking him back in his chair.

But he and I both stand.

Prentice says to Dame Maggie, "You have reached a verdict, Madame Foreperson."

"We have, Your Honor."

Jacobson and I both turn slightly to face her.

"On the first count, the murder of Mitchell Gates Jr.," Prentice says, "murder in the first degree, how find you?"

Dame Maggie starts to answer, but then it's as if she's the one who can't swallow or breathe. She loudly clears her throat, reaches down for the bottle of water next to her chair, drinks some water.

"Sorry, Your Honor. I'm a little nervous."

"*She's* nervous?" Jacobson hisses.

"Take your time," the judge says to her. Then Judge Prentice says, "Once again, on the first count of murder in the first degree, how find you?"

Jacobson tries to take my hand.

I pull it away.

"Not guilty," Dame Maggie says.

Rob Jacobson falls back into his chair as soon as the words are out of her mouth, grabs his head with his hands.

Then something quite amazing happens.

He starts sobbing.

Uncontrollably.

Like a child.

The remaining two verdicts are presented, both also pronouncing Jacobson not guilty. Then Judge Jackson Prentice III is thanking the jury for their service, even as they're all staring at Rob Jacobson.

Then Judge Prentice tells Jacobson he is free to go. But he doesn't go anywhere. He doesn't pick his head off the table. The only real movement is the rise and fall of his shoulders.

He just keeps crying.

The last sound in Judge Jackson Prentice III's courtroom, the last act of the *People v. Robinson Jacobson*, is that.

ONE HUNDRED ELEVEN

Jimmy

JIMMY KEEPS TELLING HIMSELF to turn off the television, he's seen enough. But he hasn't. So he doesn't.

He watches Jane's back-and-forth with the media, seeing how obvious it is that she just wants to haul ass out of there the first chance she gets. But she plays the good soldier to the end, as her client feels compelled to inform the world that he hasn't just been acquitted, that he's innocent, he wants to make that clear.

By now he's composed himself, after breaking down the way he did after the reading of the verdict.

"You know the old line, right?" Jacobson says. "Now where do I go to get my good name back?"

"*What* good name, asshole?" Jimmy says to the television.

Finally, and before he does turn the set off, he watches the foreperson, the woman Jane kept saying reminded her of some famous actress, talk about how convincing she and her fellow jurors found Jacobson's testimony about his father's suicide, his own suicide attempt, and his depression.

"We frankly weren't expecting to see that kind of humanity," she says.

"It wasn't humanity, honey," Jimmy says. "It was a master class in BS."

Jane calls him from her car about a half hour later, asking if he's up for meeting at Sam's in East Hampton for pizza and beer. He says he's always up for, and up *to,* pizza at Sam's. So he's in. Jane tells him she's going to invite Dr. Ben to join them.

"Good," Jimmy says. "Then you can tell him."

"If not tonight, then very soon."

"Sweet Jumping Jesus."

"Just let me breathe for a minute, okay? The trial just ended."

"Am I even allowed to congratulate you?"

"Fuck no."

For a moment it seems that she's ended the call on that line, like a mic drop. But then she says, "I haven't even told you the last thing our client said to me before I headed for my car and he headed off to do more TV."

"Did you believe those tears?" Jimmy says.

"I don't know what to believe about this guy anymore," Jane says. "What he's capable of. Or not."

"Did he at least thank you for saving his sorry ass before the two of you parted ways?"

"Not exactly."

"So what *did* he say?"

"He asked me how many times I thought somebody could get away with murder," Jane says.

ONE HUNDRED TWELVE

Three weeks later

JIMMY KEEPS ASKING ME if I plan to continue working now that I've finished the first round of chemo. Hell yeah, I tell him—tell him that there're two classes of people in the world, the ones who work to live and the ones who live to work.

"I'll be working to live," I say. "And living my effing life."

Jimmy grins. "Jane Effing Smith."

I've even gone back to training for my no-snow biathlon, scheduled for the end of summer. Tonight, as a way of sharpening my aim and especially my focus, I've used the new Walther air pistol I've bought myself as a present for winning the trial. I love the feel of the Walther in my hand. Love hitting the target with the smaller gun's BBs even more than I do with my trusty BB rifle. Like I've raised the degree of difficulty, as a way of challenging myself.

And I'm challenging myself on the trail, too, running as hard as I ever have despite all the energy that chemo has sucked out of me, getting to my spot, stopping and kneeling, extending my arm, my hand steady despite being out of breath, grouping my shots like a champion.

If I miss with even one, I go back up the trail, start running again, back to that spot, and make sure I don't miss this time.

A lot has changed since the start of the trial.

One thing has not: I can still hit what I'm aiming at, no matter what size gun I'm using.

It makes me feel like *me*.

It's nearly dark by the time I finish and return to where I parked my car near Three Mile Harbor. But I'm in no hurry to go home, so I just drive around on back roads, smiling to myself as I put on the Stones. *Voodoo Lounge*. Trying to pretend that I'm still as young as I was when I first listened to it. When I was sure so much good stuff—the rest of my life, mostly— was still ahead of me.

Rip is fine. I gave him his injection of fluids and fed him and walked him before heading over to train. I have no place to be tonight, until I decide as I do start heading home that I am badly in need of a pizza from Astro's. Too lazy to head into East Hampton and get one at Fierro's or Sam's. Like I'm rewarding myself for a kick-ass training session. So I call in an order of a half pepperoni, half sausage—you only live once, right?— and ride around a little more until it's time for me to stop and pick it up.

When I get to Main Street, I can't find a parking spot, even at this time of night, and I slowly make my way down toward the Stephen Talkhouse. There is already a line out front, stretching up the block to the hardware store, even on a Thursday night. But then out here Thursday has been the new Friday for a long time, especially once we're getting into the season.

Season to be young.

All that good stuff ahead of you.

Life, mostly.

I find a spot just past the hardware store and start walking back up Main toward Astro's.

"Hey, Jane!" I hear from a car slowly passing me. "Hey, Jane Smith. Way to go on the trial, girl!"

It's been happening like this, the past few weeks, when I'm out walking around here, or in East Hampton. I want to tell people that when it comes to celebrities, they have to set the bar higher than me. But I have to admit something to myself, if I'm being honest:

I like the attention.

The stroke.

I like being recognized, even if I'm being recognized for getting an acquittal on a client I think might have done it. And it's even more than that.

I did my damn job. Was my old damn self.

Coming toward me now I see Leo, the Aussie who runs the service station at the other end of Main.

"Good on ya, kid," Leo says.

He bumps me some fist.

"Girl's gotta eat."

I'm nearly to Astro's when I realize I've left my damn purse in the car. I turn around, start walking back to where I parked, when I see a couple crossing the street, having just left the Talkhouse.

Guy in a baseball cap, arm around an unsteady young girl in white jeans already looking overserved at a fairly early hour, the two of them making their way to the lot behind Jack's that serves Amagansett Square.

When they stop in the middle of the crosswalk, making sure a car heading east is going to stop for them, I can clearly see, because of the headlights, that the guy in the Yankees cap is Rob Jacobson.

And I think of an old Yogi Berra line that Yankees fan Jimmy Cunniff uses all the time, because he always seems to be quoting Yogi.

Déjà vu, all over again.

I unlock the car and get back behind the wheel. And wait, until I see Jacobson's Mercedes pull out of Jack's lot, making a left, heading west.

I pull out onto Main Street myself.

Following them.

Working to live.

ONE HUNDRED THIRTEEN

WHAT THE HELL AM I doing?
  Seriously.
  What in hell *am I doing?*
  I was supposed to be eating my pizza by now. Only I'm
not. I'm following the guy I just got acquitted, not even
remembering the last time I tried to follow anybody in a car
but feeling jazzed about it at the same time. Edgy. And a
little bit fearful, not entirely sure whether I'm afraid for myself or for the girl in that car and what might be about to
happen to her.
  Not sure where either one of us is going right now.
  I stay with Jacobson as he's the one taking back roads now,
having taken a left off 27 when he got to Wainscott. I make
sure not to stay too close to him, not wanting him to know
that he's being followed, even though I'm not sure what would
change if he did.
  What the hell am I doing?
  If the kid with him is in trouble, what am I going to do about it?
  Pull an air gun on him?
  I'd taken the Glock out of the glove compartment before
heading for the beach, planning to take it apart and clean it

later. But I'd left it at the house, in the drawer of the small table in the front hall. There was another Glock in the nightstand next to my bed. Also of absolutely no use to me right now.

No music inside the car now. Just the sound of my own breathing, coming fast.

And the feeling of being even more alive than I was on the trail.

Being me.

I stay with Jacobson, maintaining my distance, realizing he's on his way home as he makes one last left off Daniel's to Gibson Lane, on his way to his big house, even if he's passed much bigger ones along the way. Claire Jacobson is in Paris, or so I'd read last week in the *East Hampton Star.*

Maybe with her away, he's already turned the place on Gibson back into his party house.

The aging frat boy back at it.

Brazen enough—shocker—to be back cruising the Talk-house again for girls.

Feeling young himself.

Immortal even.

I'm not sure what my plan is here, if it is an underage girl with him. Burst in on them and confirm my worst fears about Rob Jacobson, that he's about half an Epstein?

One of my worst fears, anyway.

One of many.

I stop the car near the end of the driveway, hidden enough by the privet down here but still allowing me a view of a house pretty close to the road for this neighborhood, the back lawn far bigger.

I roll down the windows and feel the ocean breeze, smell it, hear the muted sound of the ocean from a half mile away.

I remember the night I came and parked not far from here

and saw Gus Hennessy show up for his sleepover with Claire Jacobson.

One more fun couple of the Hamptons.

I know I might be wasting my time. I am quite conscious of time these days, and how precious it is. Twelve months left. Or whatever it is. That many days and nights.

How do I put them to their best use?

I think about time *all* the time.

Do I want to spend it alone?

Or with Jimmy and Ben and Rip the dog?

I love the sound and the feel of the ocean. There could be worse places to go out. Worse ways. I know I shouldn't feel a sense of peace here, on what might be a useless, and cockeyed, stakeout of a dirtbag like Rob Jacobson.

But somehow I do.

I am here for an hour, more or less, when I hear a scream that shatters the sounds of the night, and the ocean up ahead of me.

The scream of a girl.

Somebody's daughter, the way Laurel Gates was. And Paul Biondi's daughter was.

And then her daughter after that.

I hear another scream, louder than the first.

Somebody's daughter making that sound.

I'm out of the car now, running up the driveway.

Wishing I had a real gun on me.

ONE HUNDRED FOURTEEN

AS I SPRINT PAST the Mercedes parked at the top of the drive and around the garage and into the backyard, heart pumping like I'm back on the trail, hearing one more scream in the distance, I stop briefly.

And hear the sound of laughter.

Rob Jacobson's.

My client.

Then I'm in motion again, seeing him in the light of his back patio, shirt out of his jeans, shoeless, laughing his head off now, almost like someone baying at the moon.

"Got a runner!" he yells.

I look past him, across the vast expanse of the back lawn. In the distance I see a figure, who has to be the girl with whom he left the Talkhouse, sprinting toward the dunes, stumbling, falling to the grass, scrambling frantically back to her feet, no longer wearing the white jeans she'd been wearing an hour or so before.

She looks back over her shoulder one last time and then disappears in the direction of the Atlantic.

I wonder briefly what she thought was going to happen when she got into the car. Or why she got into the car. Was it because of how famous he is now? Or how rich?

Both?

Only now she acts as if she's running for her life.

Jacobson turns and sees me just as I am about to take off running again, this time after the girl.

Far more interested in her right now than I am in him.

"Well," he says when he sees that it's me. "*This* is awkward, isn't it?"

I ignore him and take a couple of steps toward the dunes before I am brought down from behind, half tackled and half shoved forward, nothing I can do to break my fall, the air completely knocked out of me as I land on my chest, my face pressed into the wet night grass.

My midsection, because of the way I've landed and what I've landed on, hurts like hell.

I turn my head enough to finally catch my breath, force myself to roll over. Jacobson and another man, the one who must have put me on the ground, are standing over me.

I hear Jacobson say, "Looks like we both lost a step, huh, Jane Smith?" He says my full name with amused contempt.

Rob Jacobson is smiling down at me.

But I'm not focused on him.

My eyes are fixed on the other man, backlit by the full moon.

A man who's supposed to be dead.

One Rob Jacobson swore to me was dead.

"I don't believe you and Mr. Champi have been formally introduced," Jacobson says.

ONE HUNDRED FIFTEEN

THEY TELL ME TO sit on a long white leather couch, and I willingly oblige them, as Champi is the one with the gun.

Jacobson goes over to the bar at the far end of the living room and fixes himself a scotch over ice in a highball glass. I see what looks like a small splash of blood on the front of the white shirt and hope it's his blood.

Champi is seated across the coffee table from me, a gun I know is a .22 in his hand.

I point at the gun and say, "The gift that keeps on giving. Am I right, Joe?"

Champi, his blue Rangers cap pushed back on his head, says, "I should put one in your leg for starters, like you put one in mine that night on the train tracks. Still hurts like a bastard."

"I rushed the shot. If I'd had more time, I would have put one right between your eyes."

I look at Jacobson, then nod over at Champi.

"One more lie from you about him being dead. On what appears to be a very long list of lies."

"So it does," Jacobson says.

I direct my attention back to Champi.

"So tell me, Joe. Was it you who killed them all? Or were you still just cleaning up after your excitable boy here the way you always have?"

Champi tries to keep his face blank as he stares back at me. Is it guilt I see in his eyes now? Or something else? Maybe it's just the kind of indifference you see from a snake.

His answer is to just grin, and shrug.

At least one of them knows enough to keep his mouth shut.

"Do the two of you plan to kill me now?"

Jacobson pokes at his temple with an index finger.

"I've thought about it, Jane Smith. Not gonna lie about *that*. I *have* thought about it." He shrugs now. "But no," Jacobson says, "I'm not going to kill you. Despite what you might think about me, even now, and even though you might not believe it, I'm not a killer."

I look for a reaction from Champi but don't get one.

Then Jacobson is talking again. "But I *have* been thinking a lot since the trial ended about what to do about the way you fucked with me every chance you got." Winks at me one more time. "And you know what I came up with, what would be like a life sentence for you? Making you believe you freed a guilty man."

"Did I? Free a guilty man, I mean. You keep swearing up and down that you didn't do it."

He acts as if he hasn't even heard me, walks to the end of the room, toward the open terrace doors through which his date must just have run. The moon seems even brighter than ever, as if it's gotten closer. When he turns it's almost as if there's a spotlight on him.

"The whole trial," he says, "you kept bringing up O.J. I always got a kick out of that." He drinks some scotch, loudly smacks his lips. "You remember that book he wrote after he beat the rap? On the murders, not the shit later on in Vegas. *If I Did It*—that was the title. Maybe I should write a book of my own like that. Get back into publishing with a nice double-dip. Write it *and* sell it."

He drinks again.

"If *I* did it."

I look over at Champi. His eyes are still very much locked on me. The gun rests on his knee. I idly wonder how many people have died because of that gun.

Or are about to die.

"You always thought you were in charge, Jane Smith. But now I'm the one calling the shots. So to speak."

As always, when he's doing most of the talking, he's enjoying himself mightily.

But I turn to Champi now. "I'm curious about something," I say to him. "I'm curious about a lot of things, actually. But let's start with this: Why didn't you take out Jimmy that day at McCall's, when you had the chance? Why'd you wait until you ambushed him in that chickenshit way? It was you at McCall's, wasn't it?"

I see Jacobson look at Champi and slowly shake his head.

"He's not your witness, Jane Smith," Jacobson says. "I am. You don't talk to him. You talk to me. Got it?"

"Okay, I'll play along. *If* you killed the Gateses, *why* did you?"

"Well," he says, "maybe getting a thrill out of getting a daughter into the sack all this time after I did the same with the mother finally caught up with me. And they were going to tell, even though we had a deal."

He turns back to Champi.

"Now I'm the one talking too much, right?" Jacobson says.

"Your whole life," Champi says. "Even though she's not even asking the right questions. Again."

I turn back to him. "What questions should I be asking?"

"You ever wonder what happened to the Morelli kid?"

"I just assumed you threw him into the ocean."

"One more thing you got wrong," Champi says. He shakes his head. "List keeps getting longer. All the way back to high school."

"What does that mean?"

Champi again shakes his head. "I mean, you think his old man killed himself over his kid's girlfriend?"

I stare at him, then Jacobson.

"*Your* girlfriend?" I open my mouth, close it. Finally I say, "Are you the one who killed them?"

Jacobson smiles, and shrugs. "What, you want that one pinned on me, too, Jane Smith?"

He walks over to me now and leans down, his face close to mine, his breath smelling of the scotch.

"You just had to get right back up in my face tonight, didn't you? You just couldn't help yourself. And you know why? Because the whole time you were defending me, you absolutely believed I was guilty. I swear, I thought it pissed you off that the jury said I wasn't, even if a guilty verdict would have screwed up your perfect record."

One more time I can't help myself from doing something else, despite my current situation.

I slap him.

He is about to slap me back when Champi is out of his chair and grabbing his arm to stop him.

Like he's the boss now.

"For Chrissakes, will you please shut up and let me handle this?" Champi says.

ONE HUNDRED SIXTEEN

"PLEASE DON'T SHOOT MY DOG," I say to Champi after we've driven to my house and Rip growls at him from the kitchen doorway.

"Then put him in there and shut the door," Champi says.

"Does Rob really want you to do this?"

He grins. "Do what?"

"I've got neighbors."

"I've got a suppressor. Jump ball."

He's right behind me as I grab Rip by the collar and walk him into the kitchen, leaning down just long enough to scratch him behind the ear and whisper, "Love you, Rip." Then I close him in the kitchen.

Think.

But there is no room for me to try anything, no play I can make with his eyes on my every move, and he's keeping just enough distance between us that I can't even think about going for his gun.

Or my Glock, currently in the hallway table.

Let me handle this, he said to Jacobson.

One of my yellow legal pads is on the desk on the far side of the living room. Champi points to it.

"You're just gonna be one more who decided to end it all," he says. "Like that poor bastard Paul Biondi." He grins again. "And he didn't have cancer."

They know.

"Does he know, too? He has to know if you do, tight as you two are."

"Does it really matter?"

He points again at the yellow pad. "Let's get this done. I'll tell you what to say."

"Not happening." Now I grin at him. "I'm dead anyway, right? But I'm not leaving behind a suicide note, you son of a bitch."

"Sure you will."

"No."

"*Yes.* You do it this way and I won't kill your boyfriend and your sister like I already killed Cunniff." He shrugs.

I feel all the air come out of me at once.

Like I already killed Cunniff.

"You're lying," I say to Champi.

"You're confusing me with my boss," he says. He is smiling suddenly.

"This is funny to you?"

He shakes his head. "Endlessly."

When he finally says he's tired of talking, he tells me to start writing.

"No," I say again.

"Yes," Champi says. *"Now."*

I think: *Now or never is more like it.*

"I'm going to be sick," I say suddenly, leaning forward, trying anything to distract him. "The damn cancer drugs . . ."

It is in that moment that the front door opens and Dr. Ben Kalinsky comes walking in, saying, "I've got the pizza you didn't pick up."

Champi turns without hesitation and fires.

As he does, and I see Ben spin around and go down, not sure where he's been hit, just that he's been hit, I roll off the couch and away from Champi and pull the Walther air pistol I'd stuffed into the front of my jeans and underneath my baggy BC hoodie, before I got out of the car at Rob Jacobson's house, before I ran up the driveway.

Get to Ben.

But Champi first.

Then I'm aiming as well as I can, Joe Champi's face my target now. I fire, hitting him between the eyes this time even though it's only a BB gun, and hear him scream as I do.

He's on the ground now, clawing at his face with his free hand, trying to find me, firing wildly with the .22, the shots sounding like small explosions even with the suppressor, as I crawl behind the couch and get to the table in the front hall, reach up and grab the Glock out of the top drawer, roll toward where Ben is lying just inside the door.

I'm firing real bullets at Joe Champi now from my knees, hand steady, aiming for center mass.

Then the room is quiet again, except for the sound of Ben Kalinsky's faint, labored breathing.

ONE HUNDRED SEVENTEEN

One day later

I HAVEN'T SLEPT, having spent half the night at Southampton Hospital after talking to the police. I know I should be tired, looking to sleep for about a week.

But I'm not tired.

I'm relieved, is what I am.

Feeling very much alive.

And feeling lucky, for the first time in a long time.

Like I've finally beaten the odds.

At least for now.

"I believed him when he told me he'd killed you," I say to Jimmy Cunniff. "Turns out we're both hard to kill."

"Us and Dr. Ben," Jimmy says. "Champi turned out to be as lousy a shot with him as he was with me that night at my house."

"And from nearly point-blank range."

"The doc got lucky."

"We all did," I say.

We are in Jimmy's car, driving west on Route 27. We have been talking about how Champi's bullet grazed Dr. Ben on the side of his head, just above his ear.

A couple of inches the other way, it would have been Dr. Ben who took one right between the eyes.

"This is a bad idea, what we're about to do here," Jimmy says.

"You said that already."

Before I can say anything else, he holds up a hand. "No, check that. This is as bad an idea as the last time you made this ride."

"At least I'm armed with more than an air pistol."

When Rob Jacobson opens his front door, he doesn't seem surprised to see us.

Just annoyed.

"I've got nothing to say to either one of you," Jacobson says.

He starts to shut the door. Jimmy holds it open.

Jimmy says, "Step aside or I will happily knock you on your ass."

Jacobson hesitates, but only briefly, before doing as he's just been told.

"You caught your killer last night," Jacobson says. "Catch and kill, right? Isn't that what they always say?"

"So you want us to believe it was Joe Champi who killed everybody?"

"Believe what you want to," Jacobson says.

"What if I think you're the one who was killing people from here to the city?" Jimmy says.

"Well, then prove it. I'm telling you, it was Champi. From the time I was a kid, he was the one calling the shots. Like, real shots."

"Not what you said the other night," I say. "You reminded him he worked for you when you wanted to shut him up."

Jacobson smiles, one last time. "What can I tell you, Jane? I lied."

"But wait," Jimmy says. "Wouldn't that make you an accessory after the fact?"

Jimmy is clearly enjoying himself. And I have to admit, so am I.

"You know what they say," Jacobson says to him. "Dead men tell no tales."

"You sure about that?" I say to Jacobson.

I walk past him and take a seat on the same couch where he told me to sit the other night.

Then I take out my phone and place it on the coffee table and check to make sure that the volume is turned up all the way before motioning for Jacobson to take a seat across from me, in the chair where Champi sat the other night.

"Are we ready?"

"For what?" he says.

"For this."

I hit Play.

The next voice in the living room is Joe Champi's, from the last moments of his life, from *my* living room. The audio ends with Champi trying to laugh, and going into a coughing fit instead.

One of the last things he says is this: *"You asked me if I thought this shit was funny."*

More coughing, the sound getting worse as his voice gets weaker.

"You want to know the funniest part of all? They had him on trial for killing the wrong family."

Finally Champi, his voice almost inaudible by now, says, *"You don't know how crazy his family is."*

On the tape you hear me pleading with Joe Champi to stay with me.

He dies then.

There is no response right away from Rob Jacobson to what he's just heard.

Then he turns to Jimmy Cunniff before looking back at me, Rob Jacobson at a loss for words, at last. But not for long. In the next moment we're somehow all the way back to where we started.

Only he's talking to me about three different victims this time.

"Now you really do have to believe me," Jacobson says. "I. Did. Not. Kill. *Those*. People."

About the Authors

JAMES PATTERSON is the world's bestselling author. Among his creations are Alex Cross, the Women's Murder Club, Michael Bennett, and Maximum Ride. His #1 bestselling non-fiction includes *Walk in My Combat Boots, Filthy Rich,* and his autobiography, *James Patterson by James Patterson.* He has collaborated on novels with Bill Clinton and Dolly Parton and has won an Edgar Award, nine Emmy Awards, and the National Humanities Medal.

MIKE LUPICA is a veteran sports columnist—spending most of his career with the *New York Daily News*—who is now a member of the National Sports Media Association Hall of Fame. For three decades he was a panelist on ESPN's *The Sports Reporters.* As a novelist, he has written seventeen *New York Times* bestsellers, the most recent of which was *The Horsewoman,* his first collaboration with James Patterson.

For a complete list of books by

JAMES PATTERSON

VISIT
JamesPatterson.com

 Follow James Patterson on Facebook
@JamesPatterson

 Follow James Patterson on Twitter
@JP_Books

 Follow James Patterson on Instagram
@jamespattersonbooks